I looked back across the dark stretch of Agford's lawn to the house. Every light was ablaze and her blinds were pulled low, creating a milky white screen. And projected onto that screen was the most terrifying image I had ever encountered.

Agford's silhouetted figure loomed before me, twenty feet high and ten feet wide. She raised one arm and paused—the black outline of a cleaver hovering overhead—before swinging violently downward.

THE WIG IN THE WINDOW

KRISTEN KITTSCHER

HARPER
An Imprint of HarperCollinsPublishers

Library of Congress Cataloging-in-Publication Data

Kittscher, Kristen.

The wig in the window / by Kristen Kittscher. — First edition.

      pages   cm

   Summary: When their game of neighborhood spying takes a dark turn one night, pre-teen sleuths Sophie Young and Grace Yang find themselves caught in a dangerous cat-and-mouse game with their bizarre guidance counselor, who may be hiding something sinister.

   ISBN 978-0-06-211051-0

   [1. Mystery and detective stories. 2. Friendship—Fiction. 3. Middle schools—Fiction. 4. Schools—Fiction.] I. Title.

PZ7.K67173Wi   2013   2012025337

[Fic]—dc23   CIP

                                                                  AC

Typography by Lissi Erwin

15 16 17 18 19   OPM   10 9 8 7 6 5 4 3 2 1

First paperback edition, 2016

For Papa's kiddos,

Sophia and Juliette

Contents

One **Midnight Mission** 1

Two **Seeing Red** 14

Three **The Root of the Matter** 21

Four **S.M.I.L.E.!** 42

Five **Shadow of Doubt** 61

Six **Wigging Out** 70

Seven **A Blue Streak** 78

Eight **Stranger Danger** 94

Nine **Cracking the Code** 101

Ten **Awkward Encounter** 112

Eleven **Texas Hold 'Em** 121

Twelve **Impatient Bait** 137

Thirteen **Famous Last Steps** 142

Fourteen **Special Delivery** 153

Fifteen **Bottoms Up** 164

Sixteen **Exhibit (Dr.) A** 173

Seventeen **Enemy Incoming** 184

Eighteen **A Shocking Discovery** 191

Nineteen **All Locked Up** 213

Twenty **The Face in the Window** 228

Twenty-one **Rock Bottom** 236

Twenty-two **Hairtight Evidence** 241

Twenty-three **Questionable Assumptions** 250

Twenty-four **Over and Out—Forever** 276

Twenty-five **The Nightmare Begins** 285

Twenty-six **Initial Breakthrough** 294

Twenty-seven **The Art of War** 304

Twenty-eight **Amazing Grace** 311

Twenty-nine **Happy Family** 331

Thirty **Walking Tall** 339

Acknowledgments 349

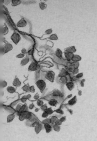

Chapter One

Midnight Mission

I thought I'd mastered the art of escape. It was our third midnight spy mission, after all. I knew to oil my bedroom window so it wouldn't squeak. I knew how many stuffed animals to shove under my comforter. I knew how to lash my black rope to the bed frame, how to ease out of the window and rappel down the side of my house. I knew when to jump to avoid the rosebushes. And I knew exactly where Grace would be waiting.

So when I lowered myself out of my window and fell backward into the fog, I was so shocked when the rope didn't tighten that I barely caught the ledge in time.

How could I have forgotten to secure the rope? That was the easiest step of all.

My fingers ached. My grip was slipping.

If I had been in a movie, it would have been easy. I'd have

dropped down, landing with a quiet thud as my impossibly long legs bent to break my fall. But I was not in a movie. And my legs aren't long. Seriously, some people's *arms* are longer than my legs.

My best hope was to jump for the rose trellis and climb down. Sun Tzu said that when you face a desperate situation, you have no choice. You must fight. I squeezed my eyes shut and took a deep breath. Then I leaped. The trellis swayed under me but held fast. For once I was grateful to be so small.

By the time I had plowed through the rosebushes and hobbled next door, Grace was waiting on the patio outside her room, perched on the railing and dressed almost entirely in black Lycra. Her long legs ducked into the mist and reappeared again as she swung them impatiently. "Sophie! I was just about to come find you," she whispered as she jumped down. "We're on for Operation Freezer Burn. The feds just sent word." Grace clicked on a tiny headlamp fastened around her black knit cap and pulled out a grainy printout of an FBI mug shot from her backpack. "Here's our man. Freddy the Freezer, aka the Italian Ice. Known for his *chilling* method of storing his victims' bodies . . ." She squinted at me and plucked a leaf from my hair.

"What happened to you?"

I looked down at myself, swimming in the folds of my dad's ratty black softball shirt. My blue sweatpants were ripped and covered with rose brambles. "I ran into some complications," I said.

"Thorny ones." Grace tried not to laugh as she helped me pick off the rest of the brambles. When she stood up again, she looked at me intently, eyes glistening. "You still up for this?"

I shivered a little as I looked down the hill at Luna Vista's rows of identical red-tiled roofs rising up from the fog. A breeze rattled through the silhouetted palm trees along our street. Things were spiraling out of control. They had been ever since Grace started getting real-time FBI bulletins and poring over Most Wanted mug shots. It didn't matter that the bulletins were actually mass emails from the FBI's community-outreach department. We were pushing our luck. But I wasn't sure I could stop the missions now—not even if I wanted to.

I looked back at Grace and smiled. "I'm here, aren't I?"

Grace grinned. "Then let's do this." She unclipped her walkie-talkie from her neoprene belt. Its sleek pouches and holsters held everything from a mini black light to a mobile fingerprint-dusting kit. "Frequency check," she said. "One-eight."

I rummaged in my backpack for my own walkie-talkie. "Got it," I said, adjusting my handset. We were old-school. Grace insisted we have military-grade equipment that she ordered from an online spy-gear supplier. Cell phones were for backup only.

"Breaker, breaker, one-eighter," Grace whispered. "Agent Yang here. Agent Young, do you copy?"

"Agent Young here." I frowned. "What about my code name?"

"I'm not calling a white girl that. I'll get laughed out of Chinese school."

"Doesn't that happen all the time?"

Grace pretended to look stern. "Watch it, shorty."

I stretched onto my tiptoes. "Hey, I'm four foot six now."

Grace could have easily pointed out that I still looked about ten, tops—especially when you factored in my freckles. She was already busy unzipping her backpack, though. "Binoculars," she said, tossing me a pair before peering through the fog with her own. She thought we should buy night goggles, but it'd be a while until we'd saved enough money. We'd only been running night missions since the start of the school year, when Grace had decided twelve was the right age to train for a real FBI career. I considered

4

telling her we could have started a whole year earlier if we counted by the Chinese calendar, but I knew she would have just rolled her eyes at me.

"Binoculars, check," I whispered. "Flashlight?"

"Check." Grace spun her flashlight like a gun and slid it into a holster on her belt. We alternated our way through the rest of the checklist like always. Extra batteries, note-book, spy pens—even ponchos, in case it happened to be one of the ten days a year it actually rained.

"What about food?" Grace finished off the list. "In case we need to extend the stakeout?"

I rattled a box of Nerds.

Grace gave me a look. She was good at giving looks.

"Never underestimate Nerds." I smiled back.

"I wouldn't dream of it, *nerd*." Grace patted me on the shoulder. "So. Here's the deal." She pulled a map from her backpack and unfurled it on the patio. It was a smaller replica of the neighborhood satellite map of Luna Vista that we kept mounted on a bulletin board in our command central in Grace's room, only without our news clippings and detailed notes. In one corner, in red pen, we had listed our "persons of interest," or possible neighborhood spy targets. Black Xs marked the houses that were off-limits. I had crossed off anyone associated with Luna Vista Middle School, like Rod

Zimball. (Who cares if people still called him Rod Pimple? He was cute now, and I wasn't about to get caught crawling around in his dad's azaleas.) Grace had put her Xs over any houses near the beach. In fact, to make her feelings perfectly clear, she'd drawn an army of skulls and crossbones over the ocean, next to her chain of Xs lining the entire coast. I couldn't blame her. When she was six, she'd nearly drowned when a rip current carried her and her father out to sea.

"The feds say Freddy the Freezer's on the loose in a suburb." Grace pointed to a house on the map. "I think it's Mr. Fabiani."

"The dry cleaner?"

"Just a Luna Vista dry cleaner? I don't think so." Grace raised her eyebrows. "No one stores that much steak in his garage freezer."

My stomach tightened. I was fairly sure Mr. Fabiani was just enthusiastic about prime rib. But considering we were talking serial killers, being *fairly* sure is very different from being sure. I hoped we'd end up spying on whoever still had their lights on, like we had the last two missions. Of course that meant paying another visit to the Wagners—the world's most boring insomniacs. Grace would probably rather continue being homeschooled by Miss Anita for the rest of her life than put up with watching Mrs. Wagner clean out her toe jam again.

Grace ran her laser pointer over the map as she detailed our route in FBI lingo consisting mostly of Greek letters.

"We'll zero in on Omega from the back," Grace finished.

As I looked at her hunched over the map, I found it hard to believe that a month ago our biggest spy achievements had been catching my older brother asking his mirror out on a date or spotting Grace's dad dancing around the living room with the family cat. Forget night missions. I was usually home doing vocab work sheets by five p.m.

"Okay. Time synch." Grace looked at her lone digital watch. Usually, for style's sake, she wore about six watches— most of which didn't work. Some were vintage, a couple were neon and plastic, and at least one rattled around on her wrist like a bracelet. If I did that, they'd whisk me off to the insane asylum. Grace Yang wears six watches, and it looks awesome.

"Twelve ten," I said.

"Twelve hundred ten," Grace corrected into the walkie-talkie. "Roger."

"Is that really how you use 'Roger'?"

"Oh, just let me have my lingo."

"I will." I smiled. "Once you let me have my code name."

7

Grace rolled her eyes at me, crouched, then led the way down the hill—diving for cover behind shadows and bushes as I followed.

How did we go from joking that Mr. Peterson's bushy mustache was a disguise to sneaking out at midnight? If I knew exactly, you can bet I would have stopped it before I was ducking in and out of shadows, heart pounding in my chest, on my way to spy on a potential serial killer. I do know that, like most things that eventually spin out of control, it all started as a joke because we were bored. One minute you're making fun of the old Barbies on your shelf, and the next you're co-hosting a wedding extravaganza for Barbie and Ken, complete with honeymoon hot-tub frolicking. Only—if you've made the mistake of joking around with Grace Yang—an hour later she has her heart set on a career as a wedding planner.

Grace stopped short behind the hedge at the bottom of the hill. She grabbed my arm and pointed through the mist.

The lights were on at Dr. Agford's.

"No way, Grace. Not Agford." I crossed my arms. "That was the deal."

When I had drawn my big black X over Agford's house on our satellite map, there was a reason I'd made it twice as big as all the rest and traced over it ten times: Dr. Charlotte

8

Agford was my school counselor at Luna Vista Middle School. She was, more specifically, the world's *worst* school counselor. "Dr. A" (as she asked us to call her), aka Dr. Awkward (as we called her behind her back), couldn't keep a secret to save her life. She'd glide across campus with half-closed eyes, smiling and tilting her head in her forced Pose of Compassion, then she'd sidle up to some poor soul dumb enough to have trusted her, gently place a hand on his shoulder, and ask loudly if he was "okay now" or if his "little problem" had cleared up. The resulting rumors usually provided the entire school weeks of entertainment. Grace claimed she understood that if I got caught at Agford's I would find myself below virtuoso nose-picker Julian Winkle in the seventh-grade social order. But, then again, Grace herself had never witnessed the devastating power of a Dr. Awk-topus tentacle touch and "check-in."

"This calls for a lights-on exception," Grace said, digging into the pouch, where she kept a black notebook. It was like she'd forgotten Freddy the Freezer had ever existed.

"When a serial killer might be on the loose?"

"Oh, Mr. Fabiani just buys in bulk." Grace waved her hand. "We'll spy on him next week . . . if *his* lights are on."

Grace had been itching to spy on Agford since the summer. It was hard to blame her. Even my parents thought

Agford was strange. In the two years since she'd moved across the street from us, no friends or family had visited. Though she positively smothered her house with kitschy decorations for every holiday, she'd never invited any of the neighbors over for a party—or even dinner. Once, when Grace stuck a misdelivered letter in Agford's mailbox, Agford had come rushing out of her house and—without ever letting her perma-smile falter—pretended to be very concerned she might not know that "in this country" interfering with mail was a federal offense punishable by up to five years in prison. Grace had resisted the urge to kick her in the shins and had bolted back home, but she never forgot it.

"Mr. Fabiani is only *maybe* a serial killer," Grace said. "But we *know* something's not right with Agford." She rattled off her same old reasons we should spy on her, some of which were pretty convincing. Whose name only gets four Google hits, all in the last two years? I'm twelve, and I get at least seven hits that are actually me.

"C'mon, Grace. You know I can't risk it," I interrupted.

"We won't get caught." Grace's eyes flashed. "When have we ever been caught?"

I arched an eyebrow. "The Valdez Disaster?"

"That doesn't count. We had the perfect excuse!"

That past summer, after we hadn't seen our neighbor

10

Mrs. Valdez for a while, Grace got it in her head that Mr. Valdez's brand-new vegetable garden housed not only heirloom tomatoes but also his wife's body. Her hypothesis quickly crumbled when—as we stood in their backyard wielding shovels—Mrs. Valdez and her mother returned home from a two-week Alaskan cruise.

"Lost soccer balls don't require excavation, Grace."

Grace shrugged. "They totally bought it. Anyway, we're real spies now. And it's much harder to get caught at night."

I had to admit there was an awful lot that didn't add up about Dr. Agford. Her hair alone merited a spot on our list of "persons of interest." It fanned out from her scalp in a translucent auburn helmet that—judging from its eye-watering hairspray scent—required some serious styling effort. Her special fondness for tacky Southwestern jewelry clashed with the suits, high heels, and pantyhose she wore to cultivate a professional look. She'd definitely had some plastic surgery, too. No one with a petite frame like that could support such colossal boobs. They bobbed in front of her like overfilled balloons. Grace and I were pretty sure she inflated them each morning. They looked uneven.

"Why do you think she's still awake?" Grace asked. She must have sensed I was wavering.

"Probably trying to fit her hair into its nighttime protective bubble."

Grace snickered. "Maybe she popped a boob."

I giggled. I couldn't help myself. Soon we were both doubled over.

"Shhh! Someone will hear us," Grace said, catching her breath. "But seriously, Soph. When are we going to have another chance like this?"

I looked up at Agford's. Her white stucco walls blended into the fog, and the yellow glow of her lights floated eerily above us. I had to admit it was tempting to find out what she was up to this late. Spying on her *had* to be more interesting than examining the Wagners' bedtime hygiene routines. And it was certainly less dangerous than getting caught in a potential serial killer's yard.

I looked back at Grace. Her binoculars were in hand. She was ready to spring into action. The next day she'd be alone with scowling Miss Anita, finding square roots and diagramming sentences. Boredom was like an unstable chemical compound when it came into contact with Grace. Too much of it, and something might explode.

"Okay," I said. "But this is a *one-time* exception."

Grace smiled as she raised her walkie-talkie. "Breaker, breaker, one-eighter. Agent Yang here," she whispered into it. "Hidden Dragon, do you copy?"

Now *that* was more like it.

"Ten-four," I said into my handset, grinning. "Hidden Dragon reporting for duty."

Chapter Two

Seeing Red

Minutes later we were crawling across Dr. Charlotte Agford's manicured lawn, trying to blend in with the shadows as we headed to a narrow side yard that led around to the back of her house. Grace stole ahead and signaled for me to follow before she disappeared into the fog.

We had crept as far as Agford's side door when I heard a gentle click and buzz. A spotlight burst on. I froze. Spy clothes are no help when some genius has managed to harness the entire power of the sun into a motion-detector light.

Grace dashed to the shadows beyond us and crouched by the hedge along Agford's back fence. I tried to follow but went only two steps before my toe caught an uncoiled hose in the grass. I went flying, smacking face-first into what I thought was a pile of dirt but which—surprise!—was an anthill.

It turns out ants wake up when a human destroys their colony with her face. Luckily they weren't the biting kind. The last thing I needed were painful, blotchy red trails of ant bites to ensure that I would never, ever win Rod Zimball's love.

Just then Agford flung open the side door. Blinded by the glare of the motion-detector light, she held a phone in the crook of her neck and squinted into the fog. "Gosh-darned raccoons!" she spat—except what she actually said was a hundred times worse.

I couldn't believe it. At school Agford always spoke in a sickly sweet falsetto, never uttering anything harsher than *gee* or *my goodness* as she discussed the importance of hygiene during *poo-burty*, as she pronounced it. Now she was cursing raccoons?

But it was Agford, all right. Her poufy helmet of hair seemed askew. I held my breath. In half a second, Agford's eyes would finally adjust to the light, and there I'd material-ize beneath the fog, outstretched on the lawn and clutching a walkie-talkie.

"I tell you, Danny, I'll rip their throats out," Agford growled into the phone.

The door was ajar, but Agford had turned inside. She grasped the phone in one hand and kicked off one of her

15

high heels. Realizing with horror what she had in store for the "raccoons," I shielded my head. A four-inch heel thrown at that range could probably crack my skull.

Nothing came. Instead Agford wriggled her toes and scratched her leg with her foot. *Please don't turn around*, I begged.

"But don't worry," Agford continued into the phone. "They won't put it together. If they find us, we'll take care of it. Simple as that," she said. She slammed the door shut just as my lungs surrendered and pushed out the breath I'd been holding.

I sprang to my feet and sprinted for home, assuming Grace was right behind me.

I was halfway across the street before my walkie-talkie squawked to the neighborhood, "This is Agent Yang! Hidden Dragon! Come in, Hidden Dragon!" I hugged it to my chest and groped for the volume control.

"Oh my God . . ." Grace's voice trailed off.

"Agent Yang?"

Nothing. I shook my walkie-talkie. All I heard was the hammering of my own heartbeat.

"Do you copy?" I tried again. "Grace?"

Dead air.

A bolt of adrenaline sent me tearing back to Agford's. I

dashed along the side yard—leaping to avoid the hose—and dove for cover by the hedge, where Grace had huddled in the shadows only a moment ago.

She was gone.

I looked back across the dark stretch of Agford's lawn to the house. Every light was ablaze and her blinds were pulled low, creating a milky white screen. And projected onto that screen was the most terrifying image I had ever encountered.

Agford's silhouetted figure loomed before me, twenty feet high and ten feet wide. Her balloon boobs wobbled as she raised one arm and paused—the black outline of a cleaver hovering overhead—before swinging violently downward.

I stifled a scream and wildly scanned the yard for Grace.

Agford's silhouette bore down the cleaver again and again.

"Um. Agent Yang?" I croaked into my walkie-talkie. My heart pounded so hard, I was sure my radio broadcast it.

"Shhhhh!" the handset hissed back.

I let out a breath. What was I thinking? That Agford would mosey out to the yard, catch Grace, then bring her inside to chop her to pieces?

"What's your twenty?" Grace's voice came over the walkie-talkie.

"Hedge. Back fence," I whispered back.

I was about to return the question when I caught a glimpse of a black shape in the flower bed directly under Agford's kitchen window. My chest tightened in panic. It was Grace. She was going to get us caught. I knew she was.

"Get your binoculars, Sophie." Grace could barely keep her voice steady. "Now."

From inside came a dull grunt and a *thwap* of a cleaver loud enough for me to hear even from my hiding spot at the back of the yard. In a daze I rummaged in the backpack. My hands shook as I adjusted the binoculars and looked toward Agford's kitchen. A slight gap in the blinds gave me a direct view.

Still holding the phone tucked between her shoulder and neck, Agford hunched over something on the floor. I chuckled, relieved. Grace was playing it all up, of course. It's not like you can murder someone while chitchatting on your cell. I was about to lower the binoculars when my eye caught sight of the cleaver.

I gasped. It sat on a large carving board, smeared with blood. Even more blood pooled in the board's gutters like a moat. Splatters of crimson covered the sink, the faucets, and the tile countertop.

Agford hoisted something up then let it thud to the

floor. On her second heave, I saw it was a large trash bag.

The director of counseling at Luna Vista Middle School had just butchered someone with a cleaver, and now she was cleaning up the body parts as if she were gathering some old odds and ends for Goodwill.

Charlotte Agford stood up. Grace must have seen it when I did. Emblazoned across her oversized chest were the unmistakable outlines of two bloody handprints. In their final moments, grasping fingers had streaked long red ribbons down her cream-colored sweater.

"Run!" Grace's voice gasped through the walkie-talkie.

By the time I caught up to Grace outside her room, we were both panting so hard, we couldn't speak.

"Do you . . . have . . . your . . . phone?" Grace wheezed as she caught her breath. She pulled off her knit cap and wiped her forehead. Her long black hair rose with static. Her eyes were wide.

I pulled out my cell. Walkie-talkies or not, I was never without my phone. I steadied my hands enough to dial—at the last second remembering to deactivate caller ID. If our parents found out we'd sneaked out of the house at midnight, the police would have two more murders on their hands.

"Nine-one-one. What's your emergency?" answered the operator.

I tried to keep my voice steady, deepening it to disguise myself. "Uh, yeah, hello, uh . . ." I wanted to sound like a guy. Instead I sounded like an idiot.

"Ma'am? Please state your emergency."

"My emergency?" There was only one way to put it. I looked at Grace. She nodded. I cleared my throat. "Murder," I said. "I just witnessed a murder."

Chapter Three

The Root of the Matter

By third period French, I had replayed the night's scenes in my head at least a thousand times—and that's not counting my nightmares. The deep-red blood clotting the cutting-board moat. The way Agford's hair bounced with each swing of her cleaver. The police cars skidding to a halt in front of her house, their doors slamming, boots pounding up her front walk. It was hard to picture Agford behind bars. Would she wear pantyhose under her orange jumpsuit? Would they even have an orange jumpsuit that could accommodate that chest?

"Le Massif Central. That's what it's called, right?" Rod Zimball's voice interrupted my thoughts.

I stared at him blankly. I suppose that was as good a name for Agford's chest as any.

"Le Massif Central?" he repeated, pointing to a mountainous area on a blank map of France. "For the quiz?" Rod's hazel eyes peeked at me from underneath his brown curls. At Luna Vista the guys weren't allowed to let their bangs hang over their eyes. It made him seem even cuter that he was so adorable *and* a rebel.

Things had started looking promising with Rod last year. He'd signed my sixth-grade yearbook: "Stay smart. Love, Rod." It took me a long time to figure out which I liked better—that he admired me for being smart or that he used the word *love*. I called it a tie and decided they were the four most beautiful words I'd ever seen in a row. A few weeks into seventh grade, he'd started passing me notes. His first was a bug-eyed caricature of our French teacher, Madame Tarrateau, her generous armpit hair penciled in like seaweed. Underneath the picture he'd coined a new nickname for her and scrawled: *"Madame Tarantula est très ennuyeuse."* ("Madame Tarantula is very boring.") Maybe that doesn't sound romantic. But it got better. We started texting at the start of October, hiding our cell phones behind our *French in Action* workbooks. Our latest thing was trying to stump each other by texting secret codes.

"Uh, yeah, le Massif Central," I stammered back. "That's right."

"Merci, Agnès." Rod smiled. Madame Tarrateau had given us all French names. It didn't matter that my name was the same in French—or that she assigned all the other girls runway-model names like Rochelle and Simone. I was Agnès. It was supposed to be pronounced "an-YES," but only Rod said it right. Trent Spinner and his charming friends called me Ay-nus.

As Madame Tarrateau attempted to wrangle the class to order, the door swung open to reveal our school principal, Mr. Katz. He looked as gray and fierce and tight-lipped as ever.

"Madame Tarrateau? I apologize. I can see you have—" He paused as a lone paper airplane came in for a shaky landing near his feet. "I can see you have your hands full, but I need to talk to . . ." My heart thumped so loudly, I didn't even hear him finish. I didn't need to.

"Sophie? Euh . . ." Madame Tarrateau frowned, searching her brain. *Euh* was the sound she made between everything she said. I think it was the French version of *uh*, but it always seemed like she was just disgusted by whatever she was saying. Finally it dawned on her. "Ah, *oui*!" she exclaimed, her tight poodle curls bouncing as she flipped one end of her long silk scarf over her shoulder. "Agnès!"

Rod looked puzzled as I made the long, slow march to

the front of the classroom. Why did *I* feel like the one who murdered someone in my kitchen?

I had just reached the front of the room when I realized that lurking in the hall behind Mr. Katz was Officer Grady, our local police deputy, who'd once pulled me over for not wearing a bike helmet. His hands were on his hips and his fat fought to break free from his polyester uniform. Standing next to him was . . .

No. It was impossible. My heart stopped. She cocked her head and opened her lips in her best imitation of a smile. "It's okay, Sophie," Dr. Charlotte Agford called out before forcing a laugh that sounded like a snort. "We don't bite!"

The class could hear her, of course. Grandpa Young could have heard her even without his hearing aid.

"It's all right, AY-NUS!" Trent Spinner added. His buddies smirked and snickered, right on cue.

My parents were already waiting in Mr. Katz's office. My dad stared straight ahead, jiggling one heel up and down like a human sewing machine. My mom raised her head and looked at me, her eyes red-rimmed and questioning. My parents were not angry. Matters were much worse.

They were disappointed.

"Take a seat, Sophie," Mr. Katz said. He sighed and

gestured to a black armchair positioned under a picture of a golf course bearing the block-letter caption EXCELLENCE. I glanced around. His office was decorated with an entire family of pictures flashing similar one-word motivational slogans, all framed in black and spaced along the room's bland gray walls.

Mr. Katz waited as Officer Grady waddled across the room and crammed himself into a narrow armchair next to Agford. His leather belt creaked in agony as he strained to get comfortable.

"I want to thank you again for interrupting your work-day, Mr. and Mrs. Young," Mr. Katz said as he laced his fingers together. "My son's a project manager at AmStar, so I'm especially aware of what a stressful time this is."

I cringed. My parents—and half of Luna Vista—worked for AmStar, a company that made missiles, rockets, and radar systems for the military. For months they'd been pre-paring for an important missile test, which was now just two weeks away. Since their last one cost many millions and was a huge failure, everyone had been working over-time. Another bungled launch, and a lot of people in Luna Vista would lose their jobs.

"Officer?" Mr. Katz said. "We're ready."

Officer Grady pressed a button on a handheld device.

"Uh, yeah, hello, uh . . ." My pretend deep voice crack-led through the tiny speakers. I wanted to crawl under Mr. Katz's lacquered black coffee table and live there for the rest of the school year.

My mother bit her lip. My father rubbed the back of his head. I stared at a pointy glass paperweight on Katz's desk. The recording continued. In the background I heard the faintest hiss. It must have been Grace's breathing. Did they hear it?

"Uh, Charlotte Agford. A-G-F-O-R-D," my guy-voice clarified. "She just killed someone."

Agford coughed delicately and shifted in her chair. I didn't dare look her way. Just smelling her perfume was enough to turn my stomach. Sometime in September I'd named the scent *eau de Lysol*.

I closed my eyes as my recorded voice blared on. It was like I thought that if I couldn't see them as they listened, they couldn't hear it. I'd been so stupid to think disabling caller ID would keep the police from tracing a call.

"Eighty-seven Via Fortuna. F as in French fry . . . O-R-T as in turd . . ."

I never had quite understood how to phone-spell.

By the time I'd opened my eyes again, my parents had sunk low into Mr. Katz's sofa, cowering in the shadow of the mountain-range poster commanding us all to BELIEVE & SUCCEED.

Officer Grady clicked off the recording, and Mr. Katz finally spoke. "I am baffled," he said, removing his glasses and resting one of the arms in his mouth. It was a practiced gesture that he must have thought conveyed the proper mix of thoughtfulness and superiority. "Over the years kids have pulled a variety of pranks, but none has found it hilarious to accuse a staff member of murder."

Who said it was hilarious? Mr. Katz could add me to the list of the Baffled. Last night Agford had hacked someone to death with a cleaver and put the pieces in trash bags, yet here she was, buoyed up by her balloon boobs, smiling her fake smile.

"Officer Grady has spent all night investigating this lie and will spend the better part of his afternoon filling out paperwork associated with it. He certainly doesn't find your midnight shenanigans hilarious," Mr. Katz continued. "Nor do your parents, who have now been pulled away from work for an entire morning." His face was getting flushed. "And how hilarious is being spied on and accused of murder, Dr. Agford?"

After years of being forced into a permanent smile, Agford's lips quivered with the strain of taking a neutral position.

"Kids will be kids, Mr. Katz. Nobody understands that better than a professional." She looked first to my parents, then to me. "But in the two years since I've moved to Luna Vista, I have to say—I've never felt quite so . . ." She fingered an ugly brooch on her suit lapel that looked like a bedazzled, cursive version of the letter A. In my mind's eye, I saw the red, bloody finger streaks smeared across her cream-colored sweater. Agford chose her next words carefully: "Quite so *hurt.*"

My mother's shoulders sank. She searched her own shoes for clarification about how and when I became such a horrible person.

Mr. Katz shook his finger at me. "Miss Young, we're all *very* curious about what you might have to say for yourself."

I opened my mouth and hoped the right explanation would find its way out.

"I thought—I mean," I stuttered. "The whole place was covered in blood!" I blurted out at last.

My mom sighed. Agford made a little gurgling sound that might have been a stifled laugh or an expression of sympathy, I wasn't sure which. When I looked over, she tilted her head at me, squinted, and smiled.

"Soph, honey," she cooed, shaking her head slowly.

I shuddered. I allowed maybe four people to call me Soph. Charlotte Agford was not one of them.

"I understand if you're not ready to apologize, sweetie, but I think we need to get a few things clear. You sneaked out of your own house at midnight, correct?"

Reluctantly, I nodded.

"You trespassed on my property?"

Dr. Agford waited for my agreement.

"You sat in my backyard and spied on me through my windows? Yes?"

"I guess so," I said.

"You guess so?" my dad erupted. "You *guess so*?" An actual vein popped to the surface of his forehead.

"I mean, that's correct," I said, fixing my gaze on the basketball hoop in Mr. Katz's AIM HIGH poster.

"When the police came, Sophie, do you know what they found?" Agford asked. There was the slightest edge to her falsetto.

I was tempted to reply that they'd found mutilated pieces of a human corpse when Mr. Katz answered Agford's question for me:

"Beets, Sophie. They found beets."

The room closed in around me. I couldn't breathe.

"Dr. Agford pickles root vegetables every year and gives

them as gifts for Thanksgiving. She's famous for it," Mr. Katz explained. "Perhaps you'd better explain your findings to the Youngs, Officer?"

Officer Grady detailed in his gravelly voice how he and his partner had indeed discovered Dr. Agford cleaning up her kitchen after preparing beets. She'd had an unfortunate incident with the blender. He smiled at Agford as he finished. "The suspect then invited us to enjoy a glass of freshly prepared beet juice. Delicious, Dr. A. Really. Thank you."

"I jar them," Agford said. "They make great holiday gifts."

"I hope I'm on your list this year," Officer Grady chimed in.

"They're amazing, Charlotte," Mr. Katz said. "Honestly, I never liked beets before."

Agford pushed her smile so wide, I feared her face might snap like a rubber band and catapult across the room. "They sure are messy, though!" She snorted as if she'd made a joke. No one else laughed.

I looked around the room. I thought of the red smears. The way Agford brought down her cleaver in such rhythmic blows. The chopping, the cutting board, the trash bag . . . it was for *beets*?

My mother spoke then, her voice small and strangled.

"It was very neighborly of you to include us last year, Charlotte."

I had a vision from last Thanksgiving of my older brother, Jake, jamming his hands into a jar of bright red lumps before waving his fingers in my face and laughing like Dracula.

Beets. Agford's beets.

Dr. Agford studied me. "You understand now, Soph, dear?"

Her voice faded into the background. My cheeks felt hot. The red droplets *were* awfully red for blood, weren't they?

"I thought it was blood," I mumbled.

"Oh. Oh, dear." Dr. Agford slowly shook her head again. She exchanged a knowing look with Mr. Katz. He gave a curt nod.

Agford turned to my parents. "I believe Sophie is depressed," she announced, folding her arms across her massive chest.

Officer Grady looked at his watch.

"Depressed?" my mom repeated. She looked pale. "That doesn't really seem like—"

"Soph, sweetie," interrupted Agford. If she had been close enough to lay her hand on my shoulder, she would have. "Needless risk taking is a sign of self-destructiveness. Not to mention anger." She nodded at her own pronouncement. "We have to ask ourselves—you, Sophie, have to ask yourself, 'What is the root of this rage?'"

The *root* of my *rage*? Agford smiled again, fastening her dead eyes onto me.

"I'm not angry," I said in a near whisper. I stared at a speck of dust on the coffee table. I felt a twinge of bitterness as I pictured Grace sitting at home, oblivious, listening to Miss Anita drone on. I wondered if it'd be any better if they knew Grace had been there. Then I imagined her parents finding out. I clamped my mouth shut.

"Denial." Agford clapped her hands together. "It's textbook." She addressed me at a volume reserved for the hard of hearing. "Sophie, you're exhibiting *very* disturbing behaviors. You need help. And Sophie? I'm here to help. We're *all* here to help." She spread her arms. Officer Grady looked like he wanted to flee, lest she suggest a group hug.

Tears welled in my mother's eyes. My dad looked at the ceiling.

"I recommend Sophie meet with me for therapy twice a week," Dr. Agford announced. Mr. Katz's posters blurred around me in a jumble of sunrises and bald eagles. Twice a week?

"We pride ourselves on the support system we offer students, Mr. and Mrs. Young." Mr. Katz touched his fingertips together as if illustrating his point.

Agford handed a tissue to my mom. She'd made it materialize out of thin air. Had she taken it from her *cleavage*?

My parents looked at me. My mom dabbed her tear-streaked cheeks with Agford's tissue. My throat tightened. I was not going to cry. I couldn't let them see me cry. Least of all Agford.

My father squeezed my mom's hand and turned back to the room. In a strained voice he thanked them all for their time. My mother added an apology so rambling that I wouldn't have been surprised if she'd also begged forgiveness for having given birth to me.

"Not to worry," Dr. Agford said when they'd finished. She turned to me, her smile as tight as a ventriloquist's. "Sophie is in *very* good hands."

As my dad told Grandpa Young the story at dinner that night, I felt as if I were being drenched in shame by one of the waterfalls in Mr. Katz's posters. Grandpa prized smarts. I'd been anything but smart. It didn't help that Jake sat across from me, on track to break a Guinness World Record for how long he could keep smirking. I almost couldn't blame him. The last time I'd really been in trouble was when I scribbled all over my walls with purple marker when I was five. He'd had to wait years for a smirking opportunity like this.

"Who the devil eats pickled beets?" Grandpa Young cocked his head. His fuzzy, flyaway gray hair made him look all the more puzzled. Relief washed over me. "We're talking about the wacky one across the street?" he continued. He put down his fork and mimed two gigantic spheres in front of his chest. "With the big bazoo—"

"You win at cards today, Don?" my mom interrupted as she shoved the breadbasket into my grandpa's outstretched hands.

"Nah." Grandpa made a face. "Navy boys are a buncha cheats." My grandpa spent his days playing canasta with other veterans down at the VFW, a club for Veterans of Foreign Wars. (Besides the Civil War, were there any non-foreign wars?) He'd gone there occasionally even before my grandma had died, but since he'd moved in with us, he walked down there all the time. It was a good thing he did; otherwise we'd have had to call in emergency fumigation experts every night. The man ripped a thundering fart *at least* every fifteen minutes. How the army ever put him in charge of stealth missions during the Korean

34

War was beyond me. Talk about literally blowing your cover.

Grandpa turned back to me. "You remember what General Sun Tzu said about spying, Sophie?" He always quoted Sun Tzu's *The Art of War* to me. You'd think a book from the fourth century BC about some Chinese military general's philosophy would be super boring, but Grandpa made it interesting. "He said," Grandpa continued, shaking his finger at me, "you have to be *subtle* about it."

My mother nudged my father so hard, he almost spilled his iced tea.

"I think Sophie's learned *more* than enough about spying, Dad," my father piped up. "Let's give Sun Tzu a rest, huh? At least until Sophie's not grounded."

"Fair enough, soldier." Grandpa turned his attention back to his chicken.

Jake spoke then. "Speaking of grounded, I don't get it. I saw Grace at the Seashell today. Why isn't *she* grounded?"

My parents swung their heads around to me. My heart stopped. I could practically hear the puzzle pieces clicking into place.

I pretended to finish chewing. How long could I reasonably do that? Thirty seconds? One minute? Half an hour? It was so tempting to tell the truth. "Jeez, Jake," I said, finally.

I did my best imitation of a Grace Yang eye roll. "Why would Grace want to spy on *my* school counselor?"

I waited for Jake to provide a four-part explanation detailing exactly why, offering as evidence the unbelievably embarrassing time he caught Grace and me hiding in the Stenwalls' bushes on a fake stakeout. Instead his eyes widened in alarm. "Oh, dude, right. Totally forgot she was homeschooled," he said. It was the nicest thing he'd done since pricking his finger to add blood tracks on the fake snow in my *The Call of the Wild* diorama last year—and I wasn't so sure that was supposed to be nice.

Grandpa chimed in. "Yang's got a nose for covert ops, that's for sure. I was just telling her about the night in '51 when we parachuted over the thirty-eighth parallel, and—"

"If you want to know the truth, kids at school dared me, okay?" I flung up my hands.

My mom and dad traded looks. My dad took another bite of his chicken and chewed for an eternity, then slowly wiped his mouth. "I never realized you were such a follower, Sophie."

I stared at my plate. I wasn't sure which was worse—how right he was or that he'd never noticed before.

Grandpa patted me on the back. "Aw, she'll make a fine

commander yet," he said as he leaned forward and—right on schedule—punctuated his sentence with a single toxic blast.

After dinner my parents condemned me to the prison of my room with no access to a computer or cell phone and no hope of getting in touch with Grace. I couldn't bring myself to do homework. I couldn't sleep. I stared at my poster of Kai Li (a Taiwanese superstar and musical *genius*) and wished he'd share some advice. After a while, though, even his smile started to remind me of Agford's.

A sound made me bolt upright. It was my closet. It hissed at me. I was sure of it.

I waited on high alert.

There it was again.

"Psssst!"

I sprang to my feet and was already half out the door when I realized I hadn't turned off my walkie-talkie the previous night. I went into the closet and pulled the door shut.

"Is that you, Grace?" There would be no code names tonight.

"No. It's someone who likes to radio little girls on their walkie-talkies at night. *Mwahahaha!*" Grace cackled. "Of course it's me. I've been trying to get you on the phone all afternoon. What's going on over there?"

I told her every detail, right down to Officer Grady barely fitting into Mr. Katz's armchair.

"But it looked just like blood," Grace blurted out. "And who chops beets at midnight?"

"Apparently she roasts and pickles them every fall. Gives them out at Thanksgiving."

"When you chop vegetables, do you typically raise a cleaver over your head and swing it downward ferociously?" Grace asked.

"All the time. Totally standard procedure."

Grace chuckled. "Seriously, though."

"Why would she murder someone on a cutting board?"

"Maybe she was done with murdering and was chopping body parts to fit them in her trash bag?" Grace suggested.

"Yeah, right. And she paused midmurder to curse out some raccoons and take a phone call," I said. "Think about it, Grace. Unless she murdered someone who didn't have vocal cords, wouldn't we have heard screaming?"

Grace pondered this in silence.

"You didn't tell them I was there, though, right?" she asked.

"Of course not," I answered, guiltily remembering how close I'd come to telling on her.

"Thank God. If Monday and Janice find out, I'm dead."

Monday and Janice Yang were Grace's parents. They were really high-powered cancer doctors. I called them Mr. Dr. Yang and Mrs. Dr. Yang to tell them apart. The two had met at Harvard Medical School when they first came over to the United States from Beijing in their twenties. Both of them worshipped Grace so much, she could have probably set fire to the house and they would have praised her match-lighting skills. They were crazy protective of her ever since she'd almost drowned when she was little. Still, they *freaked* if she was ever disrespectful. Grace once talked back to her teacher, Miss Anita, and she had to write an essay on the role of educators in society.

"No worries. You'd have done the same for me, right?" I asked.

"Are you kidding? I'd have sold you out in a minute," Grace said. Then she sighed. "Of course I'd have done the same, you *nerd*. FBI protocol. A spy never betrays her partner."

Somehow Grace's joke still stung. I fiddled with the pendant around my neck. At the end of sixth grade, Mrs. Dr. Yang had given each of us one teardrop-shaped half of a yin-and-yang pendant to wear. When you put the two together, they formed the yin/yang circle. According to

Chinese philosophy, yin and yang are opposite forces that interact with each other. Yin is dark, quiet, colder energy. Yang is active, bright, and warm energy. The two need to be in balance for harmony. I had the black yin one with a dot of white yang, and I wore my necklace every day. Grace hadn't worn her yang pendant even once. She claimed it didn't go with any of her outfits.

"Soph?" Grace's voice had grown quiet.

"Yeah?"

"Did we really imagine all of that?"

"I guess so." My voice shook a little. It shouldn't have been such a big deal. So we thought we saw something we didn't.

"So what now?" Grace asked.

I explained the terms of my grounding: no cell, no TV, no going online, two-hour study halls every day after school with Grandpa Young. "Oh, and let's not forget," I added. "My parents are making me do yard work at Agford's house every Saturday for six weeks. You know, to show how sincere my apology is."

Grace let out a gasp. Over the walkie-talkie, it sounded like a hurricane of static. "Oh, Soph. This is so unfair. That's *besides* the therapy with her twice a week?" she said. "What on earth are you going to talk about?"

I sighed. "The *roots* of my *rage*, Grace. The *roots* of my *rage*."

"Speaking of roots, see if you can find out what's up with her hair."

"Ten-four, Agent Yang."

"Roger," Grace said. I could tell she was smiling. "Over and out."

Chapter Four

S.M.I.L.E.!

My mom drove me to school the next day. It was only a mile walk, but I think she was worried I wouldn't go unless she escorted me there personally. She was probably right. As soon as we rounded the bend and I saw Luna Vista Middle School perched over the Pacific, its low white buildings and outdoor hallways looked so exposed that I wished I could leap into the ocean and drift away.

"Listen, Sophie," my mom said as she pulled into the carpool line. She tucked my hair behind my ear like she used to do when I was little. "I know Dr. Agford is a little odd. But keep an open mind, will you? She means well."

Maybe she *meant* well, but I wasn't sure she actually *was* well. All the same, I muttered an agreement, grabbed my stuff, and slipped from the car.

Almost as soon as I stepped onto the sidewalk, a cluster

of kids fell silent, then erupted into a flurry of whispers once I'd passed. Someone snickered. I tightened my grip around my backpack straps and strode ahead through the outdoor courtyard—until I nearly ran smack into S.M.I.L.E.'s bake-sale table.

S.M.I.L.E., aka the Society for Making Improvements in Lives Everywhere, was the club that Agford advised. It was made up of five members: Marissa, Alissa, Larissa, Clarissa, and Jenn. (Jenn's mom had probably shot down a legal name change to Jennissa.) S.M.I.L.E. was not only immune to the social consequences of being on Agford's radar, they *were* her radar.

Left to themselves, the members of S.M.I.L.E. would have simply been the kind of kids who lingered in teachers' classrooms after school to help change bulletin displays and erase whiteboards. But Dr. Awkward had harnessed S.M.I.L.E.'s need to please to make it look like she was doing her job. Rolling backpacks in tow, S.M.I.L.E. would march across the campus handing out brochures with titles like "Sleep Hygiene: Much More Than Clean Sheets." When they weren't raising money for questionable causes, Agford had them hosting her famous Brown Bag Lunch Seminars on peer pressure and resolving conflicts. Still, somehow they managed to have enough energy left over to know absolutely everything and grunt *oo, oo* like monkeys every time they raised their hands in class.

To be fair, they probably weren't *really* like that—and I admit some of their names were actually different—but they had soaked up Agford's attitudes so completely, I could hardly see them as anything else but carbon copies of her.

That morning S.M.I.L.E. sat behind piles of baked goods, wearing pins that each featured a very ordinary-looking brown bird (Jenn's was upside down). "Save the New Zealand Bush Wren! Buy a Tweet Treat!" a huge banner behind them announced as they handed out bird-shaped pastries. When I nearly ran into their table, S.M.I.L.E.'s president, Marissa Pritchard, was busy counting a sixth grader's change. Sensing a sudden disturbance in her happiness force field, Marissa froze and looked up.

She trained her blue eyes on me like lasers. She had no mercy for someone who'd caused trouble for her beloved patron saint. Even her straight blond hair seemed to quiver with rage. The rest of S.M.I.L.E. felt their queen's unrest. They whipped up their heads to locate its source.

Kids in the bake-sale line turned to see who had earned the group's wrath. When had S.M.I.L.E. ever *not* smiled? Membership required smiling, just as it required heartfelt annual celebration of National Happy Hugs Week.

44

Just then Charlotte Agford materialized beside the bake-sale table in a purple sweater with a plunging V-neck that (shudder!) threatened to spill out her gravity-defying boobs. S.M.I.L.E. turned to greet her, looking like baby birds themselves as they gazed up at her. Agford's eyes flitted to me; then she leaned over and whispered something to Marissa.

"We've made fifty-two dollars already, Dr. A!" Jenn interrupted, beaming.

"Now, Jenn. We don't measure success in dollars alone," Agford said. "Think of the *awareness* we've raised today."

"We need to care about the *journey*," Marissa added, her voice an eerie echo of Agford's falsetto. "Not just the destination." She exchanged a knowing glance with Alissa.

"That's right," Agford said. "Now keep selling, ladies. Marissa, you'll bring up the cash box to my office after? I'll write you a late slip." Marissa looked smug as Agford patted her on the shoulder and smiled.

I wanted to throw up, and I hadn't even eaten a "tweet treat." I ducked through the archway and was about to enter the science lab when I stopped cold. Peter Murguia was standing just inside the door. "I heard the cops found a gun in her locker," he said.

"Nuh-uh!" answered another voice. "They would have sent her to juvie!"

"I thought she called in a bomb threat," a girl's voice chimed in. "She always was a little off, wasn't she?" It was my friend Stacy Pedalski. Correction: my former friend Stacy Pedalski.

"I heard it had to do with Agford," said someone else, setting off a murmur of questions.

"You guys have got to get lives," rang out a voice above the fray. It sounded like Rod Zimball. My heart leaped.

I rounded the corner into the classroom. Rod sat facing the whiteboard. Had he seen me and turned away? If he hadn't stood up for me, then who had? All I knew was that everyone but Rod watched as I walked to an empty desk and sat down. Everyone but Rod watched as I opened my pencil case and took out a pencil and eraser. Was our love affair over before it had even started? Au revoir, secret-code texts.

At lunch Stacy and my so-called friends walked right by me as I put my books in my locker. I made my way to the cafeteria and took my place in line alone. Or rather, I took my place behind Trista Bottoms. That's what things had come to.

It wasn't like I had anything against Trista Bottoms. The universe was against her enough already. How could someone have the worst name on the planet *and* be at least two times as wide as the next biggest person in our class? I stared at her lunch tray. Steamed vegetables and brown rice filled her plate.

Trista caught my look and frowned. "What?" She cocked her head at me and uncrossed her arms. Her T-shirt read TRUTH OR CONSEQUENCES in all caps. "You never heard of a slow metabolism?"

Trista moved forward, sliding her tray along the metal track. A refrain rose up from behind us in line.

Boom, boom. Boom, boom, Bot-toms. Boom, boom. Boom, boom, Bot-toms! Trent Spinner and his friends' song sounded like a bass drum thumping in a marching band. Trista stopped. So did the refrain.

Trista's body tensed. She gripped her tray. She took two steps and paused.

Boom, boom—

She took six quick steps.

Boom, boom. Boom, boom, Bot-toms! rang out the chorus again. Stifled snickers followed.

Trista knew exactly what was happening. So did everyone within earshot. None of us said a word.

Her long, dark curls whipped around as she turned back. I don't know exactly what I expected, but it certainly wasn't what happened next. Mouth parted in surprise, cheeks aglow, Trista cast her brown eyes to the ceiling.

"Oh, my lord!" she shouted. It never occurred to me that a girl who didn't say much to anyone could have such a thundering voice.

Trista grabbed my shoulder. Her strength surprised me.

"Do you hear that?" she cried in awe, beaming.

My eyes grew wide. I couldn't find my voice.

"I said, do you hear that!" Trista extended her arms above her head and rocked her hips slowly. "My butt!" She cupped a hand to her ear and leaned toward her backside. "My butt is *singing*!"

Even though Trent and his *boom, boom* buddies had fallen silent, Trista closed her eyes and continued to sway, dancing to a groove only she could hear. Kids in line exchanged looks. A few giggled.

She stopped dead, pretending she'd just caught sight of Trent Spinner standing in line behind me. He smirked at his buddies. They nudged him as Trista stepped toward them. She spoke her next words slowly, jabbing her finger at Trent's chest as she enunciated each one.

"Does. Your. Butt. Sing?"

Trent opened his mouth to speak.

"Wait!" She held up her hand and made a show of looking around to investigate the back of his saggy jeans. Then she turned to the rest of us in mock bewilderment. "I forgot! He doesn't have one!"

A peal of laughter rang out at the head of the lunch line. It was Rod Zimball and his friend Peter. Trent glared at them. Even his buddies were fighting to hide their smiles.

"That's right," Trista said, lips pursed. "Be glad I can't find your butt." She leaned into Trent's face like a baseball umpire and yelled, "Because if I could, I'd *kick it*!"

The lunch line's Plexiglas sneeze guards were still rattling as she sauntered off. She turned back to me. My mouth hung open. I'd never felt quite as short as I did just then.

"You coming or what?" she asked.

"Me?" I said.

"Yeah, you!" she said. "Got any better options?"

Ripples of laughter rang out behind me. Did I really need any more convincing?

Trista and I walked to the far corner of the outdoor lunch patio, where she always ate alone. Stacy Pedalski and my usual lunch crew spread themselves out at their table in case we were even *thinking* of sitting with them.

Trista frowned at my lunch as she sat down. It was Pizza Boat Day. Teetering on a cardboard plate was a massive piece of French bread oozing grease and cheese. It was topped with pepperoni and paper American flag "sails" held up by toothpicks.

"I don't even want to think about your cholesterol levels," Trista said.

"I like nautical themes."

"And seasickness, I guess?" Trista said.

I shrugged and bit into the pizza boat's bow. Trista speared a piece of broccoli. Was there really such a thing as slow metabolism? It occurred to me that I'd been at school with Trista since sixth grade and never wondered anything about her. I knew *of* her—the same way everybody knew of her—but sitting across from her now, I had a hundred questions. Trista didn't look like she wanted to talk, though. She ate her lunch and looked out over the bluffs. Strangely, the loser section of the patio had the best view of Luna Vista's coast. The ocean looked calm that day, but whitecaps flared in the water. Seagulls flew overhead in the strong breeze.

"Uh-oh," Trista broke the silence. She caught sight of something behind me before putting down her fork and fixing her eyes on a splat of seagull poo.

I turned around. Marissa Pritchard and S.M.I.L.E. were gliding directly our way, Marissa's head tilted like Agford's. She waved overenthusiastically. Alissa and Clarissa pouted at us as if we were sad, abandoned puppies.

Whatever Agford had whispered to them had inspired a complete attitude makeover.

"Don't make eye contact," Trista chided. I stole a glance before turning away.

S.M.I.L.E. sat down not far from us. They began to unfold brightly colored heart-shaped cardboard boxes and spread themselves out over several tables, forming a sort of assembly line.

"Phew! Close call," Trista said. "Looks like assembling care packages is on the agenda." Trista cut up her carrots into perfectly proportioned pieces. "They got me last week," she explained. "Just sat down and started knitting sweaters for the troops. Someone forgot to tell them it's 105 degrees in Peshawar." She chuckled. Her chuckle was as loud as my loudest laugh.

I looked over at S.M.I.L.E., who, in between bites of their lunches, were marking off items on checklists as they packed their cardboard heart boxes. "Why would they . . . ?"

"Want to sit with me?" Trista finished.

"That came out wrong. I meant—"

"They're spies," Trista interrupted. She carefully folded her napkin and dabbed at her mouth. "For Dr. Awkward?" she said, answering my puzzled look. "C'mon. Without them scouting for dirt on everyone, she wouldn't even have a job.

You're one of the crazies now. You'll see."

"I'll see?"

"Even *I've* heard the rumors about you, Psycho Sophie," Trista said.

I knew that people couldn't stop talking about Agford and the cops hauling me out of class. And Stacy was always deciding *someone* wasn't allowed to eat lunch with us. But *Psycho Sophie*?

"So what *was* the deal with the cops at school yesterday anyway?" Trista asked. She might as well have posed her question directly into the school's loudspeaker.

"It's a long story," I whispered, hoping she'd take a volume cue.

"I've got time," she roared back.

Maybe it was the way Trista looked at me—or maybe it was the way her T-shirt threatened me with capital-letter consequences—but I knew Trista wasn't going to rest until she got a straight answer. Besides, the truth couldn't be worse than whatever rumors were flying. I took a deep breath and unloaded the story as fast as I could, like those guys rattling off disclaimers at the end of radio commercials.

"You thought she *murdered* someone?" Trista said when I'd finished.

A hush fell over the lunch crowd. A fork clattered to the patio. If all eyes hadn't already been on me, they were now. Trista finally lowered her voice to a stage whisper. "She's no murderer. But I meet with her every week, and trust me, she's the psycho one. Psy-cho!" She sang the last word as she swirled her index finger by her temple.

"Why do you keep meeting with her, then?"

"They worry about my self-esteem." She gestured to herself, laughing. "Boom Boom Bottoms?"

I chuckled uneasily.

Trista frowned. "What's so funny?"

"Uh, I—I guess—"

"Just kidding!" Trista burst into laughter. So did I then—for real. I could feel everyone looking at us doubled over, laughing too hard. But I didn't care. Not at all. As the seagulls squawked and scattered, I hoped Trista Bottoms liked me. It may have been the first time she invited me to lunch, but I didn't want it to be the last.

I spent all of science making up fake dreams for Agford to analyze at our first meeting as Trista had suggested. I couldn't focus on anything else. For one, Marissa's volcano project—an elaborate scale model of Mount Etna—was seriously distracting. At timed intervals it sent up plumes of smoke and spat red baking-soda lava in case we forgot to glance its way. Mine was overdue, but when the cops bring you in for making accusations, it's easy to forget to make papier-mâché.

The staircase to Agford's office felt endless. Luna Vista Middle School consisted mostly of separate one-story buildings linked by outdoor courtyards and hallways, but Agford's office was tucked away upstairs in the main administrative building. "To ensure student privacy," she'd explained at our orientation assembly. Because nothing says privacy like walking by the main reception desk and up stairs that lead pretty much nowhere but Agford's.

"Soph! Welcome." Dr. Agford's lips pulled back into her trademark dead-eyed smile as she wheeled around in her office chair. I don't know how my mom expected me to keep an open mind when the lady had a smile like that.

"Make yourself comfy." She gestured to a bright purple beanbag chair that matched the shade of her sweater. Nearby a low table displayed brochures such as *What's Happening to My Body?* and *Help! I Have Hair in New Places!*

"Here?" I said. My other option was the purple puffy sofa along the wall, but it was decorated with so many pillows that it couldn't possibly be for sitting.

"Perfect, sweetie. Now why don't we get started?"

I sank into the beanbag. When you're four foot six, the last thing you need is to sit in something that makes you feel two feet tall. I guess sitting in a purple beanbag was supposed to put kids at ease. We were probably meant to reach out and play with the gadgets and toys arrayed on her desk: stress balls, Rubik's Cubes, windup kangaroos, fuzzy dice. But who could reach them while lodged in a beanbag?

"Today we're going to work on perception. Do you know what *perception* means?"

It was funny how Agford thought seventh graders couldn't understand words of more than one syllable but thought we needed to know everything about sex. I considered reminding her that during last week's health seminar, she'd made us look at magnified pictures of genital crabs.

"Perception means seeing." I humored her.

Agford sucked at her front teeth and nodded slowly. "Very good," she said, fixing her gaze on me so unsettlingly that I had to look away for a second. "Did you know, Sophie, that preteens literally perceive differently than adults do?" She held up a picture of a woman who looked so scared, you would have thought she'd been cornered by an ax murderer. Or by Agford herself.

She didn't wait for my answer. "Kids look at this picture, and they see anger." The tone of her voice dropped from her usual falsetto, jarring me. "But this woman is afraid. See the fear in her eyes?"

I saw the fear. In fact, I felt it start to creep from my heels to the base of my neck.

"Your brain is at a tender age. Your frontal lobe, the locus of good judgment, is tiny and of no use against the powerful, primal urges coming from your amygdala."

I wasn't quite sure where my amygdala was, but I crossed my legs at the mention of it.

"Soph, I'm trying to understand how you *perceive*," she explained. "I'd like you to tell me about the other night. In detail." She clicked open her pen. "Why don't we start with what you heard, shall we?"

I hadn't seen this coming. Weren't we supposed to talk about my fake dreams?

"What I heard?" I said. The beanbag sighed as I shifted my weight. My sweaty legs stuck to its pleather surface. I wished I hadn't worn shorts.

"What you heard." Agford crossed her legs and dangled one red high heel from the tips of her toes. I could tell she was trying to look casual. Why did she care what I'd heard? I'd seen blood-spattered countertops and her silhouette bearing a meat cleaver. If she had been a guilty murderer pumping a potential star witness for details, she would have started with what I saw. So what was she up to?

"Um, I heard chopping sounds."

"*Mm-hmm . . .*" Agford's dangling shoe swayed back and forth, like she was trying to hypnotize me.

"Some thudding?" I offered. "A grunt, I think?" I felt as though any second a trap would snap shut, and I'd find myself in my beanbag cocoon hanging upside down from the ceiling in a net. "I heard you yell at the raccoons," I added uncertainly.

Agford flinched. "Yes," she admitted.

"And you were on the phone."

Agford's shoe fell to the carpet. Her chair creaked upright.

"On the phone?" Agford cleared her throat. "I don't remember that at all." She leaned down and jammed her shoe back on.

"You definitely were."

"You're so sure about that, Sophie. Interesting." Agford scribbled something on her pad. She shifted her weight in her chair and tugged at one of her oversized red hoop earrings. She cleared her throat again. "So. What did you hear me say?"

That's where she'd been going with all her business about teenage perception. She thought I'd heard something, and she wanted me to doubt it. Better yet, she wanted me to reveal what it was, so she could spin it her way. I suddenly felt as if I were sparring in tai chi class—and I was pretty sure I had the upper hand.

I shrugged. "Oh, nothing," I said. "The door slammed shut."

What was it General Sun Tzu said about all war being based on deception? *When we are near to the enemy, we must make him believe we are far away.* Grace made fun of my Chinese obsession, but ancient Chinese philosophers came in handy when you least expected them to.

"Nothing else?"

"Nope."

Agford studied me. "I see," she said.

I might have won the first round, but the battle had just begun. Convinced I couldn't have acted alone, she grilled me about why I wanted to spy on her in the first place. Weighing each of my words carefully—especially my pronouns—I navigated my way through her questions.

"So you guys entered through my side yard?"

"*I* entered through your side yard, yes." *If your enemy is superior in strength, evade him*, said Sun Tzu.

"Was it your idea to spy?" she asked.

"Yes. It was just me, remember?"

58

"So you woke up that day and thought it might be fun?"
Agford narrowed her eyes.

"It wasn't like that."

"Tell me how it was, then."

"I don't really remember," I said.

"Sophie, this was two days ago." Agford's voice tightened.

If your enemy is temperamental, irritate him, said Sun
Tzu. "Maybe it's because I'm always watching *Law and
Order* with my grandpa. I don't remember why I did it. I
didn't expect to see anything."

"But you *didn't* see anything, Sophie. You imagined a
very disturbing scene that never took place." Agford tapped
her notepad with her pen to emphasize each of her last three
words. She crossed her stockinged legs, leaned back, and
stared at me.

"So Grace wasn't involved?" she finally asked.

"Grace?" I asked.

"Your best friend. Your neighbor. The girl I see you with
just about every afternoon, Sophie." Agford slapped the pad
on the table and folded her arms. Or tried to. It just created
supersized cleavage.

It wasn't surprising how quickly Agford suspected Grace
had been involved, especially after last year's incident with

the misdelivered letter.

"I thought this was about how I perceive things," I said.

"Friends can be very destructive influences, Sophie. Especially when it comes to perceiving reality."

She had it wrong. Friends were *constructive* influences when it came to perceiving reality.

If I showed you a picture of Agford that day, her fake smile and empty eyes would leave you with no doubt about what she felt. It wasn't joy. It wasn't caring. This was the smile of a woman scared out of her mind.

And she would do anything not to be scared. That much was clear.

Chapter Five

Shadow of Doubt

"I knew it!" Grace said as she paced my room after dinner that night. "None of it makes any sense if she's not up to *something*."

The Yangs had asked my parents weeks earlier if Grace would be able to come over while they were at some doctor banquet an hour away in Los Angeles. Jake was outraged that my parents still let her. He was sixteen, so he was always outraged. Anyway, when Jake was grounded, apparently he was chained in a dank dungeon and served gruel or something like that. I think he underestimates what it's like to have a homework session supervised by Grandpa Young. Two hours of reading about the Industrial Revolution while cloaked in a fog of sulfur emissions and war stories, and he'd be begging for quality dungeon time, stat.

"Sounds like she has at least five FBI-recognized

markers of suspicious body language," Grace said. "The jittery foot, especially. I wish I'd been there to see. Did she blink a lot?"

I shrugged. "I try not to look at her eyes."

The floorboards under the carpet creaked as Grace kept pacing. I stared at her cowboy boots. If I wore those, I'd look like I was dressed up for Halloween.

"Okay, so we know she thinks I'm in on it. And she's worried about what we heard? What *you* heard. I was farther— Ah!" She'd crashed into the wind chimes hanging near my closet. They gonged wildly as she tried to untangle herself.

"Sorry. I'm balancing out my surplus of wood in that *gua*," I explained as I freed her.

"What?" Grace asked, rubbing her head.

"My reputation *gua*. It's seriously off. The metal balances out the wood?"

"I see," Grace said. She rolled her eyes.

"Are you mocking three thousand years of Chinese tradition?"

"No. Are you sure you're not, *Hidden Dragon*?" Grace patted my shoulder playfully.

Even I could admit I'd gotten a wee bit carried away with the traditional Chinese practice of feng shui. Okay, a *lot* carried away. What's not to like about the idea that you can arrange your space to bring good luck and cultivate positive chi, or energy? I'd first heard about feng shui from Grace's mom at a dinner after they had moved next door to us. Neither she nor Mr. Dr. Yang put much stock in it, but out of respect for Grace's more traditional grandmother, they'd made sure to move into a house with a favorable address number and street. Mrs. Dr. Yang added a few touches, like stationing small stone protective fu dogs at the front door and giving their pets names involving the word *luck*. I, on the other hand, not only lived at unlucky number eighty-four, but my parents stubbornly refused to put imperial lions at the front door. With those kind of odds against me, I had no choice but to undertake serious corrective feng shui measures.

I had met Grace at that same dinner at the beginning of sixth grade. She still claims she knew we would be best friends from the very start. But as I remember it, the entire night she looked like she'd rather be doing anything else. Brushing her hair, maybe. Feeding her goldfish. She posed precisely one question to me all evening: did I like the band Nux Vomica? I had never heard of them, but I'd gushed about how awesome they were and how I'd downloaded all of their albums. "They've only put out one," Grace had replied before examining her fingernails for the remainder of dinner.

I laugh about it now, but I still haven't forgotten it—especially when Grace rolls her eyes at me like she did about the wind chimes.

"We should trade families. You can be our resident chi consultant or something," Grace said. "Gramps and I can chat covert ops twenty-four/seven."

I definitely wouldn't have minded moving in with the Yangs for a month or so. To wake up to Monday Yang's laugh every morning, to talk about things that really matter, like if we all really see the same colors or if my idea of blue was someone else's green. Besides, I could seriously use the positive chi boost that would come with living at lucky-number 86 Via Fortuna alongside Lucky the cat and Chance the hamster.

"Bring a gas mask," I said. "And remember, Jake's part of the deal."

"Score. He's totally hot."

"You are disgusting, Grace Yang. Wash your mouth out with soap."

"He is! It's a fact."

For the record, unless there's a planet peopled with life-forms who lust after boys whose main talent is hocking loogies and letting them ooze out of their mouths before sucking them up again, there is no solar system in which my brother can be considered hot.

"Speaking of facts, let's get a few straight," I began. "So Agford hurls open the door, and she threatens to rip out the poor raccoons' throats."

"Right. And she's on the phone. That's what she's worried about." In the meantime Grace had stretched out on my bed and held a can of Diet Coke to her eye, as if the flimsy aluminum wind chimes could possibly have done enough damage to require a cold compress.

"Don't look at me like that," she added. "Your gow-whatever got me right in the eye. I don't want it to leave a mark. Agford might mistake me for a raccoon and tear out my throat."

"That's it!" I snapped my fingers.

Grace made a face. "What?"

"You're right about the phone. She's talking to someone, right? 'I'll rip their throats out,' she says. But to someone who can't see the raccoons, obviously. Maybe she wasn't talking about raccoons at all. Maybe she was talking about ripping *people's* throats out."

Grace put one hand around her throat as if to check if it was still intact. "So she wasn't pickling beets?"

"No, she *was* pickling beets," I replied. "The cops would have found something. Besides, it's just like Agford to spread holiday cheer by handing out jars of pickled vegetables."

I expected Grace to laugh, but she wasn't listening. "Ripping out people's throats?" she repeated. "I think you're right, Sophie." Grace ran her fingers through her long hair. She always played with her hair when she was thinking or feeling nervous. "Until you brought up the raccoons, I didn't remember," she said.

"Now you're the one not making sense," I said.

"I was so freaked out Agford was going to see you, I didn't even think about it. God, that voice! She said something like, 'If they find us, we'll take care of it.' If she's talking about people, then . . ."

"She's afraid of people finding her," I finished.

Grace nodded slowly. "Soph, our Agford case file might not be so crazy, after all."

Not long after Grace's run-in with Agford over the misdelivered mail, we had started a make-believe case file on Agford. It was the type of thing so embarrassing that—had Grace not eventually started preparing for a career with the FBI—we would have pretended never happened. When we Googled Agford and came up with no hits but the staff directory at Luna Vista Middle School—a place she'd worked

66

for only two years—we'd suspected her odd name was an anagram hiding her real identity. The only problem? Her name spelled nothing but "rad fog." Grace had trouble letting it all go, especially with all the other strange details about Agford. Maybe her name wasn't an anagram, but it did seem awfully weird—like someone had come along and lopped off a few letters from the front of it.

"Maybe not," I said.

Grace stood and looked out the window toward Agford's house. "I don't think you should go to Agford's alone tomorrow," Grace said. "Something's not right."

Her concern caught me off guard. I was used to her teasing me about my Buddha figurines or finding it amusing to launch water balloons at me during my meditative backyard tai chi sessions. Part of me was flattered. The other part wondered why I was so surprised.

"I'll be fine, Grace. If you go, there's no way our parents won't figure out we spied together," I reminded her. "Besides, don't you have Chinese school? Then lunch with Jocelyn and Natalie?"

Jocelyn and Natalie were Grace's friends from piano. Jocelyn went to Chinese school with Grace on Saturdays too. I hung out with them once. Never again. It was a sleepover that turned into an episode of *Makeover Miracle*, starring me. While Jocelyn plucked my eyebrows and piled all my hair into an updo to "add height," Grace and Natalie painted me with so much glittery eye shadow, I literally saw stars for weeks.

"I think this is a little more important than lunch, Sophie." Grace cupped her hands around her eyes and pressed her face against the window for a better view of Agford's. "At least take my cell with you. I'll borrow my dad's and—" She gasped and ducked below the windowsill. "Turn off the light!" she said. "Quick!"

I flipped the switch and joined her in a crouch. We peeked above the sill. Agford's house was dark except for the porch light, which cast illuminated rectangles across her perfect lawn.

"That car." Grace pointed. "It was there last night too." Parked one house down from Agford's was a big, dark-colored sedan. Agford always drove around in a late-model red Mustang convertible with the top up, probably to protect her precious hair helmet. The sedan definitely wasn't hers. Besides, two-car garages and roomy driveways made it rare to see cars parked overnight on Via Fortuna.

"The Stenwalls must have gotten a new car," I said.

"Andy Stenwall wouldn't be caught dead driving that beast."

"Maybe they have relatives visiting," I offered.

"Maybe."

A dark shape flickered in the driver's seat. Grace and I exchanged a look.

"Just a shadow, right?" I said. My voice cracked.

"I don't think so, Sophie. Someone is sitting in that car." Grace swallowed hard. "And I'm not sure we want to find out why."

Chapter Six

Wigging Out

Early the next morning, the house was quiet except for my grandfather's uneven snores drifting from his bedroom down the hall. My parents had gone into AmStar at the crack of dawn to keep the launch on schedule after losing a workday because of me—a fact they'd managed to mention each of the five times they'd reminded me about my Saturday yard work.

I pulled up the blinds in my room and stared across the street. The red clay tiles of Agford's roof seemed black in the dim light, and the long windows gazed back emptily at me, like Agford's eyes. It didn't matter that the dark sedan was no longer outside. Her front lawn felt menacing enough.

I rang Agford's bell at eight o'clock sharp. She opened the door so quickly that she must have been waiting and watching through the peephole. In one hand she brandished a sharp, shiny new pair of pruning shears. She held them out in front of her and pumped the handles together, grinning at the sound of their *snip, snip*. I flinched.

"Let's put you to work, shall we?" She stepped outside and shut the door, locking what seemed to be a hundred dead bolts, then led me past the half-demolished ant colony where I'd tripped over the hose. I tightened my grip around Grace's cell phone in my pocket and regretted telling her I'd be fine on my own.

I had to hide my surprise as Agford ushered me around back. Her front yard might have been flawless, but—in the light of day—her backyard was a disaster. If it hadn't been for the hedge at the back fence and, of course, the kitchen windows, I wouldn't have even recognized it. "Bit of a mess, huh?" Agford shook her head. She gestured at a tangle of brambles, pushed the pruning shears into my hands, and wished me luck.

I was supposed to remove endless climbing rosebushes that slunk their way throughout her garden and through a mess of ivy, doubling and tripling over to create forbidding dreadlocks of vegetation. In *To Kill a Mockingbird* Jem thought it was bad when Atticus made him read to old Mrs. Dubose after he ruined her flowers. I wonder how he would have liked doing forced labor for a possible fugitive.

Without gloves the work was bloody. But by then blood and this backyard were inseparable in my mind. As I worked, I imagined Agford watching me from her upstairs windows, delighting in each crimson scratch. When I looked up once, the curtains swung as though someone had just dashed away.

By ten o'clock I had cleared only about a quarter of the climbing roses, but I sat down in the shade for a break and braced myself for the two hours still ahead.

"How about something cold to drink?"

The voice made me jump. I turned to see Agford, her outstretched hand offering up bright red punch.

"A little leftover blood juice?" She laughed at her own joke, letting out a series of piggish snorts.

"Thanks," I said. What choice did I have? I took the drink. Sure enough, it smelled of beets. I pretended to take a sip, giving myself a bloody mustache instead.

Agford looked at the pile of rosebush brambles I'd gathered. "I wish you'd spied on me months ago, Sophie. Next week maybe you can help with the garage." There was the smile again, the lips that pulled back over her teeth like an animal bearing its fangs.

"I'm headed out for some errands," Agford continued. "If I'm not back before noon, just put the shears by the side

door. Watch your step, now. That hose can sneak up on you."
With that, she swiveled on her heels and headed inside,
where she again made an elaborate show of locking every
door and window before she left.

I went back to work and tried not to look at the house.
It seemed strange that Agford would leave me alone on my
first day. Suspicious, even. But, as curious as I was about
what Agford might be hiding behind those walls, I wasn't
about to risk a trap.

An hour later my T-shirt was damp with sweat. A blister
bubbled up on my thumb. I was debating slipping home to
get a Band-Aid when—suddenly—a piercing shriek rang out
across the street. By the time I had spun around to look, the
shriek had already given way to giggles. Through Agford's
side yard I could see Jocelyn, Natalie, and Grace spilling
out of a minivan, crouched over, they were laughing so
hard. Natalie wore a gauzy scarf just like Grace's. Grace was
tugging on it, trying to snatch back a picture from Natalie
and Jocelyn.

I gripped the pruning shears and hacked at the rosebushes. I knew I'd told Grace I'd be fine, but did she really
have to yuk it up with Jocelyn and Natalie right in front of
me? I mean, she hadn't even *looked* my way. The three of
them were probably headed to Grace's room to fawn over

Nux Vomica pictures or something. I ripped away a tangled rose vine. It whipped against my arm. I winced.

"Hi," said a voice behind me.

It was Grace. Though she looked carefree in her loose sundress and sandals, her eyebrows were knitted in concern.

"You scared me," I said, hoping Grace would think my flushed cheeks were from the heat. God, I was stupid. Of course Grace hadn't forgotten about me. I glanced toward the road. The minivan was gone. They'd just been dropping off Grace after Chinese school, before continuing their Jocelyn and Natalie gigglefest somewhere else. I guess they hadn't gone out to lunch after all.

"I saw Agford's convertible in town and figured the coast was clear," Grace said. "Everything okay?" She twisted one of her long French braids around her finger nervously. Each of her fingernails was painted a different fluorescent shade. I hadn't noticed them before. She'd probably painted them with Jocelyn and Natalie sometime, but I tried not to care.

"Yeah." I looked back at the house. The curtain in the upstairs window that had twitched earlier hung slightly open now. Or was that the glare? "You should go," I said. "If Agford comes back . . ."

"But this is the perfect opportunity!" Grace interrupted,

her eyes flashing. "When did she say she'd be back?"

"Oh, no. No way." I raised the shears, attacking the rose vines with a vicious snip. "After what happened last time?"

"This time we *know* she's trying to hide something, Sophie." She looked at me with pleading eyes. "Twenty minutes?"

"She locked up the house."

"We can peer in the windows, at least."

I turned to Agford's. The blue sky reflected in the windowpanes made the house seem friendlier than it had before—like maybe it wouldn't even mind if we slipped closer for a quick peek. I looked back at Grace. I was getting tired of reining her in all the time. It wasn't like I could get in much worse trouble than I already was.

"Ten minutes," I said.

"Fifteen."

"How about until we get caught and your parents disown you?"

"Deal." Grace shook my limp hand and smiled.

She crept toward the house, leading the way. Fearing she'd trip an alarm, I cringed as she tugged at the locked patio door and waved me forward to the kitchen windows. My stomach somersaulted as we pressed our faces up against the cold glass and peeked through the famous gap in the blinds. There was no terrifyingly sharp cleaver lying around. No blood spattered across the counter. Just a cereal box and a copy of *Us Weekly*. Grace complimented Agford's taste in reading before beckoning me toward the basement windows. We flattened ourselves on the ground to peer in, not sure exactly what we were hoping to find. Boxes lined the walls, and dust floated in the beams of light that stabbed their way through the dark. Not much else.

We stood up and brushed ourselves off. Grace froze. Her eyes went wide. I turned to look. I nearly screamed.

It was Agford. Right above us in the bathroom window. There was no mistaking her puffy cloud of hair. If she hadn't already seen us spying, she'd catch us both as soon as she turned around. So Agford knew her Sun Tzu, too. Had to go do some errands? Right. *When you are near, you must pretend you are far.* Nice one, Charlotte.

Grace hoisted herself up to the window. Panic seized me. I would have reached out to stop her if my short legs hadn't rooted themselves in place. I couldn't even cry out for fear Agford would hear us.

"Relax, Soph! It's not her," Grace said. "Look." She pointed.

To the right on a shelf stood Agford's helmet of hair. Or, more accurately, one of her helmets of hair. Perfectly coiffed, it flared out from its perch on a Styrofoam head.

"A wig!" I laughed.

"I guess we know what's up with that hairdo now," Grace said, giggling as she eased herself down from the sill.

"And why she never puts the top down on that convertible." I snickered.

"Ha! I know," Grace said. "Can you imagine—?" The color drained from Grace's face. "Oh my God, Sophie."

"What?"

"What woman buys a convertible when she wears a wig?"

I shrugged. "Maybe she bought the convertible before she bought the wig."

"You know what that means, don't you?" Grace gripped my arm. Her eyes were filled with fear. "It's a *disguise*, Sophie."

The back of my neck prickled. Women wear wigs all the time, I tried to tell myself. During cancer treatment. If they're old and losing hair. To achieve a certain look. Agford's wearing a wig wasn't *necessarily* a disguise. So why were my hands shaking?

Just then a dark blue sedan cruised slowly past Agford's house. Our heads turned to follow it.

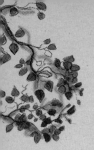

Chapter Seven

A Blue Streak

It felt like we saw the blue sedan everywhere over the next few days. A glint of blue slipped around a corner as I came out of my Monday afternoon tai chi class. In the Sav-a-Ton parking lot with my mom on Tuesday, a dark car two rows down sprang to life and jetted out to the main street. Grace was positive the same blue Crown Victoria had followed her and Jocelyn to Chinese school. Neither of us had gotten a good look at the driver yet, but Grace had gone over to the Stenwalls to drop off a coupon for her pet-sitting services and confirmed they didn't have any out-of-town guests.

Grace thought the driver had to be whoever Agford had been talking to that night. "They're keeping tabs on us," she said one afternoon. "Or maybe . . ." She hesitated before suggesting Agford might be planning something worse.

"She's a fugitive, Sophie. She thinks we know something."

"I don't know, Grace." I pictured Katz's office. My mom's red-rimmed eyes. The grim set of my father's jaw. It was easy enough for Grace to throw out wild scenarios.

"This is different than the beets, Sophie. Think about it." She put her hand on her hip. "The wig? Talking about people finding her? Grilling you about what you heard? Locking up her house like it's some secret vault?"

Dread knotted in the pit of my stomach. I realized Grace's theory wasn't that far-fetched. What else could those clues add up to?

On Thursday morning before French started, I was thumbing through my Feng Shui Planet mail-order catalog looking for something—anything—that might be able to ward off evil chi when Trent Spinner came up behind me.

"Bon-jour, Ay-nus!" he said in his cowboy French as he swept my books off my desk. Feng Shui Planet skidded across the floor and landed near Marissa's feet. "Ay-nus and Boom Boom Bottoms. Now doesn't that make the perfect team?" He fired off a machine-gun laugh. "Get it? Ay-nus? Bottoms?"

His friends Jae and Matt snickered dutifully, but only after Trent's clarification.

Trent turned to me with a fake pout. "Sorry I had to move your leee-vrays off your poop-eater, Ay-nus." He meant *livres* and *pupitre*, French for *books* and *desk*. I wished Trista took French. I would have liked to see what she had to say about Trent and his poop-eater.

As I bent down to pick up my books, someone crouched beside me. I looked up into hazel eyes peeking from behind bangs. "Forget him," Rod whispered as he grabbed my French book off the floor. My heart skipped a beat as his arm brushed mine. Had he been the one to speak up for me after all? He smelled like Tide. Tide could make millions with a male fragrance line. Or was it just the combination of Rod and Tide that was so perfect?

Madame Tarantula bopped into class, poodle curls bouncing, sparkly scarves a-flying. Insistent that we learn French organically, she refused to translate a word. Each class was an elaborate game of charades. I eyed my sad, torn Feng Shui Planet on the floor by Marissa's feet, wishing I had some better way to pass the time than call out guesses for Madame's wild gestures. "Airplane!" the class cried. "Happiness? No, interpretive dance!" we shouted out.

The bell rang, finally ending my torture. I gathered my books and headed for the door.

"I think you dropped this," a voice interrupted.

I looked up. It was Marissa Pritchard. I realized with horror that next period was lunch. She was going to invite me to sit with S.M.I.L.E., just like Trista had said. I braced myself.

Instead Marissa held up Feng Shui Planet in one hand. "Isn't this yours?" she asked. In her other hand she held out a piece of white paper. "And this, too. Whatever it is."

Spared a lunch of singing campfire songs to promote good cheer, I sighed and looked down at the black handwriting on the paper. I saw what she meant. None of the words made any sense. My heart beat faster. Rod had sent another code! "Thanks," I mumbled, shoving it into my pocket before Marissa could ask any questions.

I sneaked a look at the code as I headed to lunch. In neat and careful black capital letters, Rod had written:

GET SMART AND ANNOY THE ASKEW TREASURY. ASK FOR FREE HONEYMOON AT PAGODA. FOUR OR MORE ADDRESSES SHARE EMPTINESS OF IDEAS. ASIAN DRAGON, REST FROM YOUR QUESTS.

Three full lines—and an actual note! Nothing like the short, simple letter substitutions he usually texted. I blushed at his code-word choices. Pagoda? Asian Dragon? It's not like I ran around school declaring my love for all things Chinese. How'd he know? I ran my fingers along the half sheet of paper and imagined him huddled over his desk last night writing it. Getting a note like this almost—*almost*—made me forget everything else.

"Sophie!"

I jerked up. I'd nearly bulldozed my science teacher, Ms. Gant. In one hand she held a familiar poo-brown cone glued to a piece of cardboard and decorated with fiery orange streaks. I'd tried to make it look like a volcano. I really had. Maybe if my brown marker hadn't been so low on ink, it would have looked less pathetic. She lifted it toward me. "Is this yours?"

I considered making a break for it. Ms. Gant looked pretty spry for fortyish though.

"Did I forget to put my name on that?" I asked. "Sorry."

Ms. Gant searched my face, her blue eyes filled with such genuine concern that I had to look away. "I'm sorry too, Sophie," she said, handing me my volcano along with a project evaluation sheet. I folded it over so the bright red C minus couldn't stare up at me. Until then the only minuses I'd ever seen were attached to As.

I looked at the ground. It killed me to disappoint Ms. Gant. To let down patient, kind, wise Ms. Gant—the woman who managed to make PowerPoint presentations on the Earth's crust entertaining—seemed unforgiveable.

"I heard about your trouble." Ms. Gant frowned. "Are you sure everything's all right at home, Sophie?"

Even Ms. Gant knew? I had a vision of Mr. Katz standing at an emergency closed-door faculty meeting, pointing to a huge pretend-inspirational poster of tiny me next to an exploding volcano. DISASTER, read the caption.

My ears turned red as I nodded and managed to mumble that everything was fine. "I've just been distracted," I said. It was the truth.

At least Rod had sent me a code, I told myself as I shuffled to lunch carrying my pitiful volcano. At least I had that.

My heart soared when I saw Rod waiting for me. He was standing beyond the cashier, his tray heaped with curly fries. (Obviously a man of fine taste.) I swiped my lunch card at the register and waved. He didn't see me. He probably *couldn't* see me, behind that stupid volcano on my tray.

"Hey!" I rested my tray on the condiment bar next to him and held up the white paper. "I have pre-algebra next. Perfect for decoding, huh?" Our math teacher, Mr. Hawkins, had a lazy eye. We never knew where he was looking. It made the challenge of doing anything off task doubly risky—and therefore doubly fun.

Rod looked to see if I was talking to someone else. He turned back, confused. His eyes traveled over the volcano on my tray—the poo-brown ink, the scribbled orange flames. "Hey. Um, definitely," he said, shifting his weight. He glanced around the cafeteria as if looking for an escape route.

One minute he slips me a note and the next he acts like I'm Psycho Sophie? The sounds of the lunchroom swelled and closed around me. I was searching for something to say when Peter Murguia blew past me and clapped Rod on the shoulder. Rod gave an awkward wave as the two disappeared through the double doors to the lunch patio.

Forget codes. Boys were even harder to figure out.

My hand shook as I set down the note next to the flaming-turd volcano. I thought Rod didn't care what everyone else thought. He'd helped me with my books. He'd sent me a *code*.

"Oh, good! I hoped you'd eat lunch with us," a voice interrupted.

I turned to face a row of white teeth and blond bangs. Marissa Pritchard. Alissa and Larissa materialized at my side. They turned and waved to Jenn, who sat alone at a center patio table. This had to be the third straight week S.M.I.L.E. had put Jenn on table-claiming duty.

"That's okay. Trista will be—"

"Oh, Trista's so funny," said Clarissa, joining the group. "Isn't she sooo funny?"

"Trista's sooo funny," confirmed Marissa. "I love Trista. Where is she? She should eat with us, too."

The four of them steered me toward Jenn. I felt like a gale force wind was sweeping me away.

"Oh my goodness, what's that?" asked Jenn as I put down my tray. For a second I thought she meant my volcano, but she was pointing at my lunch. The cook in the cafeteria was all about themes, and today's offering was Dogs of the Sea. A hot dog stood on end, cut so it flared out into tripodlike "legs." Surrounded by a heap of curly fries, the hot dog was meant to resemble an octopus adrift in the ocean.

"I like nautical themes," I said, smiling to myself.

"Naughty what?" A wrinkle creased Alissa's brow. Or was that Larissa's?

"Interesting," Marissa said, looking at me intently. "In dream imagery the sea can represent anger."

I wondered if Agford gave S.M.I.L.E. weekly scripts to memorize. I pictured group hypnosis sessions in her office, the row of -issas sitting on the purple couch chanting lines about "emotional baggage" and "unresolved conflicts" while Jenn, crammed in the beanbag, struggled to mouth along. I shuddered. The scenario probably wasn't that far-fetched.

Clarissa nudged closer to me. "Marissa said you had a note. A *weird* note," she said. "Can I see it?"

I leaned away.

Alissa's eyebrows arched. "That's awfully defensive body language, Sophie," she said.

A throat cleared. S.M.I.L.E. and I looked up. Trista stood above us in a green T-shirt that read PROUD TO BE AWESOME.

"Trista!" Marissa said. "We were just talking about you and how *funny* you are."

Trista didn't look impressed.

"I love your shirt," said Larissa.

Jenn nodded. "Dr. Agford was just telling us how important it is to express confidence in ourselves, wasn't she?"

"And our bodies," Marissa added. "Confidence is important for women of *all* shapes and sizes. Why don't you sit with us, Trista? We have *plenty* of room." Marissa shoved Jenn over to create a space that easily would have accommodated three Tristas.

"I would love to, Marissa," Trista replied. "But you know, setting healthy boundaries is important for women of all shapes and sizes. So Sophie and I will be sitting waaaay over there today." Taking my arm, Trista pointed to the sun-bleached tables in the far corner of the patio. She plunked my volcano on their table as a centerpiece, then chuckled and nudged me as we shuttled off. "I *am* pretty funny, aren't I?"

I cast a glance at Trista's lunch tray when we sat down. Grilled chicken over a bed of lettuce. I was starting to think she had simply willed herself to take up more space in the world. "Thanks for the rescue," I said.

"Ah, *To lift an autumn hair is no sign of great strength,*" Trista said.

My mouth dropped. "What did you just say?"

"Nothing, I'm just quoting—"

"Sun Tzu. *The Art of War*! How do you know that?"

Trista shrugged as she unpacked a recyclable container she'd brought from home. She dumped a pile of carrots onto her plate and smiled. "When are you going to realize I know a little bit about everything, Sophie Young?"

I'd already begun to. That morning Trista had been bent over the cell phone she'd stolen from Trent Spinner, repro-gramming it to cc his mom on every text he sent. "I think she's going to be very impressed by his vocabulary, don't you?" she'd said, chortling as she detailed phases I–IV of her revenge plan.

I'd assumed Trista's skills were limited to technical stuff. Her mom was high up at AmStar. She was an actual rocket scientist, so it was no surprise that Trista's favorite hobby was taking stuff apart and putting it back together. Last year for the science fair, she'd actually built a hydraulic go-kart by herself, from scratch.

"And if there's one thing I know," she continued, pointing her fork at my poor Dog of the Sea struggling in tempestuous curly-fry waters, "it's that if you eat like that, you'll die before you're thirty!" Her shout made kids stare. I didn't even mind this time.

"That sounds pretty good around now." I sighed and shoved a fistful of fries into my mouth. "It'll shorten the misery."

"Oh, c'mon. So S.M.I.L.E. watches you for Agford. Big deal."

I wondered whether Trista would feel the same way if she had the full picture. S.M.I.L.E. could pass along plenty of useful information about me to Agford, even if they thought they were just doing recon for therapy sessions.

"Yeah, you're right," I lied. "Just a bad day." I pulled out the white paper. "Rod sent me another code. Great, right?

Then he totally snubs me in the lunch line."

Trista picked up the code. "A null cipher?" She whistled. "*I've* never even made a null cipher." She tapped her finger down the letters on the first line and counted to herself.

It was as though she hadn't even heard me. I shouldn't have been surprised. The other day I'd wondered aloud if Rod liked me back, and she'd shot me a strange look. "Why don't you just ask him?" she'd said. A second later she was explaining how the game designers of Covenant totally ripped off H. G. Wells's *The War of the Worlds*.

Trista continued, pointing at the paper. "See, only certain letters matter in a null cipher. Every second letter, every third, that kind of thing. Without software, a code like this would have taken hours."

He might've spent *hours* on the code? Hours leaning over his desk, carefully penning those Asian references in neat all caps . . . only to blow me off the next day? Grace claimed guys weren't complicated. What did she know?

Trista pulled a mechanical pencil from her back pocket. "You want me to decode it?"

"That's all right," I said. I slid back the paper and tucked it into my hoodie pocket.

"It's for the best." Trista jerked her head toward S.M.I.L.E. They'd since cleared away the poo-cano centerpiece and were huddled deep in conversation, shooting occasional looks our way. "The last thing you need is Agford knowing you're running around with spy codes."

I felt queasy as I looked down at my fries. I thought of the blue car.

"Speaking of Agford . . . ," I said.

"Yeah?"

I hesitated. "Did you know she wears a wig?"

"Hah!" Trista laughed and waved away a seagull lurking in hope of snagging some of my fries. "I *knew* something was up with that hair."

Encouraged, I continued. "It's kind of weird she drives a convertible then, isn't it? I mean, the wind . . ."

"Not really," Trista said, cubing her chicken breast into tiny pieces. "A lot can change after you buy a car. Alopecia, say." She answered my puzzled look. "Hair-loss disease some people get? Like the nice bald dude with no eyebrows who works at the gas station?"

I trailed my curly fries in ketchup as I tried to wrap my mind around Trista's logic.

"She's not going to buy a new car just because it's better for wig wearing. But . . . ," Trista continued, "it *is* strange her Mustang's such a recent model. It can't be more than two years old. The retro styling, the xenon headlights, the

90

cold-air induction system to reduce drag."

Leave it to Trista to miss the point and fixate on the specs of Agford's car. Sometimes I wondered if she spent her nights memorizing technical dictionaries.

"Wait . . ." I finally realized what she was saying. "Agford moved here two years ago. Since then she's had precisely no hair-helmet changes, so that means she's worn the wig the whole time."

Trista sucked on her fruit smoothie and nodded. "Exactly. The wig can't be less than two years old. And, unless she's a crazy woman who slaps down Gs for a new convertible when she wears a wig, she probably only started wearing a wig *just* after she bought the car. At least, based on those Mustang specs. It's not certain, though."

"Grace and I think it could be part of some disguise," I whispered.

Trista raised her eyebrows. I pushed further and told her about the phone call and the way Agford tried to discover what I'd heard. "We think she might be on the run from something," I said, sounding as breathless as Grace would. "There's this car . . ." I hesitated, realizing how crazy I sounded. "Someone's following us."

Trista looked at the horizon and slowly shook her head. The lunch crowd was thinning. It was quiet enough that I could hear the waves hitting the shore below the bluffs.

"Sophie, a few days ago you thought a woman cutting vegetables was a murderer."

"I know, but—"

"Now she's a fugitive because she wears a wig?"

My Dog of the Sea looked even sillier now as it teetered over my ketchup-soaked fries. I scrambled to explain. "She was talking about ripping out people's throats if they find her—what else would—"

"Is that what *you* think, or is that what your friend Grace thinks?"

My cheeks felt hot. Is that how Trista saw it? I just went along with Grace no matter what? I never should have told her that it hadn't been my idea to spy on Agford in the first place.

"Of course it's what I think," I said, my voice rising. I didn't sound at all convincing. "What are you implying?"

"I'm not implying anything. I asked a question." Trista pursed her lips. "A disguise is *one* explanation. Not the only one. It's strange you both jumped to the exact same conclusion."

"I don't think it's strange," I said. It was easy enough for Trista to shoot everything down. She hadn't seen how Agford had acted in the first therapy session. "I mean, we *are* being followed," I pointed out.

Trista folded her arms. "Why would Agford need to follow you? She's around you all the time."

"Maybe it's whoever was on the phone that night. They—" I hesitated. "They could be planning to do something." It had sounded more believable when Grace had said it.

"Something?" Trista made a face. "Are you saying Agford's going to have you killed because you overheard a phone conversation?"

"No—I don't know. But I'm not making it up."

"I didn't say you were. But I could go out to the parking lot right now and a quarter of those cars are going to be some shade of blue. That doesn't mean they're following you. There's always more than one explanation for something, Sophie. You know that."

I grew quiet. Trista sounded so reasonable. "Better safe than sorry," I mumbled.

But as Trista placed her silverware neatly across her plate and snapped her plastic container shut, I knew she was right.

Chapter Eight

Stranger Danger

It would have been hard to miss Grace waiting outside school for me that afternoon. She stood astride her vintage ten-speed, dressed entirely in black: black pants, black sweater set, black sunglasses—even a black chiffon head scarf that made her look like a fifties movie star. Her watches rattled on her wrist as she waved. Kids on the way to the bus shot looks toward her. I found myself hoping that Trista didn't see us. What would she think of Grace's getup?

"Going undercover?" I joked. Grace's scarf ruffled in the breeze.

"It's best to be stealthy these days," Grace said, looking behind her. She was dead serious. "But I had to celebrate my freedom. Miss Anita went home sick. If she hadn't made me work all day when *I* was sick last month, maybe I'd feel bad." She shrugged. "Want to go to the Seashell for some fries?"

"I don't want to die before I'm thirty," I said.

"Okay," Grace said uncertainly.

"Inside joke."

"With yourself?" Grace asked. "Maybe they're right about that Psycho Sophie business." Before I even had time to glare, she grinned and bumped her shoulder against mine. "Home it is."

"I've got study hall with Grandpa." I sighed.

"Oh." Grace cringed. "Right." She pushed her bike ahead quietly. "Maybe get him talking about interrogation techniques?" she offered. "I hear you can actually hypnotize a confession out of someone."

As we made our way up the hill toward town, the sun cast a glow across the hills of brush beyond Luna Vista's neat yards and red-tile-roofed houses. It was definitely fall now—Southern California fall, at least. The sky was bright blue, and the smell of manure rose up from freshly seeded lawns, attracting crows looking for easy food. The first Halloween pumpkins and decorations were starting to pop up. I was surprised Agford's house wasn't fully mummified in fake cobwebs yet. She'd gone so overboard for Flag Day, we were positive she'd hauled out a Ouija board and conjured up Betsy Ross to consult on the project.

Grace glanced around as she walked. "I can't stand it anymore," she whispered. "I think the blue car might have followed me here."

"You don't say. Even with your undercover outfit and everything?"

Grace stopped. "This is serious, Sophie," she said. "I can't believe *I'm* the one reminding *you*."

I shielded my eyes from the sun and looked back at the cars parked along the road. At least three or four of them were blue. I thought of Trista.

"Maybe we're imagining that car," I said.

"What do you mean?" Grace looked genuinely puzzled.

I kicked at a crack in the sidewalk. "Blue's a common car color. Maybe we're wrong."

"I don't think so," Grace said before I even finished my sentence.

The breeze had kicked up now that the sun was low. I shivered a little. "Trista pointed out that there's really no reason Agford needs to follow us."

Grace stopped short. "Trista?" she said.

"She has a good point. I mean, I'm around Agford all day. We live across the street, for crying out loud. Why would she have us followed?"

"You told Trista?"

"I thought maybe—"

Grace's voice flew up a register. "The girl you met, like, last week? The one who can't *whisper*?"

Grace gripped her handlebars so tightly, it seemed like she was trying to keep herself from throttling me. Was it really that catastrophic if Trista knew?

I stumbled to recover. "She thinks we're imagining things, anyway," I said.

"Do you realize how dangerous it could be if Agford finds out we're still investigating? Especially for you!" Grace fumed. "How'd you feel if I blabbed to Natalie and Joss?"

"Joss?" I wrinkled my nose. "Do you mean Jocelyn?"

Grace set her jaw and pushed her bike ahead. When Grace was mad, she simply pretended I didn't exist. It hurt more than I wanted to admit.

"I thought we should get another opinion, Grace. You know, after last time. You—we—maybe get a little carried away sometimes."

Grace balanced her bike against herself as she wound her hair into a messy bun.

"She thought we were making the same mistake twice," I continued.

"We get carried away," Grace repeated. She pinched her lips together.

"Yeah," I said, mistaking Grace's echo for agreement. "And she's not wrong, is she? We do get a little crazy."

"Yeah," Grace said gently. I relaxed, thinking she finally understood. "That's something that happens sometimes"— she leaned toward me and raised her voice—"when you're being followed by someone who wants to *kill* you!" Her bun shook loose.

I stepped back.

"But I guess Trista's the expert," Grace continued. "And I'm just crazy." She rolled her eyes and flung up one hand. It took me a moment to place her unfamiliar expression.

"Oh," I said. "I get it."

"What?" Grace asked, but it didn't sound like a question.

"You *are* crazy, Grace Yang." I nodded. "Crazy *jealous*."

Grace laughed too loud and too hard, like a little kid pretending to bust up at a joke she didn't understand. "Uh-huh. Right. I'm dying of jealousy." Her cheeks glowed the faintest shade of red. "You know why I'm jealous? I wish I were as smart as you. It was an amazing idea to spill everything to a girl whose only friend may very well *be* the school counselor."

Even Grace seemed surprised by her harshness. She looked away.

"I see," I said.

"You said yourself that Trista doesn't have any other friends!" Grace said. "She has therapy with Agford all the time. You don't think it's strange she happens to tell you to back off?"

"She didn't say that," I protested.

"Sure sounds like it," Grace said, folding her arms across her chest.

How could I make her understand that, with Trista, what you saw was what you got? We strode uphill in silence, both turning to look each time a car passed. I guess Grace had a point. I was flattering myself thinking she was jealous. She was scared. Just like me.

Grace finally stopped and waited for me to catch up. She sighed. "It's all right. I guess I'm just—"

Before she could finish her sentence, an engine leaped to life behind us. Grace jumped and grabbed my arm as we both spun around. A car pulled out from a parallel parking spot. I gasped.

It was a midnight blue four-door sedan.

Hunched over the wheel was a woman wearing dark sunglasses. The instant we saw her, she mouthed a curse, threw one arm up over her face, and slammed the gas. Her car hiccupped forward before she screeched into a U-turn and roared off.

Grace and I stared at each other.

"This is real," Grace said, as if she hadn't yet believed it herself.

Chapter Nine

Cracking the Code

"Quick!" Grace helped me onto her handlebars. I nearly lost my balance as we lurched forward and veered sharply down a side street. Grace grabbed onto my hood to steady me. "Countersurveillance escape route," she explained. "She might try to follow."

"Who *was* that?" I held on tight as Grace pedaled madly down Luna Vista's back streets toward home, weaving to avoid trash cans and speed bumps. Palm trees and hedges blurred by. My hair flew against my face. I pictured the blue car swerving into its U-turn. The squeal of tires. I prayed there was some way Trista could still be right. But it was one thing to see a lot of blue cars. It was another to see one rocket away the moment you spot it.

"I don't know." Grace panted. "But we've got to ID her, stat. You catch anything on that license plate?"

"Nope."

Grace zigzagged left into an alley shortcut, slowing as we neared Via Fortuna. We both scanned for cars. Once we thought we were in the clear, Grace helped me down. She pushed her bike ahead, my short shadow bobbing next to hers as I tried to keep pace with her smooth strides.

"She's around Agford's age, isn't she?" Grace asked. Her voice quavered. It unnerved me that she didn't bother to point out she'd been right.

I pictured the driver's hunched shoulders and messy light brown hair. "If Agford weren't made of plastic," I said. "There's no way it's her."

"You're right," Grace said. "Agford can't be at school with you *and* tailing me around town. It's got to be whoever she was on the phone with that night."

"But she was talking to a guy," I said. "'I'll rip their throats out, *Danny*,' she said. I'm sure," I said. But I wasn't sure at all.

"We might not have heard her right." Grace checked behind us again. "Besides, women can be named Danny. Like Danielle?" She wound her scarf around her neck. "On the other hand, I find it seriously hard to believe those two women could *ever* be friends."

I frowned. "What do you mean?"

"Nothing—just—they seem like totally different types, don't they?"

"I guess." I kicked a twig. "So people can only be friends if they dress alike?"

"Oh, c'mon, Sophie. You're always so sensitive. That's not what I meant, and you know it."

It sounded like that was exactly what she'd meant, but we had other things to worry about. Besides, it was stupid to think Grace considered Jocelyn and Natalie better friends just because they could trade jeans. At least, I was pretty sure it was stupid.

We flinched at the sound of a car idling behind us, but when we whipped around to look, the road was empty except for a white pickup truck slowing to park. Shouts rose up from the soccer field two streets over. I imagined skipping over there and asking if anyone would like to trade places. I'd offer to play goalie. They could be hunted down by a maniac in a blue Crown Victoria.

"Whoever it is, she knows we saw her. Maybe she'll lie low?" I said.

Grace hadn't heard me. "I bet we could take her," she said. "You could do some of your tai chi business. I could sneak up with a choke hold. My dad told me if you cut off circulation to the carotid artery, you can make someone pass out. Maybe even kill them."

I looked at Grace like she was crazy.

"Shouldn't we get her before she stages some freak accident to get rid of us?" she asked.

"Hi there!" a voice interrupted. My heart jumped before
I looked up and saw Mrs. Dr. Yang standing near her black
Lexus, waving. She wore a neatly tailored gray suit. Some
doctors wore scrubs under their white surgical coats. Mrs.
Dr. Yang wore Prada.

She peered into her mailbox as we approached. If I
hadn't known Mrs. Dr. Yang's thin eyebrows had been salon
tattooed on in an expression of permanent surprise, I would
have thought she was delighted with what she'd found there.
But she wrinkled her nose at the familiar red booklet. "Buy
one measly set of fu dogs and get junk mail for life!" she
said. Then she paused and glanced sideways at me, a teasing twinkle in her eye. "Sophie," she said, "maybe you could
use this?"

"Oh, Mom, please don't," Grace joked. "I'm still recovering from a wind-chime attack."

"I have an excess of wood." I grinned sheepishly as I
pulled out my own crumpled copy of Feng Shui Planet from
my backpack. "Metal is the best cure."

Grace and her mom couldn't keep from laughing. For

a moment it felt like any other afternoon. Maybe Mrs. Dr. Yang would invite me in for dumplings she claimed to make from scratch, but which, in fact, she bought in bulk from the frozen section at Costco. Afterward Grace and I would probably get bored and dress up their cat, Lucky, in a jaunty cape (he was patient that way), then I'd come back home to finish off my pre-algebra. No one was tailing us around town in blue cars, waiting to spring.

"Hang on," said Mrs. Dr. Yang. "Did you say metal?" She traded a knowing look with Grace. They both turned to me and smiled. "Why don't you come up a minute?" Mrs. Dr. Yang put her hand on my shoulder. "This just might be your lucky day."

I looked back toward my house. It was already so far from my luckiest day that being late to study hall with Grandpa was the least of my worries. Besides, Grace and I had to figure out a plan.

I skipped up the steps and bent over to change from my Pumas into the red silk embroidered slippers the Yangs kept for guests in the entry hall. When I stood up again, I found myself staring into the fierce glass eyes of a bright red elephant the size of a toddler.

"A patient gave this to us." Mrs. Dr. Yang handed it to me. It felt surprisingly light. "I think you'll agree it's a little . . ." She made a face as she gestured to her own simple, elegant decor.

"Much?" Grace finished.

"Red for fire." I smiled. "And hollow." The elephant emitted a happy little gong as I tapped his metal sides. I looked up at Mrs. Dr. Yang. "He's *perfect*."

"You realize you're destroying your chi, don't you?" I tripped over a stray flip-flop as I searched for a place to set the elephant down in Grace's room. Stacks of *People*, *Seventeen*, and *Teen Vogue* threatened to collapse. Clothes were strewn across her unmade bed. Apart from the sliding-glass door leading to her outside patio, every surface was plastered with posters—handbills for concerts she'd never gone to, pictures of bands I'd never heard of, and FBI wanted posters she'd stolen from the post office. A life-size cardboard cut-out of the shirtless lead singer of Nux Vomica sneered down over a collection of neglected stuffed animals.

Hidden behind Grace's door were a small whiteboard and shooting-range target practice sheet. A stash of spy gear spilled from a half-open dresser drawer.

"I think once crazy people are following us around town, we can pretty much assume both of our chis are toast." Grace swung open her closet door, kicking away shoes so she could stand in front of the satellite map mounted on her bulletin board. "Let's see, approximate Gamma sighting was fifteen hundred twenty today." She shifted some news clippings and Post-its, then stuck a blue pushpin into the map near school. "Then we've got Tuesday, oh seven hundred, near Epsilon. What else?"

"Don't forget Saturday at Agford's."

"Got that one already. Eleven hundred, in front of Omega." Grace traced her fingers over a sea of other blue pushpins and mumbled to herself. "No pattern whatsoever," she announced. She flopped on the bed. "I got nothing, Sophie."

"Seriously?" I wasn't sure whether to relax or panic. Now that we were tucked safely back in Grace's room, it did seem possible we were making too much of things. The driver had a weary look that wasn't too different from some of the harried moms who waited in the carpool line every day. And the way Grace stood in her command central muttering over the map made it feel like we were still playing spy games. Trista's question echoed in my head. Did *I* think we were being followed—or was it just Grace?

"Hey, it's not like I'm actual FBI here!" Grace propped herself up on her elbow. "Listen, I'll read up on counter-surveillance while you're at study hall. Let's radio tonight and— What is that?" Grace pointed to the white paper hanging out of my hoodie pocket.

"Oh, nothing." I pulled out Rod's code and felt a pang as I pictured myself waving it at him like an idiot. It was nothing. But only a few hours ago it had felt like everything.

Grace snatched the paper from me and squinted at it. Her face lit up. "From Rod? I can't believe you didn't tell me!"

I reached for the code, but she had already leaped to her desk to find a pen.

"He totally likes you, Soph. I mean, texting is one thing, but a note?" Grace clapped her hands together. "It's so romantic."

When she finally stopped gushing long enough for me to tell her about Rod's snub at lunch, Grace dismissed me with a wave. "He's just shy," she said. "If he was embarrassed to be seen with you, he wouldn't have helped you with your French books in the first place!" Grace ripped off a long, thin strip from the bottom of the note and handed it to me along with a fine-point silver Sharpie. "C'mon, I'll prove it to you."

I couldn't help but smile. I guessed a little distraction would be okay. I leaned over and looked at the code again, trying to count out a letter pattern as Trista had explained:

GET SMART AND ANNOY THE ASKEW TREASURY. ASK FOR FREE HONEYMOON AT PAGODA. FOUR OR MORE ADDRESSES SHARE EMPTINESS OF IDEAS. ASIAN DRAGON, REST FROM YOUR QUESTS.

"Oh my God. A pagoda honeymoon. I love it," Grace said. "This is a tough one though."

"Trista said that—" I caught myself.

"Yeah?" Grace said encouragingly. "Listen, I'm sorry about what I said earlier." She tugged a strand of hair over her mouth. "If you trust Trista, so do I."

I was surprised. Grace usually only apologized for things that had happened a minute earlier. It wasn't as if she acted like she was always right or anything like that. It was more like she'd just move on and forget.

"Well, she said . . ." I looked back to Grace. "Thanks. And if you want to tell Natalie and Jocelyn . . ."

"Are you insane? We can't trust those two!" She threw up her hands. We both laughed.

"Anyway, she said it's a null cipher," I said. "Only certain letters really mean anything. Like the first letter of every word, the third letter of every word. That kind of thing."

Grace's cat, Lucky, jumped up on her desktop to lend us his sharp intellect.

"Okay, I'll read you the first letters of each word," she said. "G-S-A-A-T-A," she began.

"G-S-A-A-T-A?" I read back.

"Yeah, you're right. That's not it," Grace said. She ran her finger across the paper. Lucky yawned and rolled on his back on top of an open notebook, his code-breaking career over before it had even started.

I leaned over her shoulder. "The second letter of every word doesn't work. Neither does the third. Maybe Trista's wrong." I smiled at the thought of Rod coming up with something even more clever.

"S-T-A . . . every fourth letter looks good." Grace called out the rest of the letters as I hurriedly scrawled them in a column on the sliver of paper she'd torn off. When I was finished, Grace held up the tiny scrap and squinted. Her hand flew to her mouth, the fluorescent colors of her fingernails clashing with the horror on her face.

My stomach fluttered. What could Rod have said that was so awful? I read it for myself:

STA
YAWA
YFRO
MAGF
ORD

SHEIS

DANGER

OUS

"Stay away from Agford. She is dangerous," I whispered. My mouth ran dry.

A shadow flickered behind me. I flinched. Grace shrieked, and we both flung ourselves on the floor alongside Grace's bed. An avalanche of magazines cascaded over us.

Lucky gazed at us from his perch on the bed, wide-eyed. One last *Teen Vogue* slid down and flopped across my face.

"Grace?" I said, my voice muffled.

"Yeah?"

"I don't think Rod sent that code."

Chapter Ten

Awkward Encounter

"That's it," I said, pulling myself up from the magazine rubble. "We're telling our parents."

"After the beets? You'll be in twenty-four/seven Agford care," Grace said. "And Monday and Janice will kill me. Doesn't that defeat the purpose?" She slid a metal box from under her bed. As she hinged it open, multiple levels of trays holding various sizes of tweezers, bottles, swabs, and fingerprint dusters unfolded. She plucked out a quart-sized plastic bag, carefully grasped the code between the tweezers, and dropped it in. "Evidence," she said, swinging open her closet door so her whiteboard faced the room. "So you said Trent dumped your books off your desk, Rod helped you pick them up, and at the end of class Marissa handed you this code. Three possible messengers." Her marker squeaked as she listed their names in bullet points.

"Unless someone slipped it to me earlier." I shuddered. How could Agford or "Danny"—if that was who was following us—have gotten close enough?

"True," said Grace.

"Well, it's obviously not Rod. If he knew something about Agford, he'd just tell me . . . I think." I couldn't believe that two minutes earlier I'd actually thought Rod had sent me a love note. I remembered his face at lunch, the way he turned around to see who I was waving the paper at. So he *hadn't* thought I was a freak. At least, not then.

"Okay, not Rod," Grace said, but she still put a question mark by his name.

"We can rule out Trent, too," I continued. "His idea of a funny joke would be to make armpit fart noises in French and blame them on me."

Grace agreed. "Marissa," she said. "It's Marissa, then."

"Marissa," I said, picturing her überstraight teeth and bangs. "And if it's Marissa, it's S.M.I.L.E., and if it's S.M.I.L.E., that means . . ."

"Agford," Grace and I said in unison.

Lucky looked up in alarm.

It had to be Agford. Grace and I went over it one more time before I headed back home. A sincere warning wouldn't be in code. If someone's pants are on fire, you don't hand them a null cipher and hope they decode it before they combust. The tailing us around all over town, the code—they had to go together. The blue sedan had driven by the Saturday we'd peered in Agford's windows. Whoever was inside must have seen us snooping. Now they were trying to scare us off.

It was working.

My new red elephant tucked under one arm, I opened our front door as quietly as I could, foolishly hoping I'd be able to slip myself and my cargo past the kitchen and into my room before Grandpa noticed I was late.

"You are sooo busted," Jake greeted me. He smelled like he'd been living under a pile of sweaty socks for the past month, which probably wasn't far from the truth.

"Is that you, Sophie?" my mom called out.

Jake bowed dramatically and invited me forward. I felt like delivering a swift tai chi heel kick to his knees.

"You're home early," I said as I entered the kitchen, still cradling the Yangs' metal red elephant. Grandpa Young sat at the table hunched over his crossword. Behind him stood my mom, arms crossed. She still wore her AmStar security badge around her neck.

"You're not," she shot back. Grandpa made an exaggerated show of looking at his watch as if he'd only just realized how late I was. "Sophie, I really don't know what's gotten into you," my mom said with a sigh. Her eyes looked tired. "Ms. Gant called today. Sounds like your Mount Vesuvius left something to be desired?"

I considered suggesting that Ms. Gant had misunderstood my symbolic interpretation of a *post*-eruption Vesuvius, its minimalist style representing Pompeii's devastation. I nodded instead.

"With everything that's going on at work right now, the last thing we need is . . ."

The basement door creaked open. "What an interesting tour, Wade," rang out a familiar falsetto that sent up the hair on the back of my neck. "I didn't realize you were a Led Zeppelin fan. Can you play all those guitars? Or are some for decoration?"

The elephant slipped from my grasp and sounded its hollow gong as it hit the terra-cotta tile and somersaulted to rest directly in front of Dr. Charlotte Agford's feet.

"Oh my," she said. She turned to my mom. "Does this have something to do with her interest in kung fu?"

"I think you mean fung shoo," my dad said.

"Foong *schwaaay*," my grandpa, mom, and I corrected all at once.

My dad picked up the elephant and peered at it oddly before he placed it on the table next to a centerpiece I hadn't seen before. "Dr. A was just stopping by to bring us a little something for Halloween." He pointed to the bowl of baby pumpkins huddled together atop a bed of straw and candy corn. Mini felt black cats peered out between them, eyes wide.

"Boo!" Agford wiggled her fingers and snorted.

My parents forced a chuckle. A chill ran through me. If there was one thing I was sure of, it was that Dr. Agford didn't just stop by to bring us a little something for Halloween. I looked back at the festival of pumpkins and cats. It looked so harmless. As harmless as Agford must have seemed to my parents. The tacky neighbor bringing hideous but thoughtful handmade gifts.

"We're always so impressed with your decorations, Charlotte," my mom said with fake enthusiasm. "Those cobwebs look spooky!"

"What can I say? I like to spruce up the place." Agford looked down in false modesty. She wore her "casual" post-school wardrobe: dark blue ironed mom jeans with a single stiff crease running down the center of each leg, accompanied by an orange, brown, and yellow knit sweater that (I think) was supposed to suggest fall leaves but instead screamed cat puke.

"Be careful up there on that ladder, though," my dad said. He turned to me. "Sophie, make sure you give Dr. A some help when you go over this Saturday."

Dr. Agford's expression darkened. I could feel her gathering herself for something, and I didn't like it. She drew in a long breath. "I've been meaning to talk with you about that, Wade," she said.

Grandpa put down his crossword and eyed her warily.

"I was wondering"—she pursed her lips—"if maybe Sophie's punishment was a bit . . . excessive?"

I stiffened. In my mind I saw the block letters of our decoded message. *STAY AWAY.* Of course. Five more Saturday work shifts meant five more Saturdays lurking near Agford's house. Five more Saturdays I could snoop around and find something she didn't want me to find.

"After all, for our therapy work together to be successful, Soph should have positive associations with me. Right, hon?" She stepped forward and reached out a hand. There it was. The shoulder touch. Her fingers felt like ice, even through my sweatshirt.

My parents traded a look. "I appreciate that, Charlotte," my mom said in a tone that suggested the opposite. "However, we think it's important Sophie learn how to make a proper apology."

Agford smiled at her as though my mom were a child who'd just said something adorable. I stared at my red elephant, his trunk raised as if giving a battle cry, and I prepared for her next move.

"Well, I don't know—" she began.

"My mom's right," I interrupted. It took everything I had to force out the words. "Don't worry, Dr. A." I smiled up at her as sweetly as I could bear. "It won't affect the way I feel about you."

Grandpa Young nodded slightly. "There's a brave soldier," he said. My parents looked at me strangely.

"I'm certainly relieved to hear that, Sophie," Dr. Agford said, her acrylic nails sinking in as she gave my shoulder a supposedly friendly squeeze. I felt like I was suffocating in *eau de Lysol* fumes. She turned to my parents, tilting her head in her practiced pose of compassion. "I guess I was thinking, too, of how much you both have had to work lately. With the launch and all, I couldn't help but wonder if that time might be better spent as a *family*."

My parents fell silent. My mother cleared away an empty mug from the counter. My dad plucked an imaginary piece of lint from his shirt. "That's very observant of you, Charlotte." His jaw tensed. "In fact, we came home early today for that very reason."

"That's right," my mother said tightly, turning back from the sink.

"Forgive me." Agford laid one palm above her boob shelf. "Please, let's forget I ever said a word! Five weeks will go by in no time."

My father held up a halting hand. "You have a point. We're under a lot of stress right now. My father's been keeping an eye on Sophie in the afternoons, but as we discussed . . ."

"The C minus . . ." Dr. Agford nodded.

"Did we really say five weeks?" my mom asked herself. Her brow creased.

The corners of Agford's lips twitched. "As I was saying earlier, Wade, I do think things are getting back on track at school for Soph. But if you two would like, I'd be happy to pop in from time to time. Give Grandpa here a break. How does that sound?"

As she leaned forward to pat me on the shoulder, Grandpa emitted a monster fart that thrupped through the air like an undone balloon, creating an invisible, sulfurous force field around me. Agford's smile lapsed as the wall of stench hit her. She struggled to paint it back on.

My father put his hand to his mouth and coughed. "Are you sure about that? That's an awful lot of—"

"Extra work? Pshaw!" Agford pretended to wave away my father's concern, but her vigorous fanning wasn't fooling anyone. "It's just until your launch next week, right? I'll stop by if I can. Always good to have an extra pair of eyes, hmm?"

Grandpa tapped one of the mini felt black cats crouching in Agford's centerpiece and pretended to smile. "Looks like we got eight extra pairs right here."

My dad shot my grandpa a warning look, then turned back to Agford. "That'd be a great help," he said. "Really, above and beyond."

"Isn't that what neighbors are for?" Agford said. "I'd better be off. I really hate to intrude on your family time."

"About the Saturday mornings . . . ," my mom said as Agford turned to leave. She and my dad exchanged a look. "Why don't we say just *one* more time?"

"You bet, Cynthia." Dr. Agford's smile grew wider. Her hair helmet was a little ruffled from her fumigation efforts, but as she turned back to me, her eyes held a triumphant gleam. "But we'll see each other plenty before then, won't we, Soph?"

Chapter Eleven

Texas Hold 'Em

"You didn't eat any of that candy corn, did you?" Grace whispered over my walkie-talkie late that night. I huddled under my covers to muffle the sound, which turned out to be a very good thing, because when I told her Jake might have taken a handful, she freaked.

"Jake's fine," I whispered. "That is, unless poisoned candy corn causes fits of niceness," I added. "He took the trash out for me when it was definitely my turn." He'd also stopped by my room to make a big deal about how he took out the trash when it was my turn. Still, even that seemed suspiciously like he was checking in on me after Agford's invasion.

Grace agreed Agford wouldn't be dumb enough to kill off her neighbors in a mass poisoning, but that was just it: We didn't know what Agford was up to. She might have wanted us to keep out of her business, but she was doing everything she could to keep tabs on mine. We needed a plan. Fast. We started brainstorming but had to break off quickly when Grace's dad knocked on her door. We had just enough time to set a date at the Seashell the next afternoon.

The Seashell at three thirty, it was. I had half an hour until Grandpa (or—worse yet, Agford) would expect me home. Not much time, but enough. Grace had commandeered a booth that faced the square, where she huddled behind a newspaper unfurled to the size of a small tent. She lifted her sunglasses and peered at me as I slid in next to her. "Better today, right?" She gestured to her gray sweater, tan scarf, and dark blue jeans.

"Grace. You're wearing a beret."

"My hair was a mess!"

I closed my eyes and shook my head.

Grace let her sunglasses fall over her eyes again and darted glances left and right. I craned my neck to check for Rod among the after-school crowd filling the booths. What would I do if he were here? It's not like I could run up and tell him not to worry, that I'd figured out Agford was scaring me away with codes.

"So. Here's what I'm thinking." Grace took a quick sip of

her Diet Coke through a bendy straw. "Miss Anita has some alumni thing at Harvard next week, so starting Wednesday I'll just have self-study. If you can stay home sick from school, then we can— Oh my God!" Grace yanked me close and flung up the newspaper over us as if it were a blanket.

"What the—" I tried to brush the paper down, but Grace grabbed my wrist. "Ow!" I cried out. The couple in the booth next to us shot us a look. I shrugged back.

"*Shhh!*" Grace stole a quick glimpse out from her side of the newspaper. "She's here!"

I peeked one eye from behind the paper. The blue sedan was parallel parked out front. I hunched back with Grace again. "Are you sure it's her?" I asked. My stomach tightened.

Grace bit her finger and nodded to the door. The driver of the blue sedan had entered, all right. She wore a gray pantsuit and blue blouse. She pushed down her sunglasses, darted a look around, then grabbed a menu from the hostess stand and looked it over. Maybe she didn't realize we were there?

"Let's sneak out the back," I whispered, lifting the newspaper over us.

"On the count of three. Ready? One, two . . ."

"Three?" offered the woman from the blue sedan as she

ripped back our newspaper like a curtain and stared down. Grace let out a little cry.

"No need to be alarmed, now," the woman said in a twang. Her stringy light brown hair framed her pale face. Her shoulders sloped and dark half-moons of exhaustion puckered under her clear blue eyes. She reached for something in her pocket. Grace dove under the table. I poised to strike my Wild Goose Opens Wings tai chi move.

The woman's hand reemerged, flashing a gold badge. I dropped my arms to my sides and tried to look casual as she plunked it in front of me. Pinned to it was a laminated ID card. "FBI," she explained at the same moment I read the card's blue block letters for myself. She glanced over her shoulder to see if anyone was investigating the commotion.

Grace popped back up as fast as she had disappeared. "FBI?" she repeated. She whipped off her sunglasses and grabbed the badge to get a closer look. She ran her fingers over its worn relief letters and squinted as she held the hologram up to the light. She gave a firm nod and set it back down.

If anyone could recognize a real FBI badge, it was Grace. Still, I checked it myself. In addition to the raised seal and hologram, the ID card bore a signature that—while barely decipherable—seemed to match her name. It certainly did look authentic.

"That's right. FBI," the woman repeated, a smile tugging at her lips. It was hard to be terrified of someone so calm. Judging from the fine wrinkles around her eyes, she smiled often—or, at least, she had at one time. Real smiles, not Agford smiles.

She gestured to the booth. "May I?" she asked. Grace scooted over. I flashed her a look of warning. She shook her head almost imperceptibly.

"I'm Agent Ralston," the woman said, her hair falling across her face as she slid into the booth and cornered Grace. We couldn't flee now. Not unless I abandoned Grace and made a run for it.

As the woman reached out to shake our hands with a surprisingly bone-crushing grip, her blazer shifted to reveal a mysterious leather strap near her left shoulder. A hidden holster for a gun?

"I'm from the Austin, Texas, bureau," she explained. She stole a glance around the Seashell and lowered her voice. "Under ordinary circumstances, you two ladies wouldn't know I exist." She cleared her throat. "Then I slipped up yesterday at your school. And I made an even bigger mistake in sending you that code, Miss Young."

I gripped Grace's arm under the table. Badge or not, this

had to be some kind of a trap. Agford was crazier than I thought. Staging an FBI meeting to throw us off her trail?

"Code?" I asked, widening my eyes. If there was one good thing about looking like I was nine, it was that I seemed innocent. The freckles added to the effect.

"Yes, code, Miss Young. The one you two deciphered yesterday?" Ralston's gentle drawl didn't show any sign of impatience, even if her actual words did. "I'm impressed with your military-spec walkie-talkies, ladies, but we feds have no trouble breaking that encryption. I've been listening in all week. And I heard your talk last night." She looked apologetic as Grace blushed, then explained she'd slipped the code between the pages of my Feng Shui Planet catalog in my mailbox because the "Bureau's surveillance team" had determined I would check there quickly.

The smell of greasy burgers added to my rising nausea. I tried to keep my expression neutral as I studied the woman. Her jacket was a little too big for her wispy frame. A fragile FBI agent. A fragile FBI agent who follows kids, eavesdrops on them, and puts creepy codes in their mailboxes that scare them half to death. Nothing felt right about that. Still, if Agford wanted to keep us from spying, weren't there less complicated ways?

Ralston waited for the whine of the milk-shake blender

to subside, then added, "I hope you'll forgive me. We often resort to unconventional methods to protect innocent civilians, especially when we need to keep our investigations undercover."

Now I *really* didn't understand, but Grace slapped her hand to her head. "Of course! Why didn't we think of that?"

Ralston shook her head almost gloomily. "I was worried you two ladies wouldn't be able to crack the code. Never occurred to me it'd make you two want to investigate her *more*. Guess you can tell it's been a while since I've been around any kids." She chuckled softly.

"And the blue Crown Victoria!" Grace continued. "Standard government issue. I can't believe I didn't put it together."

Grace really bought this woman's story, didn't she? What if she said too much? I dug my nails into her arm.

"Ow!" Grace cried out as she yanked her arm away. She flashed Ralston an apologetic look before turning to me. "Relax, Sophie. The feds do stuff like this all the time. They can't have amateurs interfering. When they don't want to blow their cover, they do whatever they can to keep the civilians out."

Ralston looked impressed—or surprised? I couldn't tell which. "To keep them *safe*," she corrected. "The truth is we've been tailing you for protection ever since you called nine-one-one. I was hoping we wouldn't have to say a word. But when I heard y'all on the walkie-talkies making plans last night, I had no choice."

I scanned Ralston's face as her words settled over me. Her eyes seemed soft, almost understanding—like Ms. Gant's. Grace practically knew more about the FBI than I did about feng shui, and she was confident. She'd been right about the car, after all. Maybe Ralston slipping us a code didn't make sense, but it definitely made more sense than Agford cooking up some fake FBI encounter at the Seashell complete with a badge and a Texas accent. If Ralston was really FBI, though, that meant . . .

"So we're right?" Grace interrupted my thought before I could finish it.

Ralston tucked her lips together and gave a slight nod. "I can't tell you much, but two years ago a female suspect in her forties went on the run." Ralston flinched at a sudden clattering of dishes from the kitchen. She leaned in closer. "We have good reason to believe Dr. Charlotte Agford is that woman."

My mind projected an image of Agford's dead-eye smile and the beet-red smears down her cream sweater. The sound of my heartbeat drowned out the background murmur of the Seashell's afternoon crowd.

"Two years ago?" Grace repeated. "That's about when Agford moved in."

Ralston nodded slowly. "Exactly. If you hadn't called nine-one-one, things'd still be about as clear as a Texas river. Now we're finally getting somewhere."

It took me a moment to understand what she was saying. "I thought the police had already—"

She interrupted me. "Local law enforcement can't find their own behinds with flashlights in both hands," Ralston said, letting out a soft chuckle. "They ran a background check. Came up with nothing. That was the end of the story."

"Except that it wasn't," Grace said, breathless. She scooted forward in her seat.

Ralston looked over to Grace and frowned ever so slightly. "That's right. The bureau's system flagged the background check as highly irregular." She smoothed down her blazer lapel proudly as if she'd managed the feat herself. "Turns out the name Agford didn't exist until two years ago."

"That's what we suspected." Grace looked at me smugly before turning back to Ralston. "So she murdered someone for real?"

The couple next to us spun around again.

I felt uneasy. How does a person just make up a name for herself with no birth certificate, nothing? And, if we had witnessed a real murder, how did Agford get away with the lies about the beets?

"I'm not at liberty to divulge further details," Agent Ralston said.

"I knew we were right!" Grace said.

It was times like this that I wished Grace could keep a poker face. My doubts about Ralston were fading, but I still didn't buy that the FBI's "unconventional methods" would really include sending a code to middle schoolers.

I cleared my throat and looked at Agent Ralston. "Why aren't you telling all this to our parents instead?"

Grace glared at me. Ralston looked at me a long time, drumming her fingers on the table before she let out a long breath. "Now, Miss Young, I hate to sound impolite. And I hope you can forgive the question. But, in your experience, are parents good at keepin' secrets?"

They certainly weren't. Even if they lied, you could sense they were covering up something. And, despite Agent Ralston's honest blue eyes, I could feel her navigating around some hidden truth. The FBI not telling your parents a fugitive has it in for them? That was a recipe for disaster. Or at least a lawsuit.

"Not particularly," I said. "But—"

"You see," Ralston interrupted, "while the particulars suggest this Dr. Agford matches our suspect perfectly, if we're wrong, we can't have rumors about an innocent citizen flying round a small town like this. I'm sure y'all understand?"

"Why can't you just see it's her?" I asked.

"The boobs!" Grace shouted, nearly toppling her Diet Coke. Her beret flopped to the table. Startled, Ralston darted another nervous glance around the café. Several diners stared back. Grace lowered her voice to a whisper. "That's it, isn't it? She got plastic surgery, so you can't tell it's her. That and the wig, of course."

"Positive identification does present a challenge," Ralston answered. "Now I've said more than enough. If the suspect finds out I'm talking to you—it's a matter of life and death, you got it? This ain't a game. It's already too risky for me to be here right now."

"I knew it," Grace blurted out. "I mean, she's a fugitive, so clearly there's already a warrant out on her. If you ID'd her, you should be able to make the arrest, pronto."

Ralston raised her eyebrows. I supposed she wasn't used to twelve-year-olds who seemed to have read the entire FBI procedure manual. I expected her to compliment Grace, but instead she folded her arms and remained quiet. I noticed her blazer was frayed a little at the sleeves. An old yellow stain that looked like mustard dotted her lapel.

"You must have gathered some DNA in Texas, right?" Grace barreled on, either ignoring or not noticing Ralston's sudden silence. "So I guess you get something with her skin cells—that can't be too hard—and then, bam, match 'em up, and on to the next case." She shook her head. "God, your life must be so cool."

A hard edge crept into Ralston's voice. "You let me worry about procedure, Miss Yang. Y'all are in enough danger as it is."

"Enough danger?" I echoed.

Worry clouded Agent Ralston's pale features. "I wasn't kidding around when I sent you that code," she said.

I swallowed hard. The next morning I'd be at Agford's again. I pictured her blood-red juice. The way she brandished the pruning shears in my face. *Snip, snip.*

Agent Ralston read my thoughts. "Miss Young," she said, "I want you to know we're watching twenty-four hours a day, seven days a week. Anything happens, we're at your side faster than bee-stung mustangs. You got that?"

I nodded. My throat felt like it was closing.

"Sophie knows martial arts," Grace said. "Well, tai chi. But that's a martial art."

"Much better for self-defense than guns, even," I added, looking pointedly at where I'd seen Ralston's hidden holster.

"Is that so?" Ralston asked. I couldn't tell if she was actually impressed or just humoring me. "Well, I'm grateful for your help, ladies. But you'll need to leave the real work to us professionals now." She looked at Grace especially. "This mission . . ." Ralston's neck tensed. "This mission can't fail."

"So you're going to arrest her?" I asked. If only they could lock Agford up before tomorrow morning. Maybe I could fake a crippling flu until the feds swooped in.

Ralston nodded, looking pleased. "If it's her, yes."

I let out a long breath. Could it really be over? I imagined my parents, so guilt stricken that they'd believed Agford instead of me, practically falling over themselves with apologies. I'd spend my weekends on the couch, feet up, chowing down on Doritos while flipping mindlessly through the channels. My parents wouldn't even make me relinquish the remote to Jake. Fu dogs at the entrance? Sure! Grace wants to sleep over on a school night? You bet!

"It'll take some time, of course," Ralston added. "But I

don't need to tell you that. You know exactly what happens when you jump the gun."

"A couple days or so," I said. "Right."

"Well, no . . . ," Ralston said. "I reckon we'll need more time than that. We need to gather evidence. As I'm sure Miss Yang here already knows, that evidence has to be legally obtained. In other words, we can't steal it."

"Maybe more like a week." I nodded. I could handle that.

"I'm sorry," Agent Ralston said. She slid her hand forward on the table as though reaching out to me. "I know it's hard to be patient. This is scary business you're in the middle of. But if our case ain't airtight—if she gets off on a technicality—this woman might disappear again. We'd have to start from scratch. Even worse, if she finds out we're on her tail, there's no telling what she might do."

"But the more time it takes . . . ," Grace piped up. "Isn't it just more likely something will go wrong?"

"It's a chance worth taking, Miss Yang," Ralston said, her jaw flexing. "Slow and steady. It always wins the race."

Not in every race I'd witnessed. Apart from that fable with the hare and the tortoise, fast won every time. And let's not forget that bunny took a five-hour nap midrace or something. What was this slow-and-steady business when my life was on the line? *Speed is the essence of war*, Sun

134

Tzu said. You couldn't tell me the FBI didn't know about the General.

"So how long before you have enough, do you think?" I asked.

Agent Ralston sighed. "I wish I could tell you. I just don't know. Could be two weeks, could be a month, could be three months. It's just a matter of what we find out and when." She scanned the restaurant quickly. "I've been here too long already. Never know who's on the lookout." She slapped down a business card. "Y'all can contact me here if you need me."

The card had the FBI seal in the upper left corner and listed the Austin field-office address as well as her direct line and email. Grace ran her fingers over the raised logo.

Ralston reached into her jacket pocket. Our eyes widened a moment before she pulled out a pen. She slid back the card and scratched off her phone number. "Phone calls can be monitored, even from a landline. Use email instead. Nothing can break FBI email encryption. Helped write the program myself," she said with a sniff. Ralston looked at us, her lips pulling into the slightest frown. "You're gonna keep your heads, right, ladies? I need you to promise me that." Her gaze was urgent.

I promised. What choice did I have? Grace nodded, too,

but I could tell her thoughts were already far away.

"Now, listen up." Ralston leaned forward. "I'm not going to let anything happen to you two. What was it my daughter always used to say? 'I've got your back.' That's it." She smiled. "Ladies, I've got your backs. I really do."

Chapter Twelve

Impatient Bait

"Months? It can't take months. They're the FBI!" I moaned to Grace as we made our way home along Luna Vista Drive. Maybe my dad was right when he grumbled about government inefficiency.

The sun was still out, but the wind gusted. I zipped up my hoodie. Grace had given up on the beret. Her black hair flapped behind her as she strode ahead of me. My legs felt too unsteady to walk any faster.

"Did you see her gun? I totally saw her gun," Grace said, breathless. "It was, like, right there."

I turned to look for the sedan. The road was empty. Then an engine rattled, and the familiar blue car rounded the corner and idled by a stop sign. I couldn't quite get used to being reassured by it.

"Government sure gives them crappy cars, though."

"Shhh!" Grace said as she twisted around to check for Ralston.

I rolled my eyes. "I don't think her hearing's supersonic."

A basketball thumped behind the gate of a one-story Spanish-style house we passed. Shoes shuffled on concrete; someone laughed. Life moved on cheerfully here in Luna Vista among the flame-red bougainvillea and swaying trees. On the other side of the street, a dad pushed a stroller, cooing at his kid. He had no idea an FBI agent was playing cat and mouse with a fugitive right here in town.

"You think she's a sharpshooter?" Grace asked. "She probably is. I wonder if she trained at Quantico."

I didn't know what Quantico was, and I didn't ask. "I hope Ralston's sharpshooting is better than her driving," I said.

Grace prattled on as she kicked a pinecone ahead of her, offering up an endless stream of imagined run-ins between Ralston and mafia kingpins, drug lords, serial murderers, and kidnappers. "What do you think Agford did?" she asked before providing her own terrifying answers. I tuned her out. I had to—for my own sanity.

"Don't you think they'd want to move faster?" I interrupted.

"You heard her. They don't know that she's definitely a fugitive, Sophie." Grace *sounded* as reasonable as Trista, but she sure wasn't.

"C'mon," I argued. "The FBI is looking for her. She said, 'If they find us, we'll rip out their throats.' And what about the wig? And the convertible?"

Grace slowed her pace and spun her beret around one finger. "Ralston's been eavesdropping on our walkie-talkie sessions," she said. "She knows what we've found. It obviously wasn't enough. You heard her. The evidence needs to be *airtight*."

"I just don't understand how it can be that hard," I said, almost under my breath. It wasn't like Grace was listening. In fact, you'd have thought she'd joined the bureau ranks, the way she was acting. Apart from the beret spinning, that is.

"What if the FBI busts in and arrests some middle-school counselor?" Grace's watches rattled on her wrist as she threw up her hands. A squirrel scurried up a nearby tree. "You think *you* have a public-relations disaster at school? They'd be dealing with worse than therapy and yard work, Sophie."

"Wouldn't it look worse if some innocent middle-school *kid* got butchered by a fugitive they were tracking?" I shot back.

Grace shook her head. She ran her fingers through her hair. "The FBI's not going to let that happen," she said.

"Grace, nobody but us knows the FBI is tailing Agford," I said. "If Agford killed an innocent kid and they captured her after, it'd just look like the murder had tipped them off. They'd be heroes, practically."

Hold out baits to entice the enemy, Sun Tzu said. The truth of my own words sunk in. Could we really be bait for Agford? The FBI could pluck a hair from Agford (maybe not from the wig, but still) and run a DNA test if they really wanted to know if they had their woman. Couldn't they at least get fingerprints matched? Instead they were settling in for a months-long operation and hoping a four-foot-six twelve-year-old would Wild Goose Opens Wings her way to survival if the going got rough. Something else was happening.

"You're talking about you and me, you know," Grace said, her voice growing quieter. "We're the innocent kids."

"Exactly." I looked up the road toward Agford's. I couldn't believe that tomorrow I was going to be there alone.

"But it goes against every protocol," Grace continued. "I haven't even read about *one* case . . ." She stopped midstride and turned to me, her eyes wide. "Oh my God. You think the FBI has accepted that that might be how this all shakes out?

They're just waiting until . . ." She clearly couldn't bear to finish.

We stood in silence outside my house. The sky glowed pink. Behind us Mr. Valdez was out in his front yard with a hose, overwatering his lawn again. As usual Mr. Maxwell wore his short shorts and tube socks while he surveyed his geraniums.

"Nah, you're right," I said. "We're just kids. The FBI wouldn't let that happen."

But I didn't believe my own words. I pictured Agent Ralston's eyes. They were such an honest blue, maybe I could have overlooked the worry that clouded them. Agent Ralston knew something we didn't. Her fear ran deep. "This mission can't fail," Ralston had said. Were Agford's crimes gruesome enough that Ralston's higher-ups had decided they'd risk the worst to catch her?

"We can't just stand by and let this happen," Grace said, as if she'd heard my thoughts.

I looked behind us at the empty street, then at Agford's house.

"No," I said. "No, we can't."

Chapter Thirteen

Famous Last Steps

"I know it's a long shot, but it's our best chance, Sophie," Grace said as she waited for me in my backyard the next morning, bundled up in a blue down parka, knit cap, and striped leggings that matched her scarf. The fog had drifted in from the coast overnight again, and it was still early enough to be chilly—though not exactly chilly enough to merit Grace rolling out her entire winter collection at once. In a few hours, the sun would be beating down as usual—just in time for my last Saturday work shift at Agford's.

"In fact, it's probably our *only* chance," she added. "If you can get your hands on even the tiniest proof she's not who she says she is, the feds can strike sooner."

"No pressure." I let out a nervous laugh.

"No pressure." Grace patted me on the shoulder. "Seriously." She unfurled a sketch that she'd drawn of our three houses and marked an X by her living room window. "I'll be practicing piano here." She added a dotted line to Agford's. "I should have a direct view. As long as you're cleaning the garage, like she said."

The day before, Grace had convinced her mom it'd be a good idea to skip Chinese school and practice for the all-day piano competition she had in LA that Sunday. It didn't take too much convincing. Grace was so bad at piano that all her friends were years beyond her. At events she'd sit in a row next to her eight-year-old rivals while Mrs. Dr. Yang joked that Grace was "head and shoulders" above the competition.

"So. I got seven fifty. You?" Grace glanced at her black digital watch. It looked lonely on her wrist.

"Seven forty-nine," I said.

Grace adjusted her watch with a beep. "You ready?"

"As ready as I'll ever be." I shuddered.

Grace pressed something hard and plastic into my hand. It looked like the detached handle of a toy gun. "Pepper spray," she explained, still clutching my hand. "One shot in the eyes, and she'll be blinded long enough for your Dragon Spits Fire thing or whatever."

"Dragon Emerges from Water," I said. "It's my best move."

"Yeah. That. Anyway, it'll buy you time to get away if anything happens." Her parka rustled as she rubbed her arms for warmth. She looked at me intently, then adjusted her light blue knit cap and handed me her cell. She'd pilfered her dad's again for the weekend. "Forget the FBI," she said, raising her binoculars with a flourish. "*I've* got your back."

"Thank God someone does," I said. Of course, Grace and I both knew she had my back only until around eleven, when she'd be leaving to go to Natalie's birthday party in Los Angeles. Grace would be staying over there until early Monday, since Natalie was going to the same competition.

Grace leaned around the side of the house to peer at Agford's with her binoculars. "I'm not the only surveillance team on the case. Oh—I think he just nodded." She saluted at a white truck parked just one house up from Agford's. I'd noticed that pickup truck right after we'd caught sight of Ralston in her sedan the first time. It must have been one of her agents.

"A white pickup? Is that the best they have?"

"Standard FBI procedure, Soph. If the stealth team zoomed around in Crown Vics, the target would be tipped off in no time. Same thing with the agents. They throw off suspicion by using all types—senior citizens, nuns, parents pushing strollers, you name it. Anyway . . ." She handed me the binoculars. "Maybe you have other backup, but I think you'll agree I am *much* cuter."

I adjusted the focus and took a look. Grace wasn't kidding. In the truck's cab sat a frog-faced, bulky, thick-necked man with short black hair and a single, extremely bushy eyebrow framing the top of his dark aviator glasses. At least he looked strong, which was more than I could say for Ralston. He shot another quick glance our way, then turned to rummage in his glove compartment.

"Maybe just a tiny bit cuter," I said, smiling. "But if ol' Agent Unibrow gets busy with his tweezers, he could give you a run for your money."

Grace shoved me teasingly. For a moment I almost forgot where I was about to go. Then she grew solemn. She grabbed my shoulders and leaned in before sending me off. "You can do this, Hidden Dragon."

I made my way down Agford's front walk. Her dark windows reflected my own house back to me as if the fake cobwebs hanging there had captured real prey. In fact, it was the very fakeness of Agford's over-the-top display that was the most chilling. At her house it seemed not only possible but *likely* that the goofy pirate skeleton might thrust his bony hand out and grab me by the throat. Or that real victims' bodies were rotting underneath those plastic tombstones etched with corny names like Ima Goner. I stepped over a cluster of pumpkins, took a deep breath, and pressed the bell.

"Sophie! I almost forgot." Agford practically sang out her greeting. "Your last visit." She winked. "Glad we could work that out with your parents."

Her eerie good cheer sent a shiver through me. I thought back to Ralston at the Seashell. Her clenched jaw, her urgent tone. The words echoed in my head. *Y'all are in enough danger as it is.*

"Aren't things coming along nicely?" She pointed to her graveyard and a fake witch "flying" from her tree. "I'd ask for your help, but I've got something else in mind for you," she said, her falsetto slipping slightly. "Wait for me by the garage." She disappeared through the front door.

My heart leaped as the garage door growled open and Agford's car engine roared to life. I jumped to the safety of a bed of impatiens, only to feel silly when Agford parked her convertible in the driveway. She frowned at her trampled plants and gestured to the mouth of the garage that gaped before me. "What a mess, huh?"

Agford watched me take in the scene. The smell of damp

concrete and mildew filled the air as fat spiders loitered on *real* cobwebs in every corner. Layers of grime and grease coated the floor. Spotting the walls were cloudy brown stains that looked like dried blood.

I looked back at the street and felt my stomach drop. The white truck was gone. Had Ralston's agent driven off when Agford had backed out her car?

"Something wrong?" Agford said, studying my reaction.

"Not at all," I said, pasting on a smile.

"All righty, then." She handed me a bucket and scrub brush. "I'll be inside if you need me!" She flashed a grin like the skeleton's and swiveled away in her Easy Spirit sneakers.

I dragged the bucket into the garage. Pincher bugs scuttled for cover. Garden tools—all jagged saws and sharp points—were mounted along the wall like a collection of medieval weaponry. Agford wasn't crazy enough to ambush me in the house when my parents *knew* I was there. Was she?

I scrubbed away layer after layer of black grease as Grace's jarring chords clanged down, stopping and restarting every once in a while when she—I hope—paused to check on me through her binoculars. I knew I was supposed to find out more. But how? I looked around. All at once, it hit me. *This* was our best chance? What, had Agford hidden her old driver's license in the empty flowerpots? Clamped an old picture of herself between the grips of her abandoned ThighMaster?

By noon it was official. My first real spy mission was a total bust. Grime coated my hands and forearms. My bony knees ached from rocking against the hard concrete when I scrubbed. I dumped the pitch-black water down her drain, then knocked at the garage door to the house to let Agford know I was leaving.

The door creaked open. I couldn't believe it.

"Dr. Agford?" I stepped into the laundry room. I listened. Water was running upstairs. I took two more steps. "Hello?" My heart raced.

"'Build me up! Buttercup!'" Agford's warbling voice floated downstairs as she burst into full song. She must be showering. I shuddered.

She had no idea she'd forgotten to lock the door. *If the enemy leaves a door open, you must rush in*, Sun Tzu said. My heart pounded in my ears. Maybe there was still a chance. I had time to look around. Not much time, but enough.

I drew in a deep breath and rounded the corner to the kitchen, expecting to see the blood-spattered tile that had etched itself into my brain that night. But it seemed like a plain old kitchen. The scent of Agford's god-awful perfume mingling with a moldy odor from the trash can was the only sign it was definitely hers. Even though it was lunchtime, fluorescent lights were on, coating the room in a sickly glow. A half-empty coffee mug sat on the counter next to a crumb-speckled dish. For just a moment, I actually felt sad as I pictured Agford standing at her counter alone, hovering over this plate as she chewed a dry piece of toast and stared into space.

"'I need *you*! More than anyone, dar-ling,'" shrieked Agford above the running water. I scanned the room wildly. The counters were bare. A magnet on the fridge pinned up a flyer for a bra sale at the Preppy Plus Boutique. I saw a pen by the phone and grabbed it. If Agford made it down before I could escape, I could say I was just leaving a note. I didn't know what would be worse—seeing her in a towel or getting caught. And what would her real hair look like anyway?

I slid open a drawer that housed some twist ties, rubber bands, and a few odd cooking utensils. I don't know what I was expecting. A neon sign flashing her real name would have been nice.

The water shut off. Agford's humming seemed to speed

up, like a horror-movie sound track swelling as the killer approached. The countdown was on. I flung open a cupboard: spices. Another one: Tupperware and soup cans. Where were the blood-soaked machetes? I'd discovered her boring old silverware drawer when my pocket let out three piercing beeps. The cell phone. We'd forgotten to switch it to vibrate. Grace must be texting me.

Agford trailed off midchorus. A door clicked open. I couldn't run; she'd hear my footsteps. I reached down to muffle my pocket and tiptoed toward the door, sighing in relief as I reached the laundry room. I glanced behind me and gasped.

A telltale trail of my black, smudgy footprints extended all the way to the kitchen.

Frantic, I yanked off my sneakers, strung their laces together and tossed them over my shoulder. Then I shuffled around in my socks like a maniac to wipe away my footprints. The black grease only smeared in wide arcs. I felt like an artist working with charcoal. *Famous Last Steps*, I named my masterpiece in my head. Mixed Media: Black Grease on Linoleum.

Agford's footsteps creaked overhead. My arms and hands developed wills of their own, grasping at everything in sight I might use to clean the mess. A Post-it pad? An eraser? Didn't this woman own a sponge? At last, just as I heard the thud of Agford's tread on the stairs, I spotted a thick roll of paper towels. I unraveled a generous handful and spat a loogie into it that would have made Jake proud. I crouched down and—using the flawless scrubbing technique I'd honed over the course of the long morning—furiously mopped the floor as I backed out.

The floor sparkled white again. I was going to escape. Agford would never know. You would have thought I'd be pleased. Instead I wanted to curl up into a ball and sob. I'd risked everything, and all I had to show for it was a wad of spit-dampened paper towels.

I sprinted to my house and collapsed in a panting heap on my back lawn. Something sharp stabbed at my backside. I reached behind me and felt a long, thin bulge in my back pocket. The pen. I must have shoved it into my pocket while I was cleaning up. It was a fancy pen, made of a heavy metal that might have been silver. Some curlicue decoration was on the cap. It was just nice enough for Agford to notice it was missing.

I sighed and pulled Grace's cell from my pocket. The screen blinked back at me:

Mission accomplished?

I held out the phone and texted back.

Mission failed

I lay on the lawn and stared at the pale blue sky. Drained of color and clouds, it looked almost as empty as I felt.

Chapter Fourteen

Special Delivery

My heart pounded every time the doorbell or phone rang that weekend. I knew Agford would come with a full report for my parents. She'd demand her pen back. There would be questions. More worries. More reasons for Agford to get me alone. I wondered if I should go back and throw myself at her mercy first.

But Agford never came. In fact, Agford's house was very quiet Sunday. I only knew she was home once I saw Agent Unibrow on surveillance, waddling down the street nearby. Between him and Officer Grady, I'd concluded the government really ought to look into some better fitness programs. Let's hope Unibrow was a good shot. He sure wasn't going to be able to run fast enough to save me—if they were even planning on saving me in the first place.

Not being able to talk to Grace all weekend was torture.

Not that I would have been able to see her anyway. Inspired by Agford's "observations," my parents had been all about family time that weekend. We didn't go to the beach. We didn't try to catch a movie. My parents had something else in mind.

They bought a puzzle for us to do together.

A one-thousand-piece puzzle consisting entirely of blue ocean and sky. Grandpa took one look and retreated to the TV room upstairs, where he shouted out answers to *Jeopardy!* reruns on the Game Show Network. My parents were enthusiastic but got sidetracked by phone calls from work. Pretty soon it was just Jake and me, joking as we tried to distinguish between a zillion shades of blue and jockeying for the end pieces. Something about it felt like old times—back when he and I would play laser tag and have epic rock-paper-scissors marathons. Of course, pretty soon he was back in the garage playing the same two notes on his bass like he always did. Later he sneaked into my room to topple over some of my Buddha figurines, because he thought it was funny to mess with my chi.

If my school counselor hadn't been a wanted fugitive, I would have been dying to go to school on Monday.

Agent Ralston's blue-sedan security detail followed several car lengths behind as I rode my bike to school Monday

154

morning. I wondered if she'd follow if I kept riding. Maybe I could even make it to Malibu and hide out in the hills until the feds swooped down and solved it all. Grace was right. They were the pros. I was just the one who left smeared footprints everywhere.

No matter where I walked at school, it felt like S.M.I.L.E. was always there, their lips pursed like Agford's. That day they were handing out flyers on beating stress that pictured a smiley face literally beating the word *stress* with a club. They gave me five. "For my whole family." I wouldn't have been surprised if they had established a nonprofit to raise funds for my psychiatric care by now.

I carried my tray out to the patio for lunch. I hadn't seen Trista since lunch on Thursday. I wasn't sure I was ready to—or if she even wanted to hang out. I had the feeling she'd rather spend lunch with *Car and Driver* than shoot down persecution fantasies about Charlotte Agford. Only they weren't fantasies now, were they? In any case, I'd bought a side of steamed vegetables to go with my "Jurassic" chicken nuggets in the shape of stegosauri, hoping she'd take me a little more seriously.

As I sat down, Trista gave a curt nod hello and shoved aside a book on something called "photovoltaic cells," which she'd filled with Post-its. Her T-shirt read: I DO MY

OWN STUNTS. No kidding. Trista did her own everything. The last time Trista asked someone for help was probably when she was learning to tie her shoes.

"Was it a null?" Trista said, after she finished the last forkful of her salad. "The code?" she added, when I didn't answer right away.

"Yeah. Thanks for the tip." I bit into a watery broccoli floret.

"Thought so," Trista said. I followed her gaze as she looked over at Rod and Peter's table on the other side of the patio. Rod's dimple looked adorable as he laughed and listened to Peter tell a story. That was what I liked most about him. He always seemed to be listening. If only the code really had been from him.

Trista scratched the back of her neck and shifted uncomfortably on the bench. "So he ask you out or something?"

I nearly spat out the broccoli again. It had never occurred to me that Trista would actually ask about Rod. Should I lie or spill the whole story?

"No," I said, finally.

"Oh." Trista slowly folded her napkin into quarters while she searched for something to say.

"It wasn't Rod at all." I felt as though I'd stepped off the bluffs themselves.

Trista cocked her head. The seagulls caught wind of my chicken nuggets and began squawking and flapping.

I leaned in. "In fact, what would you say if I had proof Charlotte Agford isn't who she says she is?"

Trista frowned. "All from a code?"

"From the FBI directly."

"The FBI," Trista repeated. Her lips twitched as she tried to keep a neutral expression. She was humoring me. Or was she? She reached for the pen on her sketchbook, clicking it open and closed a few times before she spoke again. "Well, I'd say . . ." She looked at me very seriously. "I'd say we'd better be sure they're FBI."

I breathed a little easier. She believed me. I even felt a tiny spark of pride that she and I'd had the same thought. "Exactly," I said. I went ahead and told her the rest of the story, only holding off on my break-in at Agford's Saturday. Trista spun her pen on her fingers as she listened.

"You actually called the FBI out on not telling your parents?" Trista asked when I finished. She looked impressed. "Bold." She dropped her pen and shooed away a gull.

"Something doesn't seem right, though, does it?" I said, fiddling with my straw. "That's why . . ." I hesitated, then told her about our worries and my failed mission to Agford's. "I think I got out without her knowing, though."

"Hope so. Where did you say Grace was? A birthday party?"

"No—I mean, that wasn't until later." I blushed. "It's not how it sounds."

"Sophie, you're in the quicksand, and you're in deep," Trista said. "But the thing is, you can—" She stopped mid-sentence and scowled.

A millisecond later I felt a gooey *splat!* against my lower back just as a gull passed overhead. I turned around to curse the bird, but instead my gaze met Trent Spinner's. In his raised hand was a plastic spoon smeared with the remains of chocolate pudding.

"Something's coming out of your anus, *AY-NUS*!" Trent shouted. He erupted into his machine-gun laugh as a thick drip of chocolate pudding oozed down the seat of my shorts. His friends, Matt and Jae, clutched at their sides, practically hyperventilating, they found it so funny.

Trista's eyes grew dark. She looked directly at Trent Spinner. "As I was saying, the thing is," she said to me as quietly and calmly as I'd ever heard her say anything, "you can do *something about it*."

My ears still blazed red, and my breath was tight, but I nodded. *"If you know the enemy and you know yourself—"*

"You need not fear the result of a hundred battles!"

Trista shouted. "Sun Tzu!" She held out her hand for a high five.

Trista ushered me off to the science lab, where she whipped together a mix of ammonia, peroxide, and water that had my "ay-nus" stain out in no time. Before I knew it, we were on our way to the gym. Mr. Katz had called for another of his Special Assemblies, which weren't so special, considering he called for one just about every other week. For Mr. Katz, the Special Assembly was a magic formula capable of curing all school problems in twenty minutes. Bullying? Racial insensitivity? Let's hire someone to give a talk in the gym. And voilà!, as Madame Tarrateau would say, problem solved.

I didn't think anything of it until Dr. Charlotte Agford clip-clopped her way up to the microphone in her cream-colored suit, stockings, and hideous turquoise pumps. Pinned to her lapel was the same bedazzled brooch embossed with the silver A that she'd worn in Katz's office.

Trista frowned. My temples began to throb. No good could come of this. I looked toward the gym door, wondering if there were any way to scramble over a row of forty kids sitting in bleachers without attracting attention.

Agford sniffed and tilted her head. "So, ladies and gents.

I'm here to—Matt, honey, please sit down, the people behind you want to get a better look at me." Her snort at her own joke sounded like a bomb explosion when amplified by the mike. A shriek of feedback followed. It was almost the same pitch as her unbearable falsetto.

"Before I get started here, I just wanted to say, seventh grade, make sure you go to room twenty-four tomorrow at noon. This week S.M.I.L.E.'s Brown Bag Lunch topic is on eating disorders, and we'll be watching a film on bulimia."

Trista made a face and erupted into a loud, fake coughing fit. Marissa passed her a throat lozenge. The irony of watching a movie about barfing up your lunch *during* lunch was definitely lost on her.

Agford ignored Trista. My muscles tensed. That wasn't like her.

"You're probably wondering," Agford began, "who the guest speaker is for today's Special Assembly." She pulled the mike from the stand and paced in front of the bleachers. She wasn't smiling. Agford smiled when she talked about body odor, for God's sake. Why wasn't she smiling?

"*I* am. I am the guest speaker," she said curtly. She stopped directly in front of my bleacher section and pivoted to face the crowd. "Recent events have led me to believe we need to discuss a topic we've never before had to address here at Luna Vista Middle School." Agford's eyes locked themselves on mine. "Today we are going to talk about *trespassing.*"

Blood rushed to my head as murmurs rippled through the crowd. I heard someone whisper my name. The members of S.M.I.L.E.—even Jenn—paused their note taking to stare at me.

Agford began to pace again. She cleared her throat. It took effort to speak in those soprano scales. "Trespassing, you say. Why would we need to talk about trespassing?" Agford didn't even pretend to look anywhere else but directly at me. She narrowed her eyes. For once they weren't empty. They flashed with rage.

S.M.I.L.E. raised its hands and waved them, their matching yellow bracelets for who-knows-what-cause spinning on their wrists.

"Marissa," Agford said, never taking her eyes from mine.

"Maybe we've recently had trouble with some people not respecting others' privacy?" Marissa smiled like she was baring her teeth.

"That would be a very good reason, wouldn't it?" Agford said. "Perhaps *some people* have had trouble maintaining boundaries. Can anyone give an example of a privacy violation?"

S.M.I.L.E.'s arms shot up again. In a fake show of fairness, Agford called on Trent Spinner.

"Hacking into someone's MyFace account!" Trent Spinner yelled out. He looked at his friends. An inside joke, no doubt.

"Yes, Trent, gaining access to online accounts is definitely a violation of privacy. It's like breaking and entering. Any other ideas?"

Trista raised her hand. Agford's gaze flicked to her, then to me. She turned to S.M.I.L.E.. "How about you, Jenn?"

"Going through someone's locker," Jenn said. She glanced back at the rest of S.M.I.L.E. for approval. They looked unimpressed.

"Going through someone's locker . . . ," Agford repeated, studying the painted lines on the hardwood basketball court as she pretended to consider this. "Now that would be disrespecting someone's *property*, wouldn't it?" Agford snapped her head up to me so fast, I wondered how her wig had kept up. "What do you think, Sophie?" she spat. "Is it ever acceptable to intrude upon another's personal, private property?"

The gym fell silent. Even the kids on the outer fringes

of the social scene—the girls who still liked ponies, the boys who still trafficked in Pokémon cards—seemed to understand what Agford was up to. They only knew the half of it.

I sat paralyzed.

Agford cocked her head. "I didn't catch that?"

"No," I croaked.

"No? Any idea why some people have such trouble maintaining boundaries?"

Trista let out a sarcastic huff. Agford glared. She didn't wait for a response from me, and I didn't give one.

"Regardless of the reasons someone might disrespect another's property"—she swiveled and began pacing anew, her heels hammering out a slow rhythm on the hardwood floor—"I think we must all keep one idea foremost in our minds. One idea. And it is that, in *all* cases"—she stopped and turned to find me in the crowd—"trespassing has consequences."

It finally came then, the smile. Dead-eyed and wide.

Wide enough to swallow me and Trista both.

Chapter Fifteen

Bottoms Up

I swayed unsteadily as the crowd poured down from the bleachers and made their way to the gym doors. Even the sixth graders kept their distance, as if stepping in my vicinity might be fatal.

Black spots crowded my field of vision. I felt like I needed to sit down.

"That's right, people!" Trista shouted at the empty space the crowd had left around us as if she were directing traffic for a presidential caravan. She grabbed my arm and led me forward. "We need some breathing room," she said, waving her arm at nothing. "Move it, move it!"

Kids shot us looks like we were insane. Trista ignored them. She turned to me and scowled. "That woman is *not* going to get away with this. No way."

"Trista, we have to be careful."

Trista clapped me on the shoulder. "I got this. Carpool line tomorrow morning. Be early," she said. "You're not gonna want to miss it."

"Miss what?"

Trista had already turned to walk down the hall.

"Miss what?" I called after her.

She wheeled around and grinned. "You dragged me into the quicksand," she shouted. "Now you gotta trust me."

Trista sauntered down the hall and disappeared around a corner before I could say another word.

"That's the thing civilians never remember about war . . ." Grandpa Young pulled off his baseball cap and laid it on the kitchen table next to my social-studies textbook. Though the book looked perfectly normal, over the course of the last week's study sessions I'd concluded it was actually a direct portal to Pyongyang, 1952. Grandpa couldn't even look at its cover without a story coming on like a sneeze. I was on my one hundred and eighty-third reading of the same paragraph about the Emancipation Proclamation.

It wasn't only Grandpa's stories that kept me from focusing. My mind was caught in an endless loop of worry. If Trista was planning revenge, Agford would think I was behind it. And then what? *There's no telling what she might do*. There I was again, back to Agford.

"Firepower's nothing. Words are more dangerous than missiles," Grandpa continued. He leaned back in his chair, his eyes searching the ceiling. "But silence—now there's the best weapon of all. I'll tell you what, Soph, when the enemy talked, we sat back and listened. Not to *what* they said, but to how and why."

I thought back to Agford at the assembly. If words were missiles, it didn't matter that she'd launched a full-scale assault: She never ran out of ammunition.

Just then my pocket vibrated. I faked a coughing fit, leaned over, and pulled out the cell. It read:

Bathroom window in 5. Dad needs his cell back.

"Grandpa?" I coughed again, for consistency's sake. "May I use the restroom?"

He looked up. "Forward march!" he cheered.

I looked down at Grace from my perch on the bathroom windowsill. I'd just unloaded the whole Agford assembly story. She sat hunched into her jacket among the shadows, fuming. Until then I'd felt more humiliated than anything else. Now I felt my rage at Agford surging. That is, until Grace finally spoke.

"But you said she hadn't seen you!" she hissed. "Jeez, Sophie. It should have been a simple in-and-out."

I almost fell off the sill. She was mad at *me*? It took me a second to find my voice.

"What happened to 'no pressure'? You were the one who said I should try to get in the house if I could!" I said.

"Soph, you were supposed to *look* for evidence, not *leave* it. I knew there was no way you could have cleaned up all those footprints." She flipped her hair over her shoulder.

I thought of the way Trista had looked when she'd asked me where Grace had been.

"Wait, why didn't we send you over?" I shot back. "You're the FBI superagent. When's the last time you took a risk? Oh, that's right. Piano recital, was it? A little Minuet in G while I was practically licking up Agford's garage floor? Or maybe by then you were already at Natalie's party?"

Grace looked caught off guard.

I couldn't stop myself. "Maybe you'd benefit from therapy sessions with a raving maniac?" I added. "Or would you prefer your parents give her an open invitation to stop by anytime?" My words came out harsher than I wanted them to. It reminded me of those phases I go through when, no matter what, everything I say to my parents sounds like I hate them.

Grace clenched a rubber band in her mouth as she fashioned her hair into a ponytail. She tugged at it and looked away.

"I'm sure she'd be happy to run a whole school assembly to mock you," I said. "Or send her S.M.I.L.E. clones to spy on you."

Grace held up her hand. "I get it, Soph. Okay?" she said. "I'm worried for you—all the time. And I just want to *do* something. But think about it! I'm practically under twenty-four-hour house arrest, and I'm not even in trouble. You really think I wanted to go to piano? To Natalie's stupid party?" She seemed small below the windowsill, the rosemary bushes buffeting her on either side. With her head angled up to me, she looked unfamiliar.

I pictured Grace's life over the past few days. Her parents cheerfully dragging her around to piano competitions and lunch with family friends, the long hours spent graphing equations and conjugating *ser* with Miss Anita while I squared off with Agford. I'd thought it was easy for her to be tucked safe and sound in her fortress at 86 Via Fortuna with all her "lucky" animals and good chi she didn't even appreciate. Maybe I'd been wrong.

"It's harder than you think, you know," Grace said. "At least"—she paused—"for me."

"Well, I could do without the judgment," I said. "And maybe you could listen more?"

"You're right." Grace unfolded her arms. "From here on out, I shut up."

I couldn't help myself. I laughed.

"Okay, I *try* to shut up." Grace curled her lips closed around her teeth for all of ten seconds. "Oh, that's never going to work. I just—I don't do well on the sidelines, Sophie."

"We're letting her get to us, aren't we?" I said. *"Only the army animated with the same spirit throughout its ranks can reign victorious,"* I quoted Sun Tzu.

Grace squinted at me.

"We can only win if we work together," I translated.

"Gotta hand it to Chinese philosophers," Grace said as she pulled herself closer to the ledge and smiled.

"So what's the next step?" I asked.

Grace shrugged. "I take my marching orders from you these days, General Sun Tzu."

"Do I detect a note of sarcasm?"

"Maybe just a little." Grace grinned. "But only a little. I promise."

"Give me a day to draw up battle plans."

"All I ask is that you put me on the front line."

"You got it, Agent Yang."

The next morning I stood in front of Luna Vista Middle School half an hour before first period, worried about what Trista had in mind. It wasn't long before the sun rose higher and the carpool line hummed with SUVs and minivans. Students bearing unwieldy instrument cases and mangled lunch bags poured forth. Marissa and her friends arrived as a set, looking like displaced flight attendants as they strode along the sidewalk, their matching rolling backpacks in tow.

I caught sight of Trista and jogged over. She fumbled in her pocket and flashed me a smile. "And . . . cue music," she announced, nodding toward the street.

A high-pitched siren wailed. Heads turned. Parents unloading sugar-cube California missions and rainforest dioramas from trunks leaped to their driver's seats, sure they'd accidentally triggered their car alarms. That is, until they realized the siren's source.

"Hold on, ladies and gents," Trista commentated for my benefit only. "For your enjoyment: Act Two. This is a little something I like to call: the Panic. . . ."

All eyes found their way to Agford's cherry-red Mustang convertible as it motored up. A wide-eyed Agford punched every button on her dashboard as she tried to stop the racket,

170

but the alarm cycled through its many orchestral movements: from the High-Speed Police Chase sonata to the Whooping Crane Etude in high E and Staccato Horn Rendition of "La Cucaracha."

Trista raised a finger as though conducting the score herself. "Wait for it, now. . . ." An ocean gust kicked up as the sirens reached their climax. "Oh, here we go. . . ." *Frrip!* Agford's automatic convertible top peeled back like a broken accordion as Trista pumped one fist high above her head.

Sheets of paper flurried like white confetti, spiraling skyward in the updraft. The crowd let out a collective gasp—half in awe, half in horror—as Agford's helmet of hair, too, took flight. Trista hid her smile as it flopped to rest, unnoticed, in a storm drain while every member of the Luna Vista Middle School community beheld the real hair of Dr. Charlotte Agford. That is, if the matted brown rat's nest on her head could even be called hair at all.

As Agford screeched off, Trista's guffaw rang out above the chorus of laughter. "And *cut*!" she said as she slapped me on the back. "It's a wrap, people."

Grinning, I turned to her. But she'd already slipped away. I found myself staring at Marissa instead. "Oh, no!" she exclaimed, staring at Agford's scattered belongings. "Ladies!" she called to her fellow flight-crew members. As she launched into a run, I did what I had to. I dropped low into Snake Creeps Down, my leg extended. Marissa toppled forward. S.M.I.L.E. shrieked and swarmed to the rescue as I raced for the street, seizing Agford's wig and every loose scrap of paper as though a birthday piñata had just opened.

Something told me this was better than a birthday.

Chapter Sixteen

Exhibit (Dr.) A

A hiss of whispers rose up as I walked into science fifteen minutes late. Before class I had sneaked across the soccer field to the trail that led down to the beach and stashed Agford's wig and papers in a hole under a sage plant. No way that evidence would be safe in my locker.

Ms. Gant looked up for only a second before she resumed passing back the quizzes from the week before. Her mouth was tight and small like a hyphen. "You'll have to check in with the attendance office first, Sophie," she said. "I've already marked you absent." Handing me my quiz seemed to disappoint her as much as me. C plus. I wondered if this was what Trent Spinner felt like all the time. I'd start flinging pudding at people, too.

As I meandered back from the attendance office and down the empty outdoor halls, I spotted Marissa Pritchard standing in the courtyard locker area. Her back to me, she gestured to her head as she spoke. What was she doing out of class?

When Marissa turned, I had my answer. She was talking to Dr. Agford, who appeared to have retrieved her backup wig from home. (It seemed even poufier and more bullet-proof than the other, if that was possible.) Marissa pointed to the front of the school and shrugged. Agford stiffened. No doubt they were discussing Agford's little morning mishap. I quickened my pace and rounded the corner to the science room.

Groups were scattered around the classroom with magnets and batteries working on a lab when I entered. I'd have to face Ms. Gant to retrieve the handout and be partnered up.

"Hey," a voice whispered behind me.

I turned around. My heart skipped a beat. It was Rod.

He smiled and hinged his hands apart, miming Agford's faulty convertible top. "You got her back for the assembly, didn't you?"

I grinned mischievously. "Whatever would have given you that idea?"

Rod flashed back a knowing smile. "Oh, I don't know. Maybe because it was awesome?"

My skin tingled. Who needed a science lab? I'd just transformed into a walking electromagnet. "In that case . . . maybe it *was* me."

Ms. Gant's voice rose above the din of the classroom as she circulated among the tables. "I'd better be hearing the sound of hard work! I expect your write-ups by tomorrow, don't forget."

"Hey," Rod said quietly. He looked down and shifted his weight in almost exactly the same way he had in the lunch line on Friday. "Have you gotten any of my texts?"

"Texts?" I felt my breath catch. He had used the plural, hadn't he? As in, not just one, but multiple texts. Possibly streams of texts. Somewhere there was an inbox filled with texts from Rod. "Oh, gosh. My parents took my phone away. You know." I gestured, as if that could begin to explain the past week.

"Oh, right." Rod shoved his hand into his pocket. Was it me, or had he blushed just a bit?

"But they wouldn't read them," I lied as I imagined my parents poring over them. Thank goodness they were probably too preoccupied with work. "I mean, not that you texted anything, you know . . ."

"It's cool," he said. "With everything that's going on, I just wanted to make sure . . . if you need anything . . ."

Want to help me catch a fugitive? I was tempted to ask. But I didn't. I knew better. When it was all over—and it would be all over—I'd tell him everything.

"Just let me know," he whispered quickly, swinging back around just as Ms. Gant approached his group's table.

I floated through the rest of the morning. When I was supposed to be multiplying polynomials, I was imagining the headline in the *Luna Vista News-Press*: "Local Sleuths Foil Fugitive." My fantasies moved quickly from there to my future beach wedding with Rod. Except then Grace couldn't be my maid of honor, since she hates the ocean. Maybe a mountain meadow location? By third period I'd just accepted a professorship at Oxford. Asian Studies, of course. Rod wouldn't mind staying home to be a house husband and care for our identical twin girls.

I forgot all my fantasies the instant I discovered Charlotte Agford standing at my open locker during break, arms folded as she watched Mr. Hiller, the head of maintenance, empty its contents. He pulled off my schedule from my inside locker door to peer behind it. It ripped in half.

"Oopsy-daisy," Agford said in her falsetto, her eyes meeting mine. She pretended to consult her notebook and turned to Mr. Hiller. "Next is two eighty-three. Bottoms,

Trista." She flashed me a grin. "We're conducting *random* locker searches," she said, before clip-clopping down the outdoor hall.

Trista was too smart to keep anything incriminating in her locker. I didn't even worry much until lunch. However, when I brought my UFO burger and ETTs (Extraterrestrial Tater Tots) out to the patio and steeled myself for Trista's rant against Space Day's unhealthy fare, she wasn't there. I pictured her sitting opposite Agford in a bare interrogation room with a spotlight and an overflowing ashtray as Agford tried to get at the truth. It was more likely Trista was locked behind Mr. Katz's door, staring at a poster of an eagle exhorting her to excellence.

S.M.I.L.E. sat down at the table next to me as I ate lunch alone, not even giving me so much as one of their usual Agford sympathy pouts. Marissa turned to another -issa—Clarissa, I think—and said very loudly, "*Someone* needs to do something about her passive-aggressive behavior patterns, don't you think?"

I turned around. "*Someone* missed the English class on irony," I said. They ignored me. Eventually they rose, put on homemade plastic yellow aprons that read DON'T MESS AROUND! (Jenn's was cream-colored), and formed an unsolicited litter patrol, making a grand show of avoiding my table. I wolfed down my last bites and went on a mission to find Trista.

I found her, all right—bursting out of Katz's Den of Inspiration, grinning. When she saw me, she slapped me a high five. "Guess who's suspended?"

"Nah. Not me," she said, when she saw my expression. "Trent Spinner," she shouted. "After I reported him messing around in the parking lot yesterday, it so happened a search of his locker turned up evidence that he tampered with Dr. Agford's car. Crazy coincidence, isn't it?" She beamed.

I smiled back. Leave it to Trista to get back at Agford *and* Trent all in one prank. The sixth graders Trent gave wedgies to all the time would have lined up to ask for autographs if they'd known Trista had gotten him suspended. I couldn't help thinking of Rod, though. Would Trent earn congratulations on his "awesome" prank instead?

Before we shuttled off to class, I managed to tell Trista I'd picked up the wig. "If the FBI can link anything in that car to their suspect, by tomorrow I think it'll all be over," I said.

"They'd better arrest her at school," Trista said. "I've got to see it for myself."

I raced out of pre-algebra last period and made a beeline toward the field, darting a glance behind me to check for

S.M.I.L.E. spies. One or the other of them had seemed to be tailing me all day. I'd even caught Marissa trying to peer into my open backpack in French. It was obvious she and Agford had been talking about the wig. No doubt Marissa was operating under orders.

I'd just passed the bike racks when a sound made me nearly jump out of my Pumas.

"Psst!" Grace peered behind a pillar. She was dressed in a drab T-shirt and jeans, actually blending in for a change.

My hand flew to my heart. "You've perfected the sneak attack, haven't you?"

"You think?" Grace looked proud. "Thought I'd come report for duty, General. You know, in case you need school backup."

"Did you see Ralston on the way over?"

Grace shook her head. "Didn't see her yesterday either." She frowned. "But that meaty guy with the eyebrow drove right past me in his truck on his way down here, so the backup is definitely around."

"I think I've finally got some evidence," I said. After a quick check to be sure the coast was clear, I led Grace across the soccer field to the beach trail. When she saw where we were going, Grace stopped short. The surf was practically nonexistent, the only sound a tiny static hiss as the waves lapped at the shore far below. Still, Grace refused to take a step closer.

I looked back at the school. Agford's office window was on the second floor, overlooking the field and trailhead. "I stashed it all just a few steps down the trail. Nowhere near the beach. I promise," I said.

Grace eyed me suspiciously but followed. I held her arm and coached her along as lizards hopped for cover. It didn't matter that the bluff trail ran at least a quarter mile above the beach. To her, the damp salt air must have felt like waves closing around her. She breathed deeply and took a few wobbly steps before finding a surer footing. When we reached my hiding place, she sat with her back to the ocean.

I dug out the papers and wig and held them up.

"Oh my God, how did you . . . ?" Grace's mouth turned into a perfect O. She let out a little laugh, seeming to forget the waves below.

"Long story," I said, handing her the wig. She took it from me as if it were a wad of used toilet paper.

"Tell me on the way home," Grace said, reaching for her backpack. "We shouldn't be handling evidence. I've got a full kit at the house."

"Across the street from Agford? No way. It's safer here."

"Hard to believe," Grace said as she cast a look at the

ocean behind us and shivered. She didn't argue, though.

As much as I wanted to tell Grace all about Agford's total humiliation, I hesitated to bring up Trista. But I shouldn't have worried at all. Grace bent over in silent, shaking laughter, and tears ran down her cheeks when I described the look on Agford's face when her convertible ripped open. "I can't believe I ever doubted Trista," she said. "How'd she do it?"

"She knew they sell remotes for convertible tops and made it work with the Mustang wiring. She's good, isn't she?" I said.

Grace nodded. She wrinkled her nose and peered at the wig more closely. "One hundred percent acrylic," she announced, reading a label inside the wig.

"That describes Agford, all right," I said. "You think there can be something in all this?" I began sifting through the various scraps Agford's convertible had liberated: some grocery store coupons, receipts, a letter from Mr. Katz about changes to the academic calendar.

"I can't believe it!" Grace exclaimed.

"What?" My breath quickened. I realized how close we were. If we found just one link, tomorrow Agford could be modeling her orange jumpsuit in jail.

"She bought underwear at Victoria's Secret," Grace said, using her fingernails like tweezers to hold up a receipt.

"Never let me set foot in that place again."

"Grace, this is serious!"

"I know, I know, but so is buying anything at the same place Agford shops!"

I shook my head, absentmindedly sliding my yin pendant back and forth on its chain. I noticed a tiny mileage logbook among the papers and picked it up. A folded piece of newspaper fluttered down. "This is weird," I said, turning it over. It was a ripped-out photo of a girls' cheerleading squad, dressed in orange and white. I almost tossed it back in the pile, thinking it was from our local paper, until I remembered. "Luna Vista is the Lightning, right?" I asked.

"What do you mean?"

"The high school's mascot. It's not a cat. It's a yellow lightning bolt."

"Soph. I'm homeschooled. I've no idea."

We squinted at the logo on the girls' jerseys. "It's definitely a cat of some sort," I said.

"The Luna Vista Tabbies," Grace joked. "I'm not wrong, am I? That does look like a T next to the cat."

"T for Texas?"

Grace nodded slowly. "Well, it's sure not T for Luna Vista."

Two gulls glided together across the horizon, silhouetted by the sun. Above us on the field, Coach Knight blew his whistle and counted in rhythmic shouts.

"This could be it, Grace. We have to get this to Agent Ralston," I said. "Wherever she's been hiding."

We made our way up the trail, agreeing to ride our bikes home separately. Each of us would keep a lookout for Ralston's blue car or the white pickup. If we weren't able to spot either, Grace would secure the evidence in a secret drop location and email Ralston the location from home. Thank God one of us still had email access. Until next quarter, I wasn't even allowed to go on the computers at school.

"When you see her, ask Ralston if the FBI has any other cold cases we can wrap up for them," I said with a smirk as we reached the top of the trail.

"Roger. Ten-four," Grace replied. "Over and outta here—" She pumped her fist and jogged off across the soccer field. In the late afternoon sun her shadow loomed before her like a giant.

Chapter Seventeen

Enemy Incoming

"How many times I got to tell you?" Grandpa Young shouted to someone at the door. "I'm not gonna buy anything."

My family had just had dinner together for the first time that week because of all the long hours my parents had been putting in before next Thursday night's test launch. It figured we'd eat together the one night I needed to be glued to the walkie-talkie for Grace's Ralston update. I was handing dirty dishes to Jake, who seemed to believe cleanup duty was actually a regular hip-hop gig showcasing his ability to rap along with one out of every eighty words blasting through his headphones. If he didn't occasionally strike painfully awkward hip-hop poses, we all would have assumed he was listening to a highly inappropriate phonics-based reading program.

"What's up, Dad?" I heard my father intervene in the foyer. "My God! Please come in. So sorry. Sometimes, you know . . ."

"That's quite all right, Wade" came Agford's reedy falsetto.

I froze.

"Old age does bring its challenges," Agford added with a little cluck.

I pulled off Jake's headphones before his next rap eruption, but it was Grandpa who shouted instead. "Enemy incoming! Double torpedoes!" he boomed.

As my dad led Agford into the kitchen, I reminded myself to find Grandpa later and hug him.

"Charlotte! Nice to see you," my mom said uncertainly as Agford handed her a decorative glass jar filled with—of course—blood-red beets.

"I thought I'd pop over and bring your gift early this year, since Soph left her assignment book in my office today." Agford waved a notebook I'd never seen in my life and scrunched up her face. She was having more and more trouble imitating a smile. "Besides, Sophie and I didn't quite finish our discussion earlier, so I thought . . . you two don't mind if I spend one quick moment with her alone, do you?"

"If that's all right with you, S—" My dad couldn't finish before Agford had slung her arm around me and steered me halfway to the stairs. What could I do? Take her out with Wave Hands Like Clouds?

Grandpa Young shook his head at my dad. "I'm telling you, Wade, it's *domestic* defense you should be working on. Increase the burn velocity on that missile interceptor. That's your trouble." Grandpa slapped him on the back.

"Sure thing, Dad," my father said, exchanging a look with my mom.

If only they understood what Grandpa really meant.

Agford's headache-inducing "perfume" cloud roiled in her wake as she walked around my room and surveyed its decor. She ran her fingers along the books on my shelf, pulling out Sun Tzu's *The Art of War* and glancing at the cover before sliding it back in the wrong place. She held up my Hello Kitty piggy bank and squinted at it, tapped the lid of my *I Ching* fortune-telling sticks, and poked at my brass Buddha figurine. I made a mental note to order incense from Feng Shui Planet to counteract her Lysol stink. It was going to take weeks to restore proper balance.

Agford's eyes crawled over my wind chimes, my bamboo ink-and-wash painting, and my twin bed's red comforter, finally coming to rest on my poster of Kai Li. She nodded slowly at it, as if interpreting highly conceptual modern art.

Agford broke her long silence. "I'm going to need my wig back," she said, still staring at the poster.

I kept my expression as neutral as possible and said nothing. *Be subtle to the point of soundlessness.*

"Now's not the time for games, Sophie," Agford snapped. She walked over to the bed and sat down next to me.

I met her eyes. I did not blink.

"I have it on good information that you have some things of mine." Agford's voice fell to a hoarse whisper. "Those items are *very* important to me. I need them back."

"I think Marissa and her friends picked up your things after the—the—"

"The malfunction?"

"The malfunction."

"Or the vandalism?" she asked, studying me. The bed creaked as she stood up and paced the room again. Her dark eyes flitted from surface to surface.

I pulled myself into a casual, cross-legged pose and watched as Agford tried to hide the desperation of her search. A burst of giddiness overcame me. I had to focus on the seam of my bed-spread to contain myself. It was like the time Grace and I were struck with a giggling fit right as my cousin Beth took her wedding vows.

But Agford stopped midstride. Her face lit up. I followed her gaze to the antenna of my walkie-talkie peering out from under my Feng Shui Planet catalog.

She picked it up slowly. I braced myself for her anger. It didn't come. Instead she fiddled with the dial and looked lost in thought.

"You know, Sophie? You remind me of myself some-times," she said gently. She smiled then—not her usual bared-teeth smile but a faint, fond smile that unnerved me. It almost looked real.

"Myself as a child, I mean. Even younger than you are now." Agford sat down on my bed again and tilted her head. Warmth flickered in her usually cold eyes. Even with our suspicions about Agford, I'd sometimes catch myself think-ing of her decorating her fake Halloween graveyard all alone and—for just a second—I'd wonder if she could really be behind anything bad. Was it possible the FBI couldn't prove their case any faster because she really *wasn't* their woman?

"Me and my younger brother, we had walkie-talkies, too," she continued. "They had a Morse code function, and we used to stay up late sending each other messages when our mom thought we were asleep. It made life seem more *exciting* somehow."

That Agford had ever been a kid—that she could have been someone's little girl—seemed impossible. I tried to picture her watching cartoons, playing tic-tac-toe with her brother, snuggling stuffed animals. I guess she couldn't have always been slathered in makeup and weighed down by the entire Southwest's reserve of turquoise jewelry. I felt the littlest bit sad that I couldn't imagine her any other way.

"But you have to grow up, Sophie." She leveled her eyes at me. "Games can cross lines. Games can hurt people. They *do* hurt people." Her voice fell to a rusty whisper. She held up the walkie-talkie. "Is that what this is for? Games?"

I felt myself snap to attention. It was like Grandpa said about gathering intelligence in the war. You have to forget *what* someone is saying and focus on *why* and *how*. Agford couldn't get to me anymore—not with childhood memories, not with smiles, not with anything. Grace would have already contacted Ralston by now. I wouldn't be surprised if the feds seized Agford tonight, so they could catch her off guard.

I fastened my eyes on hers. "Game?" I said. "No, it's definitely not a game."

Agford pressed her lips together. She stood up. "I see." She tucked the walkie-talkie into her blazer pocket. "I think your parents will be interested in this. Maybe Grace's parents, too." She studied my reaction. "In fact, I'm headed over to the Yangs' now. I promised them we'd discuss the pros and cons of public school versus homeschooling."

I stared back blankly, but inside I screamed. What if Grace hadn't stashed the evidence yet?

"That's so sweet of you." I smiled, hoping it looked more natural than it felt.

"Oh, really," Agford said as she turned to leave. "It's my pleasure."

I watched from my window as Agford strode down our front steps. My pulse quickened with the clopping of her heels. There was nothing I could do to stop her. I closed my eyes and pictured her heel catching on the stair, her outstretched arms windmilling, her teeth smacking against concrete. I opened them again. Onward she marched, arms swinging like a determined soldier's. She was almost to Grace's driveway. I pressed one hand to the glass and prayed.

Chapter Eighteen

A Shocking Discovery

ater that night I waited in the dark under my covers, fully dressed in black shoes, pants, and a long-sleeved T-shirt. I'd had to ransack my closet, but I'd managed to embrace a little spy style for once.

After Agford had left to share her walkie-talkie discovery with my parents and, no doubt, suggest that I spend the remainder of my life alone in a damp cell inhabited by flesh-eating spiders, I'd slid open my window. When my parents' last murmurs finally faded and I heard nothing but the breeze from my open window brushing against my wind chimes, I crept out of bed, lashed my trusty rope to the bedpost—tying a double knot for safety—and strung it down the house.

"Thank God you came," Grace said as she let me in the sliding-glass door that led from her side yard to her room.

"It was awful. So awful." Her hair was pinned back, and white spots dotted her face.

"What happened to you?"

"You mean this?" Grace pointed to her face. "Just zit cream," she explained. "That woman makes me break out." She shooed Lucky off the bed and swept away a pile of magazines to make room for me. Patches of blank wall yawned like missing teeth among Grace's usual floor-to-ceiling collage of posters, representing the spaces where her FBI wanted notices once hung. The cardboard cutout of Nux Vomica's lead singer still sneered, but he looked a little lost. I breathed in, checking for Agford's *eau de Lysol* scent.

"She got everything, didn't she?" I opened the door to Grace's closet command center. There were no maps, no clippings, no whiteboard. Nothing but shoes and belts and clothes falling off hangers.

"What? No! Who do you think you're dealing with here? They don't call me Amazing Grace for nothing."

"Who calls you Amazing Grace?" I shouldn't have asked. It was probably some private joke with Jocelyn and Natalie.

"You, from here on out." Grace grinned as she crouched by the bed and tugged at something underneath it.

"But the posters?" I pointed.

"Precautionary measure," she said, leaning down to toss aside one of her brown boots before fumbling under the bed. She slid out her rectangular steel forensics box and unlocked the padlock with a flourish. She wriggled on a pair of latex gloves, snapped the elastic to ensure they were adequately snug, then held up a clear Ziploc bag dated and labeled EXHIBIT A: WIG. It contained what appeared to be a furry exotic pet but was, at second glance, clearly Agford's hair helmet crushed beyond recognition.

"Grace! You were supposed to stash it!"

"Amazing Grace. Remember?" She shook her head. "Determining a secure location takes time, Sophie," she said. "Plus, everything's fine." Grace unraveled a sheet of plastic film and laid it over her bed to protect the evidence, forgetting that I'd riffled through everything a couple hours earlier. As she began to pluck papers from the box with oversize tweezers, she detailed the horrors of Agford's visit. Agford had waltzed into the house and cornered the Yangs in a long discussion about Grace's studies. Although Grace's parents homeschooled her because they wanted her to be able to enjoy lots of extracurriculars without having the pressure of juggling a lot at once, sometimes they worried that Grace wasn't learning as much as she would at a regular school. Probably sensing she could prey on those fears, Agford insisted upon seeing Grace's room to determine whether it provided suitable study conditions.

"I had no choice," Grace said. "I had to go all-out Chinese."

"Let me guess. Spontaneous piano recital?"

"Of course." She smiled mischievously. "You know she thinks we dance around our house in cone-shaped rice-paddy hats and bang gongs or something, so I figured I might as well act the part."

"And?"

"Worked like a charm. After six awful run-throughs of 'Greensleeves,' she couldn't wait to leave."

"Nice." I slapped her a high five. "I wish I could have seen her face."

"I know. My parents couldn't figure out *what* was up with me. I bet she'll be back, though." She shuddered, seeming to forget that I'd had to put up with close encounters of the Dr. Awkward kind pretty much every day.

"Don't worry," I said. "She'll be arrested before then."

Grace's face creased with worry. "About that . . ." She swiveled her laptop screen around to face me. "Things have gotten complicated."

It was an email from Agent Ralston:

*****AUTOMATED RESPONSE*********************************

I am currently out of the office on vacation. For

urgent matters, please contact the main switchboard

at (870) 555-1000.

*****AUTOMATED RESPONSE*********************************

"Vacation?" I said. I pictured Ralston, neck roped with fragrant leis, lounging ocean side with an umbrella-garnished fruity cocktail in one hand and *People* magazine in the other. "Vacation?" I repeated. "How could she?"

"*Shhh!*" Grace jabbed her finger at the door in warning.

"But, *vacation?*" I hissed.

"Don't panic. Ralston has to have a good reason for this."

"Like what?" I asked. "Unbeatable airfare to Tahiti?" I closed my eyes and practiced my tai chi breathing. *In. Out. In. Out.* I thought of the dark circles under Ralston's eyes, her drooped shoulders. I'd taken them as signs of worry and lack of sleep. But she wasn't worried about her safety. Her conscience wasn't tortured by some dark plan the FBI had hatched to use innocent kids as bait, either. She was just overdue for some R & R on sun-drenched sands.

Grace let out a heavy sigh. "She's FBI, Sophie. Maybe

she's realized Agford's not her woman," Grace said. She sounded downright disappointed.

"Then she hopped a plane for the islands without mentioning we can relax now? I don't think so." I got up and tried to pace, but Grace's magazines and clothes made it like running an obstacle course.

Grace rubbed the top of Lucky's head. "Let's think about it. When's the last time you saw Ralston?"

"Monday morning," I said, remembering her sedan trailing me as I rode to school. For all I knew, she had been going to the airport to split for Club Med. "But I saw Unibrow lurking outside Agford's last night, I'm pretty sure. And didn't you say you saw him when you biked down to school today?"

"Yeah. So, see? They're still on the case. Maybe he's in charge now."

"She's got nitwit on the case while she's sucking down mai tais? You think that's okay?"

"How do you know he's not a genius? Maybe he's smart *and* all muscle," Grace said.

"All muscle? Apart from the man boobs, you mean? He's giving Agford some serious competition."

Grace rolled her eyes. "You're totally overreacting."

"*I'm* overreacting?" I laughed in disbelief. "Now there's

a change. Grace, this is, like, the one time you should be freaking out."

"What's that supposed to mean?"

"The FBI has abandoned us with a fugitive who knows we're on to her, Grace."

"I wouldn't say abandoned exactly . . ." Grace tugged at a loose strand of hair.

Maybe my words were finally sinking in. "All Ralston's baloney about the operation taking a while? She needed to keep us out and buy time for her vacation. Then she leaves this doofus running the show while she's at the beach without even telling us!"

"*Shhh!*" Grace hissed again. "If you wake up my parents, we're dead."

"No, that's exactly what we have to do." I moved toward the door. "Let's wake them right now. Let's tell them everything."

Grace hopped up to block my way. "They're not going to believe us," she said. "What are they going to do anyway? Go to the FBI? They'll deny everything. You heard why Ralston didn't want to tell our parents. They want to keep this undercover."

It was the first reasonable thing Grace had said since we'd read the message. I sat down on the bed. Lucky cocked his head at me. "Maybe . . ." I flipped Grace's laptop back and stared at the message. "Maybe we can figure out who the FBI thought she was and work backward from there to prove the connection."

Grace nodded slowly. "You mean cut Ralston out of the equation and go directly to the police? I don't know, Sophie."

"I thought you said the FBI doesn't usually make arrests, anyway. The police do," I said. Then I pictured Officer Grady wedged into the armchair in Mr. Katz's office, gushing with compliments about Agford's beet juice. I sighed. "That's not going to work, is it?"

"Maybe it's worth a try," Grace said. She sat cross-legged in front of her laptop and began to type.

"I think we're going to need more than Wikipedia, Grace."

"Yeah? Well, look." She pointed to the screen. "Every high school in Texas, organized by county. We gather the ones that begin with T . . ."

"And check the mascots." I clapped my hands together. "This could work."

Grace clicked to one high school home page after another. Soon we'd found three "T" schools with cat mascots.

"No tabbies though." I smiled.

"Uh, negative." Grace gave Lucky a pat as he rubbed his face against her knee.

"Hang on," I interrupted. "Ralston said she's from the Austin FBI office, right? So there's got to be a way to check which counties that office covers."

Grace's face lit up. Within seconds she was on the FBI's web page. "Yep. Austin has jurisdiction over Bastrop, Blanco, Burleson, Burnet . . . fourteen counties in all," she said. Before long we'd narrowed down our list to just a few schools. "Okay, Tucker High School. Burnet County," I said, holding my breath as Grace clicked. My hopes rose.

Grace's computer speakers blared the first few notes of a marching-band song. She slammed her hand on Mute and looked at the door. On the screen furry cartoon beasts with long duck bills danced and banged bass drums. "What *are* those?" Grace made a face.

"Platypuses, maybe?"

"Oh-kayy. On to Troy High, then."

Troy High was the Trojans; Temple High, the Cowboys. At last we stumbled onto the Tilmore High School Tigers in Tilmore, Texas, not far from Austin. On the home page stood a roaring silhouette of a tiger superimposed over a bold, chunky orange T. I held up the ripped newspaper from Agford's car next to the screen.

"Perfect match," Grace said.

I nodded. "To a T."

She groaned at my lame pun.

"So now what?" Grace asked.

I hardly heard her. My vision narrowed until I saw nothing but the stern, squared corners of the orange Tilmore High T. I stood up straight. I felt a surge of anger—or was it power? We had Agford in our sights. It was time to plunge forward. *The possibility of victory lies in the attack,* Sun Tzu said. But how to attack?

"She works at a school now," I said. "Maybe she has the paper because she worked at a school then, too. Search 'Tilmore High' and 'murder,' maybe?"

Sports headlines littered the screen. Grace read aloud: "'Tilmore High Murders the Fort Hood Ferrets, Thirty-two to Seven.'"

"That's what happens when you name your team after a small rodent," I said.

Grace's fingers tapped on her keyboard. "Let's try 'Tilmore, Texas, Investigation,'" she said. A list of articles from the *Austin American-Statesman* scrolled onscreen. Now we were getting somewhere. Even Lucky seemed uplifted. He do-si-doed between the legs of Grace's desk chair, capping off his unexpected square dance with a neat allemande right with his tail.

I leaned over Grace's shoulder to read:

SWIM-MEET TRAGEDY INVESTIGATION UNDERWAY

(TILMORE—April 8) Investigations into the electrocution of five Tilmore High and three Kenwood High students in Tilmore High's newly built Olympic-sized pool at the league-championship swim meet March 30 are underway, reported Vernon LaGrange, Tilmore High's principal. Deborah S. Bain, assistant superintendent of the Tilmore Independent School District, confirmed that electrical wiring work in the athletic facility's new pool had only recently been completed before Tuesday's fatal accident.

The hair at the base of my neck prickled. Grace ran her hands over her hairpins. Neither of us spoke as we skimmed the horrifying headlines of the associated stories. "Parents Watch from the Stands as Children Drown," and "Team Captain, 17, Dies in Heroic Rescue Attempt."

It seemed an odd coincidence that Agford had a newspaper from a high school where such a gruesome accident took place.

Grace's hands were trembling. If we ran across many more stories like this, she wouldn't even go to the pool with me, let alone the beach.

"It's just an accident," I said, hoping to distract her. "Maybe we should search something with 'crime'?"

Grace shook her head. She pointed to the last in the list of related articles.

MANSLAUGHTER CHARGES IN POOL ACCIDENT

(TILMORE—April 12) The fatal electrocution of eight high school students on March 30 was the result of gross negligence and fraud, authorities have now determined.

Daniel Slater of Slater Construction, the company that performed all electrical work at Tilmore High's new pool complex, has been indicted on eight counts of involuntary manslaughter and fifteen counts of fraud. School administrators are still determining how his unlicensed company won repeated bids for lucrative district contracts despite frequent staff complaints about unfinished or substandard work.

"I can assure you we are making every effort to investigate the cause of this tragedy," said Assistant Superintendent of Schools Deborah S. Bain. The Tilmore Independent School District

paid more than $2 million to Slater's company over the past three years.

A picture accompanied the article. A heavyset man, his stomach straining against his jeans and leather belt, lifted his jacket to hide his face as he pushed his way through a crowd of reporters.

"No way," Grace said, finally recovering. "She was a guy! No wonder the feds can't tell it's her."

"Danny," I whispered.

"I know. I wouldn't have pegged her for a Daniel, either."

"No, silly. The phone call. She's not a guy. She was talking to one! *Danny*." I tapped my finger on the screen. "Daniel Slater."

"Danny Slater," Grace repeated. She rubbed my fingerprint off her laptop screen with the sleeve of her pajamas.

"Google Slater. There's got to be more on him."

Grace typed. I marveled at how easy it was. The bits and bytes containing the secret of Agford's real identity had always lurked somewhere out there, waiting to be uncovered. A few well-chosen clicks and, like a combination lock releasing as the tumblers slipped into place, Grace's laptop might very well serve up the truth.

"Hang on," Grace said, pointing. "What's this?"

FIRE KILLS LOCAL OFFICIAL

(TILMORE—May 2) Prominent local school administrator Deborah S. Bain is presumed dead after a fire ravaged her two-story colonial home in Tilmore in the early morning hours Sunday. Neighbors awaking to billowing smoke and 10-foot flames heard a woman's cries and called for help. Although firefighters prevented the blaze from spreading, it destroyed Bain's home. The cause of the fire is still being determined, but Fire Chief Robert McAllister reported Bain was likely asleep in bed when it began.

"Deborah dedicated her whole life to the welfare of our kids," neighbor Beverly Mathers said, weeping. "Now everything is in ashes." Deborah Bain gave more than 20 years of service to the school district in a variety of roles, most recently as assistant superintendent of the Tilmore Independent School District. The district attorney offered no comment about whether her death will hamper the case against Daniel Slater, a contractor accused of involuntary manslaughter for his role in the Tilmore High pool tragedy last month. Bain's office had closely coordinated with the district attorney in the preliminary investigations.

"Unless Agford's a zombie, she can't be Deborah Bain," I said with a chuckle. "Although that certainly would explain a lot, wouldn't it?"

"And, while I may be unaware of some major advances in plastic surgery, I'm pretty sure it can't turn *that*"—Grace clicked back to the article and accompanying photo of Daniel Slater and his bulging belly—"into a busty middle-aged woman."

I let out a long sigh. A moment ago my heart had been racing with the thrill of the hunt as we neared our prey. Now the jumbled details muddied my brain. A woman dead by fire. A contractor who didn't do repairs. A horrible swim-meet tragedy. All of it was awful. All of it was strange. Yet none of it traced back to Agford.

"Just when it was starting to feel easy," Grace said glumly. She flopped back onto her bed and stared at the ceiling. "We're not even very good Googlers, let alone private investigators, are we?" A gob of white acne cream smeared across her fingers as she brought her hands to her head. She glanced at her alarm clock. "Jeez. It's two a.m. You should go back," she said.

"Maybe just one more search?" It felt strange to be the one pushing her forward.

"Let's give Ralston a chance to reply," Grace said, sitting up again. "Maybe she will. If not, we'll call the number on her email. Who cares what she said about secure phone lines at this point?"

Lucky rubbed his chin on the corner of Grace's laptop. As she swatted him away, my eye caught one of the headlines on the screen.

"There's something else. Scroll down," I said, leaning in to read the headline.

SUICIDE SUSPECTED IN BAIN HOUSE FIRE

(TILMORE—May 15) Just one day before her death in a devastating house fire, Deborah Bain was interrogated by authorities about her possible role in Tilmore High's gruesome swim-meet tragedy last month, sources at the district attorney's office revealed Friday.

Tilmore High Principal Vernon LaGrange confirmed that investigations revealed Bain's office had awarded indicted private contractor Daniel Slater more than $2 million in construction bids for work that was not satisfactorily completed. The district attorney neither confirmed nor denied reports that Slater and Bain were related, but the *Statesman*'s research indicates Deborah Bain's middle initial S might stand for Slater, and that the two may be half siblings.

Interviews with Bain's coworkers and neighbors suggest Bain was distraught over the investigation. Authorities now suspect her death was a suicide. However, the investigation has been impeded by the lack of remains on the scene.

"A perfect match for our woman, and she's been incinerated." Grace flung up her hands.

"Is that what that means? Lack of remains?"

"Yep. No Deborah Bain. Just ashes. The police can't do a thing."

I pictured a bewildered group of cops standing among heaps of ash, their pencils hovering above blank notepads. "Wait a minute. If there's no body, then how do they know she really died?"

Grace didn't even hesitate before busting out a forensics lecture. "Well, in these cases, they usually match teeth with dental records, but sometimes, if the fire burns hot for a long time . . ." Grace's eyes widened. She leaped up and grabbed me by both shoulders. "You're a genius!"

"So maybe she . . ."

Grace nodded. "It makes sense. She fakes her death in the fire, hits the road, and she's home free. She doesn't leave a trace."

"That's why it's so hard for the feds to know if Agford is her! They didn't get DNA from her in the first place."

"Exactly! And check out the article dates: Agford moved here two summers ago. That would only be six weeks or so after the fire." Grace hunched back over her computer in search of more articles on Bain.

Slowly we pieced the full story together. We didn't find anything else on Bain's death, but there were piles of articles on the swim-meet tragedy, each one accompanied by haunting photos of "the Tilmore Eight" and their grief-stricken families. Even the national news media had picked up on the story. Bain had contracted with her brother's company, Slater Construction, to complete work at all the schools in the Tilmore district. Slater Construction had cut corners to make huge profits they either spent or squirreled away in offshore accounts. The electrical work for the Tilmore High pool lights was done by untrained workers the head foreman had picked up off the street. None of the required inspections had been carried out.

So, one day, as kids were hopping into the pool to begin warm-up laps for the championship swim meet, ten thousand volts of electricity pulsed through the pool's waters, because some wiring in the lights had come loose. The proud parents who filled the bleachers looked on helplessly as their children's bodies convulsed in the blue water. The captain of the swim team had jumped in to save his girlfriend. They both died, arm in arm. I couldn't bear to read about it.

"You really think we should go to the cops instead of waiting?" Grace asked.

I imagined bursting into Officer Grady's office with a scrap of newspaper and an acrylic wig, claiming Agford was a wanted fugitive who'd made off with millions, then faked her own death in a fire.

"God, you're right. We can't prove a thing." My shoulders slumped. I felt the same way I did during my tai chi sparring sessions. Just when I thought I'd mastered my Seven Star Punch or Cloud Hands, my instructor would calmly block and counterattack.

"Let's check if Unibrow's truck is out there," Grace offered. "We could see if he can get in touch with Ralston at least?"

I humored Grace. But neither Ralston's bulky right-hand man nor his white pickup were anywhere to be found. Grace tossed her high-powered binoculars on the bed as if it was their fault. "I don't think he'd even know what to do with it all, anyway," she said.

Lucky the cat, eager for more investigation, darted around the room stalking imaginary prey. If only it were still all a game. I watched as he disappeared into a toppled cardboard box in the corner.

"Hey," I said, sitting up. "Do your parents lock your door that goes from your garage into your house?"

"Nope. But I told you already, Soph." Irritation crept

into Grace's voice. "I'll stash the evidence. You don't have to worry about her breaking in."

Lucky peered out from the box, watching us curiously from the safety of its shadows.

"That's not what I mean. My parents don't lock ours either. The garage door is secure enough. And you know what? Agford left hers unlocked on Saturday. I don't think she ever locks it."

"What are you saying? We break in?"

"We know she's Deborah Bain. We just have to prove it. And I'm not waiting around for Ralston to cruise back from the Caribbean to do it." I scanned Grace's room. "I've got an idea. Where's your phone?"

Grace looked at me uncertainly. "Right on the desk. Why?"

"If you know the enemy and you know yourself, victory will never stand in doubt," I replied. The bed creaked as I stood up.

"You quote Sun Tzu one more time, Lucky and I vomit in your lap." On cue, Lucky reemerged from his investigations and stood at attention. He cast me a warning look before leaping to Grace's dresser to run a slow-motion slalom course around her various nail-polish bottles and empty Diet Coke cans.

"Is Miss Anita still going to her Harvard alumni thing?"

"Yes, thank God. Self-study from tomorrow till Monday."

"Perfect. You and I are going on a mission tomorrow, Agent Yang. Together."

As Grace raised her hand to give a salute, a loud clattering rang out. We turned to see Lucky atop Grace's dresser, wide-eyed amid the wreckage of nail-polish bottles.

A door creaked open down the hall. We froze. Lucky, the coward, dashed for cover under the bed skirt.

"Grace?" Mr. Dr. Yang's voice croaked.

As Grace shooed me away wildly, I leaped for her cell phone and slid open the patio door just wide enough to slip out.

"One p.m. tomorrow. Meet me here," I whispered just before Grace's door swung open to reveal a groggy Mr. Dr. Yang in red-and-white striped pajamas, looking concerned. I flattened myself against the wall outside and held my breath. I didn't dare run, for fear Mr. Dr. Yang would hear me.

His worry turned to anger. "What are you doing?"

"Miss Anita—" Grace protested.

Mr. Dr. Yang muttered something in Mandarin I couldn't make out. "Hand it over," he said in English.

And just like that, Mr. Dr. Yang snatched Grace's laptop—and our hopes—away.

Chapter Nineteen

All Locked Up

Bleary-eyed, I headed to meet Trista in the alcove behind the art room at break the next morning. She looked surprisingly alert, considering I'd woken her up at two a.m. Maybe it was just because she was wearing a bright orange T-shirt. "Here you go." She handed me a crumpled brown lunch bag. "You're going to go through with this crazy plan no matter what I say, aren't you?"

"You sure it'll work?" I whispered. At least one of us should try to be subtle.

"You wake me up in the middle of the night for this *and* you want it to work?" Trista shook her head at me. Then she smiled. "Of course it does. Stanley, Craftsman, Genie, LiftMaster. I found the frequencies online and programmed them all," she explained. "Even rode the bus once around the block this morning so I could test it out."

I peered in at the universal remote, picturing Trista's bus chugging down Luna Vista Drive as a synchronized sequence of garage doors flung open.

"It was a real hit," she said with a chuckle.

"I bet. You've got Grace's cell number, right?"

She nodded and patted one of the bulging pockets of her cargo shorts. "And check this out." Trista flashed a plastic vial. "Eye drops. If I can't keep her overtime in therapy last period, watch out! I'm going to cry me a river. You sure you don't want me to let the air out of her tires?"

"Nah. Too suspicious." I got on my tiptoes to clap Trista on the shoulder. "You're a good friend. You know that?"

"And you're crazy, Sophie Young," she said, breaking into a smile. "Crazier than I ever thought you could be."

When the bell rang for lunch, Madame Tarrateau was still standing at the front of the room, arms extended, flashing her impressive tufts of underarm hair as she simulated either a jet preparing for takeoff or the Crucifixion, I wasn't sure which. I didn't wait to find out. I slung my backpack over one shoulder and headed for the door. If I was fast, I might reach the bike racks before I had to fight upstream against the lunch hordes.

I passed Trent Spinner's crew lurking near the archway

to the courtyard, looking aimless without their captain to chart a course to the cafeteria. Students emptied from classrooms, shoes scuffling, shouts rebounding against the lockers. My backpack snagged on something. When I turned to free it, I was greeted by Marissa's round, blue eyes. My backpack strap was looped through her arm as if it were an old lady she wanted to help across the street.

"Our Brown Bag Lunch Seminar is on peer pressure today. You should join us," she said, pulling back her lips in a smile that reminded me of Agford's. My blood ran cold.

"Dentist appointment," I said with a shrug. Marissa's eyes traveled to the lunch bag sagging in my hand. I smiled tightly and yanked my backpack free.

I zigzagged my way down the hall, calculating the odds that Marissa was en route to report my suspicious dentist appointment to Agford. As long as Agford didn't clip-clop down from her lair to check on me in orchestra or PE, I'd be home free. But if she did . . . I sneaked a glance over my shoulder before I rounded the corner to the bike racks. I had to risk it.

As I pedaled my bike over the crest of Luna Vista Drive, I felt as if I were taking flight. Wind rushed against my face as I coasted downhill. I imagined it was the uncontainable energy of yang. Trista was right. I was crazy—crazier than even *I* thought I could ever be.

Grace was waiting for me in a lawn chair on the patio outside her room. Two neat braids poked out from under her blue baseball cap. If she hadn't been wearing a denim mechanic's jumpsuit, she might have looked like a vacationer soaking up some sun. A name patch on her left pocket read *Earl* in a loopy script.

"Where'd you dig up that outfit?" I asked.

"Oh, I borrowed it from Jocelyn's older brother. Told him it's for a costume party. All systems go?" Grace grabbed the small black backpack that held her spy gear.

"As long as that door is unlocked," I said, tossing her the crumpled lunch bag and her cell phone. "You alone?"

"My parents are at the clinic until at least four," she said, inspecting Trista's modified garage-door remote as though checking the chambers of a gun. "I'm supposed to be writing a report on the dangers of internet addiction. Longhand."

"Didn't get your laptop back, huh? I wonder if Ralston replied."

"Not yet." Grace sighed. "I logged on to my dad's computer for, like, half a second to check—but I can't push my luck right now. Not after last night."

It wasn't until Grace and I nestled behind a thick hedge near the street to watch and wait that doubts crept in. Marissa could have told Agford already. I pictured her and the rest of S.M.I.L.E. marching in lockstep up to Agford's office like aliens returning to warn the mother ship. What if Agford was on her way home? It would only take her five minutes—especially the way she drove.

Grace hitched back her sleeve. Six digital watches ran up her forearm, all peeping and chirping as she set them. "Ninety minutes tops, right?" she said as she unfolded a piece of notebook paper. Assuming Agford's house wasn't laid out very differently from ours, Grace had divided the floor plan into imaginary sectors in dark pencil lines. "Ten minutes for each of these three sectors, maximum," she said, pointing to the open areas of the house. "But at least an hour for the basement, don't you think?"

I wasn't even irritated that Grace repeated my plan as if it were hers. We were a team, and a team doesn't waste time worrying about who should get credit. Besides, my second wind was fading and I was suddenly feeling too tired to argue. I nodded. "I say we split up. You take upstairs; I'll take downstairs. Trista will text when she can't keep Agford any longer. Is your bike ready?"

"The tires are pumped, and it's right in the garage. It shouldn't take me more than fifteen minutes to bike to the station if we find anything good." Grace's eyes flickered with worry as she turned back to Agford's house. "You think Unibrow or Ralston's other agents are watching?" she asked.

I ignored the feeling in the pit in my stomach. "Whatever," I said. "We have nothing to lose."

"If they stop us, we sure do," Grace reminded me.

The bulk of the thick-necked FBI agent we'd seen lurking around Agford's house had once reassured me. Now I pictured him leaping out to stop us as we launched our kamikaze break-in. It'd be like running into a brick wall.

"Don't worry about it," I said, surprised by the sureness in my tone. I drew in a sharp breath, aimed Trista's universal remote, and pressed. Agford's garage door whirred open.

Grace and I turned to each other. "I gotta hand it to Trista," she said.

I nodded. "It almost feels too easy, doesn't it?"

"Almost," Grace said. She tugged on a pair of her latex gloves. Her hands trembled very slightly.

"You sure you still want to go first?" My hands were shaking, too.

"When's the last time I took a risk?" Grace grinned. "It's my turn, right, General?" She tucked her braids into her

218

baseball cap and pulled it low. "Meet you at the side door in five, if the coast is clear."

"Be careful, Agent Yang."

"I'll try."

Grace jogged up to Agford's gaping garage door, put her hands on her hips, and pretended to inspect the automatic garage-door mechanism. Her workman's disguise was bad. Really bad. I held my breath and hoped no one walked by.

I breathed again once Grace disappeared into the shadows. Agford's garage door hummed shut. That was our signal. The interior door was unlocked.

I counted to two hundred. If Ralston's agents were still surveilling Agford's house, they would sweep in on Grace right away. I waited until I heard nothing but the breeze rattling through Agford's sycamores. Then I made my move.

Agford's side door swung open just as I arrived. I looked up, almost expecting to see Agford towering over me with a gleaming machete, her wig askew. But there stood Grace, striking a fake fashion pose and gesturing to her feet. Slippers of red silk embroidered with gold peeked out from under her denim jumpsuit. The Yangs' house shoes for guests.

"Nice look," I whispered.

She tossed me a matching pair. "And practical," she said. "You won't leave any trails *this* time."

We looked like lost houseguests as we shuffled around in our slippers on Agford's fake wood floor. Apart from the dishes rising out of the sink like the leaning tower of Pisa, Agford's kitchen looked just as it had on the weekend. The same rotten smell seeped from the trash, mingling with the vague traces of her disinfectant-scented perfume. I felt the same twinge of sadness. Sometimes it really did seem like she was just a weird, lonely lady, rattling around in her empty house. No friends to speak of. Not even a dog.

"Ahhh!" Grace cried.

"Ahhh!" I echoed as she toppled backward into me, arms windmilling. A fly took refuge in a patch of sticky brown residue on the counter, no doubt planning a second surprise landing on Grace's face.

"It's a fly, Agent Yang. Pull yourself together!" I whispered.

"I thought there was a booby trap!" she hissed back.

"Tell me you didn't just say *booby*."

We laughed nervously.

I pointed to the basement door across the kitchen. "Let's meet down there in half an hour," I said. "Unless Trista texts first."

Grace gave a thumbs-up, started the timer on one of her watches, and disappeared upstairs.

Agford's house was a cluster of sharp angles and empty space, as though it were trying to somehow balance out every poufy pillow that graced her office at school. A square glass table stood at the center of her dining room, blanketed by a thick layer of dust. Frenzied geometric shapes stabbed their way across a painting that hung above the hard, gray sofa in the living room. Black bookshelves lined the room; the pink covers and curlicue scripts of Agford's trashy romance collection gave the room its only softness and color.

I tiptoed through the dark, empty rooms. Each time I opened a cabinet, I expected sirens and iron traps to snap around my snooping hands, leaving me to wait in shackles for Agford's inevitable return. But there was only emptiness. No mail lingered on desks. No photos were on display. Even the drawers in Agford's office were bare, except for a few pens and legal pads. I suppose fugitives don't settle into town with moving trucks bearing treasured belongings from the good ol' days, especially when they've burned their own houses down. Still, shouldn't Agford have gathered *some* possessions over the last two years? It sure would have made much more sense if she'd channeled her passion for bright orange pumpkin flags and giant pastel bunnies into her interior decor, where they wouldn't attract attention.

I pulled open another file drawer in Agford's office. Empty. The cabinet thrummed as I slammed it shut. Upstairs Grace's footsteps creaked hurriedly back and forth. Maybe she was having more luck.

Finally I gave up and shuffled back to the kitchen. I stared at the door next to the refrigerator. The basement was waiting for us. It had been waiting for us ever since my first Saturday of punishment, when Grace and I had pressed our faces against its windows and strained to see into the darkness.

I opened the door. I don't know what I expected, exactly. A flock of rabid, fang-gnashing bats shrieking as they swarmed around my head, maybe. Certainly not the silence that greeted me instead.

I ventured onto the first wooden step. The scent of damp concrete and rust was cool and refreshing compared to the disinfectant-heavy odor of the house. The door behind me creaked gently as a faint cross draft blew against it.

Halfway down the stairs, I paused and looked around. Pale light tried to push past a few cloudy half windows near the ceiling, illuminating the most beautiful scene I'd laid eyes on in weeks. Dusty shelves clung to the walls, packed with musty books, Mason jars, and bags of old clothes. Dented archive boxes struggled to contain manila folders. Each box, each rusty tool, shimmered with promise. I staggered forward, drunk with anticipation. I'd start with the bottom shelves. Grace could reach the top ones.

I had slid out the first box and was about to turn and shout for Grace when the gunshot rang out. I flung myself flat on the hard concrete and covered my head. Was I hit? Maybe adrenaline had numbed me.

"Sweet moves, Agent Young!" Grace's voice echoed above me.

I lifted one arm and peeked up. Grace laughed and jerked her thumb to the basement door. It hadn't been a gunshot at all—just the door slamming behind her. I let out a long breath and rolled back on the ground as she thwacked down the steps in her red slippers.

"Oh my God . . . ," Grace said as she took in the sight of the overflowing boxes. She reached up and pulled one down from the highest shelf. I squatted, sifting through layers of junk as if I were panning for gold.

"I think I've found every pine garland and oversized bunny ever manufactured," I said.

Grace wiped her hands on her mechanic's jumpsuit and sighed. "There's got to be something of Bain's in here, though, don't you think? A letter? A checkbook? She can't have burned *everything*."

But each box turned out to be more worthless than the last. We found old *Consumer Reports* magazines, some paperbacks, a Crock-Pot, tacky figurines of gnomes and fairies, and empty picture frames. I rubbed my nose and sneezed.

Grace checked one of her watches. "Two fifteen," she said. "I thought Trista was going to text when she started her session with Agford." She sighed.

"What's that supposed to mean?"

"What's *what* mean?"

I shot Grace a look. "She's on it, okay? We can't give up yet."

"Who said anything about giving up?" Grace grinned back. "Young and Yang do not give up."

"That's right," I said as I flipped the lid off another archive box.

Five, ten, then fifteen minutes passed. Still nothing. Soon we'd have to make our escape. Empty-handed. Grace grunted as she tried to shove a box back onto one of the high shelves.

"Hang on," I said, boosting myself up the side of the shelves to see what was blocking the way.

A heavy, leather-bound book covered in a blanket of cobwebs and dust had wedged itself in the grate of the shelves. I tugged it loose. It smacked to the concrete floor. The beveled edges of a large orange T poked out through the dust.

Grace flipped her baseball cap around backward and picked up the book. She gingerly opened it to the first page and gasped.

"Is it what I think it is?" I asked.

"Tilmore High School. Tilmore, Texas," Grace read. "A yearbook."

"Ow!" My knees cracked as I jumped back to the floor.

"You all right?"

"Never been better." I leaned over Grace's shoulder. "Can you believe this? Flip to faculty/admin photos." It almost seemed too easy.

"Deborah Bain." Grace could hardly utter the words as she pointed to the photo. "Deborah Bain!" Grace thrust the book at me. "We did it!" She gave a little yelp of joy.

But the woman in the picture looked nothing like Charlotte Agford. She was a dried-up witch of a woman, as bony and angled as the inside of Agford's house. Her Roman nose jutted out over lips so thin and tight, I wondered if I just imagined they were there. Dark bangs hung down one side of her forehead at an awkward angle, framing her jaw, while the rest of her stringy hair lay limp on her shoulders. A multicolored sweater from the eighties sagged over her flat chest. It was a far cry from her pastel suits or even her weekend jeans, but it did remind me of the autumn-themed cat-puke sweater she'd worn the week before.

Still, one feature proved beyond any doubt that it was Agford. Staring back at us from below Bain's crooked bangs were two eyes so lifeless, they could belong to no one else. Those were the dead eyes that floated above Agford's Cheshire cat grin. Those were the eyes that had crawled over every last possession in my room—that had watched me from across Agford's desk at each therapy session. I'd never been happier to see those dark, soulless pools and feel the hairs rise on the back of my neck.

We stared at them as if in a trance.

"It's really her, isn't it?" I whispered.

Grace bit her lip and nodded. "I think we've done it," she said.

Suddenly I felt light. I stood up straighter. "Ralston can stay on her stupid vacation forever," I said. My voice reverberated against the basement walls. "Young and Yang are on the case."

"That's right." Grace beamed, then pretended to glance

at her watches. "And I believe Agent Yang has a pressing appointment with the Luna Vista police."

She led the charge up the basement stairs, slippers shuffling. She stopped short at the top.

"What's the matter?" I asked.

Grace jiggled the doorknob. "Oh, nothing," she said. "The door's sticking a little." She tried again. The knob refused to budge more than an inch in either direction.

We stared at it.

"Let me try," I said at last.

Grace stepped aside. I turned the knob. It wriggled from side to side, its rattle sounding suspiciously like a chuckle.

"Don't panic," Grace said, her voice flying up an octave. "Everything's fine."

Chapter Twenty

The Face in the Window

"Tools," I said, rushing back down the stairs, slippers smacking. "She has tools!" I knocked over a ceramic pot. It cracked in half.

"Careful!"

"Maybe you want to help instead of direct?" I shot back.

"Maybe you want to not break everything?" Grace threw up her hands.

We used what we could find to try to jimmy the door. Nothing was out of the question. Hooks from Christmas ornaments. Rusty scissors. There was one horrifying moment when, imitating the countless TV robbers I'd seen break into houses with credit cards, I almost lost my school ID through the crack in the door. We turned our attention to the half windows that peeked above ground.

Grace boosted me up. They were sealed shut, every last one.

"We should call Trista," I said. "It's a risk if she's still in Agford's office, but she might be able to do something."

Grace hesitated, then handed me her phone.

I dialed Trista's number. Nothing happened. I squinted at the phone, shook it. I pressed the power button, then pressed it again. I held it up higher. No service. Not even one tiny bar.

Even if Trista had tried to text, she wouldn't have been able to reach us. The cell phone flashed the time: 3:30. Last period had long since ended. Agford would be on her way, if she hadn't slipped home already. I shuddered at the thought. "Trista must have tried to call," I said. "She would have warned us by now."

Grace grabbed back her cell and walked the perimeter of the basement, holding the phone high in hopes that one little green bar would appear. Again, nothing.

I looked around again. Double wooden storm doors at the end of a small ramp in the corner led outward and upward into Agford's backyard.

"I think they're our best shot," I said, hoping I was right. We took running starts and threw our meager weight against them. They creaked, giving way a few tantalizing centimeters before falling back. They must have been pad-locked from the outside.

Grace began to pace. The rhythmic *thwack-thwack* of her slippers against the concrete drowned out my thoughts. We needed an escape plan. Yet I could only sit there, hyp-notized by the shuffle of Grace's rose-embroidered slippers.

Slippers.

Our shoes were at the side door. If we didn't figure out how to escape before Agford came home, there they'd be, their tongues flapped open, the only time in the recorded history of the world that tongues of shoes would actually tattle on someone.

I groaned as I sat on the basement steps.

"What?"

"Our shoes." I pointed at Grace's slippers. "So much for not leaving a trail."

"She's not going to come through the side door," Grace said. She tugged at one of her braids and looked at her feet. She sighed. "But we're toast, anyway, even if Agford doesn't catch us. As soon as my parents come home and find out I'm gone . . ." She plopped down on the steps next to me. She took off her baseball cap and wiped her brow. "I can't believe I agreed to this," she said.

I was sure I'd misheard her. "What's that?"

"This dumb plan. I can't believed I agreed to it," she repeated.

"*Agreed* to it?"

"Yeah." Grace flung her baseball hat on the floor as she stood up. "This was *your* plan. Remember? I said we should wait for Ralston to come back. Instead you're all, 'My friend Trista, she can do anything!'" In Grace's version of my voice, I sounded like a five-year-old who'd sucked in a balloonful of helium. "Ever since you started hanging out with her, you think you're a superhero or something. 'My friend Trista, she can make a remote for Agford's garage. My friend Trista . . .'" Grace let out a sarcastic huff.

"That's right," I said. "Trista *can* do anything. I bet she doesn't scream when she sees a fly either. Maybe she can even figure out how to walk into a basement without locking herself in it." I heard the quaver in my voice as it echoed against the concrete walls. I looked at Grace. "Some agent."

Grace's mouth tightened into a hard line. She narrowed her eyes. "Yeah, some agent," she said. "You know who you should have brought? A four-hundred-pound giant who can't whisper."

"Classy, Grace. Great way to talk about someone you've never met."

"And where'd I get the description from, then, huh?"

I folded my arms. "Maybe we should have brought Jocelyn and Natalie. We could have experimented with eyeliner." Grace was fuming, but I didn't care. "Not everyone can look like they just stepped off a fashion runway, you know," I added.

"That's for sure," Grace said, looking me up and down. I was wearing my standard jeans-and-hoodie uniform, except for the slippers, of course.

"I don't think . . . ," I began. I struggled to keep my voice steady as I spoke my next words. "I don't think I've ever met anyone more superficial in my whole life."

Grace's face went slack. She staggered backward. "Superficial," she repeated in a near whisper. Her nostrils flared, and her voice flew into a high whine. "I'm superficial because I don't quote Chinese philosophers and string up wind chimes for my chi? I'm superficial because I read *Teen Vogue* and don't wear the same jeans three days in a row? You know what's superficial?" Grace's cheeks flushed nearly as red as our slippers. "Thinking people are superficial if they're not just like *you*."

A box tumbled from one of Agford's shelves and slammed to the floor. I felt as if it had crashed on top of me instead. I wondered if it was too late to take back what I'd said.

"You know I don't think that, Grace," I said quietly.

"How would I know?" she fired back. "I don't have thoughts. I'm just a superficial airhead!"

"Oh, you have thoughts, all right," I said. "You have bright ideas." If she wasn't going to back down, neither was I. "Like wearing black and creeping around at midnight. Like spying on Agford. I can't believe I protected you when we got caught! We wouldn't be here at all if it weren't for you. Come to think of it . . ." I didn't want to say any more, but the words pushed past the lump in my throat before I could squelch them. "I was never in any trouble until I met *you*."

Grace stood very still for a long time. Then she turned her back.

"I never wanted to hang out with you in the first place. You reminded me of a little mouse," she said. "I just felt sorry for you." She shrugged. "And I was bored."

It felt like the concrete floor had opened up beneath me like a trapdoor. I thought about the way Grace had acted the first night we met, at dinner with the Yangs right after we moved in. Her chin in her hand. Never making eye contact. The way she stared at her flaking nail polish. No matter what she'd claimed since, the truth was obvious. She hadn't even wanted to *talk* to me, let alone hang out. I was just some mousy girl she could push around. I wondered if that was what I was to Trista, too. And Rod? Did he see me that way?

"If we ever get out of here alive," I said, my voice choking to a whisper, "get used to boredom."

"Good," Grace said after a long silence. The cold edge in her voice hurt even more than the word itself. "I'll never have to look at you and your boring Old Navy T-shirts again," she said, her lower lip trembling. "I'll never have to listen to you wonder whether the northwest corner of your room needs a babbling fountain to clear out your bad feng shui. And I will never, ever have to listen to stupid quotes from some ancient Chinese philosopher. You're obsessed!"

"Just because you know nothing about your background doesn't make me obsessed." I clutched my arms tightly around my chest.

Grace jutted her chin forward. "I know more than you ever will. It's who I *am*. You never get that! Are you any less Irish because you don't know anything about the life of Saint Patrick? How would you feel if I was always spouting off stories about Irish faeries and dressing like a leprechaun while I danced jigs? I can't believe I've put up with it for this long. And your Mandarin accent sucks, by the way."

"At least I can read characters, and that's without five years of Chinese school."

"Good for you, Sophie. I bet Rod Zimball really digs white chicks who want to be Chinese. You think Rod's texting you because he likes you? He's just bored like me."

Grace couldn't have meant that. Not the girl who once braved her worst fear to walk all the way down to the beach with me just so I could run into Rod.

"People usually hate in others what they themselves are," I said quietly.

"Let me guess. Sun Tzu, circa 3000 BC?"

"Sophie Young, circa 2000 AD." I glared at her.

Grace looked at her watch. God, it was stupid to wear six watches. Really stupid. I can't believe I ever thought Grace made it seem cool.

"Getting bored again?" I spat. "Being locked in a fugitive's basement not exciting enough?"

"Counting the minutes until Agford comes home and finds us. Because then I won't have to—" Grace gasped, her eyes widening in horror. I turned around.

A face loomed in the window above us.

Chapter Twenty-one

Rock Bottom

The face peered in, its features twisted into a menacing squint. Not until I recognized the curves of its round cheeks did I catch my breath again. Relief poured over me.

But Grace had never met Trista before. She backed away slowly.

With Trista's frown filling the window frame like a horror-movie close-up, it was no wonder Grace assumed we were done for. She drew in a sharp breath as Trista leaned back and revealed her full army camouflage. At least it appeared she was wearing full camouflage until I realized she'd just thrown on some green sweatpants and a turtleneck under a bulky green cargo jacket. Her many pockets bulged—with tools, I imagined.

Grace was reassured when she saw my expression. "Let me guess," she said. "Trista Bottoms?"

"Yep." I waved to Trista and gestured to our ridiculous Chinese slippers. "Shoes!" I said, pointing to the side door.

Trista rolled her eyes and displayed one of my Pumas. Of course she'd already snagged them. I wouldn't have been that surprised if she'd commandeered a helicopter for our escape while she was at it.

She reached into one of her cavernous cargo pockets and pulled out several pieces of metal in various sizes. Centuries passed as she fumbled with the parts. What was she doing? I was about to point her to the wooden storm doors, but she had already slipped out of view. She must have headed for them.

Grace and I waited in silence.

"I can't believe this," Grace whispered. "We're waiting for a seventh grader with hands like oven mitts to pick a lock."

"If a certain someone hadn't shut the basement door behind her, maybe—"

"The wind blew it! It could have just as easily been you."

Something thudded upstairs. Agford. All she'd have to do was peer out her window and she'd see a twelve-year-old in camouflage breaking into her basement.

But the thudding hadn't been from upstairs. It was Trista, tugging at one of the double doors. Within seconds they groaned open, sending in a shaft of dusty light that appeared like a direct portal to heaven.

Grace reluctantly accepted Trista's offered hand. I hoisted myself out behind her.

"Run! I'll catch up," Trista said.

Grace had already sprinted away barefoot, her slippers in hand. I followed. Trista caught up to us halfway up the hill, her pockets jangling with tools. No sign of Agford yet.

"I ended up letting the air out of her tires after all," Trista said, panting. "When you didn't text back, I knew something had happened."

She explained that she had ranted, raved, and sobbed during her therapy session, but Agford had ended it right on the hour. Fortunately Agford had shuttled off to advise an after-school S.M.I.L.E. meeting, probably to plan for their new "Look on the Bright Side" antidepression poster campaign while Agford probed them for an update on Operation Wig Retrieval. Marissa must have kept the dentist appointment mum. When Trista texted and didn't get the confirmation signal we agreed on, she'd walked to her house nearby, improvised her army-camouflage getup, gathered her protractor, magnets, batteries, wire, and other tools in case they came in handy, then headed for the nearest bus

238

stop. Fifteen minutes later she'd arrived at Agford's. "I don't do bikes," she explained. I could just picture Trista in the bus's front priority seating in her camouflage getup. She would have crossed her arms across her chest and frowned, daring the other passengers to so much as look at her the wrong way.

"Thank God you came. How'd you ever get that lock open?"

"Electromagnetic resistance. Like in our science lab this week? It's perfect for combo locks. Wrap a battery-powered solenoid around a ferromagnetic core to create an electromagnet, then . . ." I understood only the gist of Trista's explanation. Something about how when she twisted the dial of the combination lock, the magnet helped her feel resistance at the right numbers. Then she arranged the numbers into different sequences until one worked. "Piece of cake," she said.

As we reached Grace's patio, Grace was already slipping into her room.

"That's it?" I said. "You're just going to walk away?"

Grace ignored me and shut the patio door firmly behind her.

"You're welcome!" Trista's shout reverberated against the glass door. "Really, anytime!"

The patio door slid open again. Grace reemerged holding the yearbook in front of her like a tray. The wig and papers sat atop it.

"You're still going to the cops, right?" I asked.

"Who, me? *Superficial* me? I'm sure you and the rocket scientist here can work it out." Grace's cheeks flushed red as she shoved the yearbook at me. "After all, everything was just fine before you met me." Her braids flicked like whips as she pivoted on her heels and stormed back into her room.

Trista stared at the closed patio door, then back at me. She let her backpack fall with a thud. "Seriously?" she said. "An hour in a basement and you two fall apart?"

I sighed. The evidence bag containing Agford's wig had ripped, leaking foul traces of her perfume, but that wasn't why I felt nauseated. I turned to Trista.

"Oh, no." She took a step back. "Haven't I helped enough?"

I gazed back across the street. For a moment I thought I saw my reflection in one of Agford's dark windows.

Standing alone in the shadow of towering trees, I looked like a tiny, little mouse.

Chapter Twenty-two

Hairtight Evidence

I walked home in a daze. Agford's fake curls peeked from their plastic bag and rustled in the wind. Agford could have greeted me at the back door, plucked back the evidence, and sat me down for study hall, and I wouldn't have even cared.

Jake stood in the kitchen, arm resting on the wide-open refrigerator door.

"You got another guinea pig?" he said, staring at Agford's wig. "Mom's going to be so pissed." He glugged milk straight from the plastic jug and let out a moist belch. "And news flash: You can't keep 'em in plastic bags."

"Shut up." I marched past him to my room, slammed the door, and cranked up Kai Li's "Dragonrider." So what if Grace thought I was a poseur? At least I revered a culture, not some government agency that had just been outclassed by a bunch of twelve-year-olds.

I pictured Grace as she slid her patio door shut. The thin, straight line of her mouth. Her empty eyes. Walking away was that easy for her. If she could walk away, so could I. She could go trade stupid celebrity gossip with "Joss" and Natalie when she wasn't locked up with Miss Anita all day in her lucky house with all of her lucky animals. I'd never again have to watch her roll her eyes whenever her mom talked about things that really mattered, like what happens after we die or why people dream. So what if I had to spend every dinner listening to my father drone on about ball bearings in missile sheaths while Jake bopped his head to his hidden iPod?

I'd have to go to the police myself. What was it Trista had said after Trent's pudding attack? *You can do something about it.* I could—and I would.

I couldn't blame Trista for refusing to go to the cops in my place. "I'm not getting on their radar this early," she'd explained. She pointed out that after the Beet Incident, chances were slim the cops would believe *any* kid rushing to them with evidence about Agford. "Give the FBI a chance, Sophie," she said. "They've been on it, what, five days?"

I looked at the wig on the bed. Jake was right. It did look

like a guinea pig, one of those with all the cowlicks that made it look like it had just woken up.

I had to hide the evidence somewhere while I figured out the next steps. It was study-hall time. Agford could waltz over to check on me at any minute. Could I tuck the stuff under my bed? Lame. That's the first place anyone looks. Besides, it would block proper energy flow during sleep. In my closet? That wasn't much better.

My eyes rested on the massive red elephant in my northwest *gua*. He stared back at me, trunk raised, a fierce gleam in his glass eye. I remembered the cheerful gong he gave when I tapped his side the day Mrs. Dr. Yang unloaded him on me. Red for fire—and better yet, hollow. He really *was* perfect.

My fingers found a seam near his neck. I discovered that his head twisted right off, and his sides could split apart. I nestled the evidence in his stomach and recapitated the poor beast. He stood with his head now slightly cocked, daring someone to so much as step in his vicinity.

If only I could send him down to the police station instead. At this point, they'd probably take a large, metal red elephant more seriously than me.

Grandpa finally came home from the VFW at dinner-time, smelling of beer and overly jolly about his canasta victories. He must've drunk a bottle or two—or three—to celebrate his freedom. He, Jake, and I sat at the kitchen table around our individual chicken potpies. I burned my mouth with the first bite. In retaliation I jabbed my fork into the top crust, all the way through to my plate.

Grandpa's eyes widened. "Whoa there, soldier," he said.

"Looks like someone had a bad day," Jake said with a fake pout.

I stood up, dumped the pie in the trash with a thud, and walked back to my room.

"Nah, leave her alone," I heard Jake say just before I shut my door. "It's probably that time of the month."

Back in my room a moment later, I stood at my window and gazed out. The neighborhood looked peaceful. White houses glowed against the dark sky. Swept driveways welcomed mothers and fathers home from work. Rows of trash cans stood sentry in front of each house except mine. (You don't even want to think about what leaving trash in front of your house overnight does to your chi.)

Across the street at Agford's, a light clicked off in an upstairs window, and a TV sent its ghostly blue flickers across the plastic tombstones on her lawn. Agford was probably fluffing up her backup wig as she tuned in to *Dr. Phil*

reruns. Meanwhile, somewhere in Texas, parents shuffled off to bed past empty rooms where their kids had once slept.

Until I noticed I was tracing the outline of the yin pendant around my neck, I had forgotten I was still wearing it. I resisted the urge to yank it off and throw it away. Grace had never worn the other half anyway. I'd order a new pendant from Feng Shui Planet—a complete yin/yang circle. It wasn't good to be running around off-balance anyway.

The skin on the roof of my mouth had begun to peel where I'd burned it on the potpie, exposing a tender layer of flesh. My tongue poked at it; I couldn't leave it alone, just like I couldn't stop thinking of Grace. Right then she was probably lounging on her bed, doodling on her binders and chatting with Natalie. Maybe she was dotting her face with her stupid acne cream. I hoped the musty basement air had clogged her precious pores. If there were any justice in the world, a pus-filled zit would have exploded its way to her forehead's surface with all the fury of Marissa Pritchard's Mount Etna.

But there wasn't any justice in the world. Deborah Bain was sitting across the street watching TV in a house paid for with embezzled money and the lives of innocent kids. If I did nothing, and the FBI failed, she'd sit there forever, floating through life buoyed up by her balloon boobs and pretending she had a clue how to help middle schoolers deal with life.

A shadow twitched along the side of Agford's house. Her motion-activated light burst on, illuminating the bulky frame of none other than Agent Unibrow. He blinked in the unexpected spotlight. If the FBI hired jokers like this, it was no wonder we had beaten them to the punch.

The agent lumbered to the street toward his white pickup, then pretended he was out for a pleasant moonlit stroll. I was annoyed to find myself thinking how right Grace had been about FBI surveillance agents. Unibrow's ripped gray sweatpants and jacket really did make him seem like just a regular guy out for a walk.

I looked back at Mrs. Dr. Yang's elephant. I could give it time, like Trista said—but how could I be sure I had time? Agford was desperate. She wasn't going to stop at fake counseling visits to the Yangs and humiliating assemblies.

I heard Jake shuffling around his room next door. Grandpa was in the family room upstairs watching TV. Outside my window Agent Unibrow was nearing his pickup. In a few seconds he'd be gone again. But there was something I could do. There was something I *had* to do.

I ran to the front door, flung it open, and strode down

the front walk. Unibrow, the genius, didn't notice me until I stood right behind him.

"Hey," I called out.

Startled, he jumped back. His muscles stayed tensed, even once he'd seen it was miniscule me standing in front of him.

"You filling in for Ralston while she's away?" I asked.

He looked at me, lips parted. Either he was a mouth breather like Officer Grady or he was very bad at hiding surprise. It was probably both.

"Yup." He hitched up his pants authoritatively.

"You can get in touch with her on a secure line?" I asked, hoping that was the lingo. I needed to sound like I meant business.

"Yup," he said. I wasn't even sure if the man could say anything else.

"You tell her we have everything we need for a positive ID on Bain. One hundred percent match."

"You have evidence?" The agent gave a little snort as his single bushy eyebrow shot up. Of course. I was just a dumb little kid with cute freckles. What did I know about evidence?

"I said I did," I snapped.

His eyes flitted to Agford's front door. "Good," he said.

247

"Meet me at the end of the street in five minutes with it." His Adam's apple bobbed as he spoke. He reminded me of a fat, squat bullfrog. "We'll want to move fast."

Right. I was going to hand over evidence to a half-wit who couldn't even stake out Agford's house. I wouldn't have trusted that guy to blow his own nose. I resolved to take it over Ralston's head, if I had to. I could call the Austin field office.

"Um, Agent . . ." I waited for him to fill in the blank. He didn't. "You are Agent . . . ?"

He cleared his throat. "Stone," he said. "Agent Stone."

"Agent Stone, I hope you'll understand. I only deal with Ralston," I said, hating how high and babyish my voice sounded. "Our email link has been compromised." I supposed that was one way of describing a confiscated laptop and a destroyed friendship. "So if she can't meet in person, she should send instructions using the same code as last time. I need to know I'm dealing with Ralston directly." I crossed my arms and pushed up on the balls of my feet, hoping it made me look a little bigger.

Unibrow sighed. He might as well have rolled his eyes at me. "And what should I tell her that you have?" he asked.

"Airtight evidence," I said. "That's all she needs to know."

As I walked back, I cast a glance toward Grace's. The two protective fu dogs at her front door glowed in the warm light flooding from the family room windows. I couldn't help thinking they belonged at my front door instead.

Chapter Twenty-three

Questionable Assumptions

"How was the doctor?" Marissa greeted me as I came into first-period science Thursday morning. She wore her blond hair in a strange updo that made her look middle-aged.

"Great." I stepped to the side to clear my path.

She moved in front of me again. "You said you were going to the *dentist*."

I shrugged. "Doctor, dentist. Whatever."

Marissa narrowed her eyes. "Have you heard of pathological lying?"

"Oh, I'm *very* familiar with it, Marissa," I said. "And it looks like it's contagious."

Marissa's mouth hung open as I pushed past her. It wasn't until I took my seat that she finally collected herself.

She sat down behind me. I felt her eyes on the back of my head.

Ms. Gant wrote on the whiteboard in red: "Reminder: Science Fair, Monday 4:00 p.m." I was going to trot out the same experiment I had done in fifth grade. I'd soaked my baby teeth in orange juice, water, and Coke for three weeks and charted the effects of decay. Trista was trying to build a solar panel that would harness the power of a panel twice its size. God only knows what Marissa was planning. Probably teaching rats to smile and tap-dance.

Someone poked my shoulder. I turned around to scowl at Marissa, only to see Rod smiling back from the desk across the aisle.

"What's your project?" he whispered. With the sun streaming in from the windows, his hazel eyes almost looked green. Even my fight with Grace seemed far away for that second.

"Still thinking about it," I whispered back. No way was I going to bring up my baby teeth. "What about you?"

Marissa butted in. "Ms. Gant is *trying* to start class," she said as loudly as she could. Ms. Gant didn't react. Marissa sighed so heavily, her bangs fluttered. Rod rolled his eyes. I rolled mine back.

"How to fight ocean pollution." He jerked his head

toward Marissa. "But I should have done something on the dangers of *cloning*." I stifled a laugh. I could almost remember how life was before we'd spied on Agford, when the most I had to worry about was whether he really liked me.

"Okay, class, in your seats," said Ms. Gant.

As Rod turned back and everyone settled down, I suddenly felt overcome with exhaustion. During the few hours of sleep I'd managed to get, I'd dreamed I was back in the basement again, only this time it had filled with water up to my chin. Grace and Agford stood at the top of the stairs, watching calmly as the water rose over my head. When I tried to swim, I discovered I was paralyzed from the neck down. I woke up with a jolt just as the water lapped at the thick cable of exposed wiring above my head.

I had put out the trash that morning and checked the mailbox for a code from Ralston. Empty. I had checked again after breakfast. Still nothing. I had even turned down Jake's rare offer to drive me to school, figuring that riding my bike would make it easier for Agent Stone to approach me. I could have saved myself the trouble. In the end I decided to give Ralston until dinnertime to contact me.

Ms. Gant cleared her throat and rolled up the sleeves of her crisp button-down shirt. "Let's see . . . who's absent today?"

"Trent Spinner's still suspended, Ms. Gant," Marissa said in a singsong.

As Ms. Gant nodded and called roll, I thought about next period. Instead of going to second-period orchestra, I would have to trudge upstairs to Agford's office for our therapy session. My hands began to sweat. There's nothing Agford could do to me at school, I told myself. Not with this many witnesses.

"I'd like to offer some words of caution as you finish up your science-fair projects," Ms. Gant began. "All projects require my approval. That means if you changed your project, you need to see me again. As a reminder, no projects involving flames or other combustible materials are allowed. While we're lucky Joe McDougal lost only his eyebrows and eyelashes last year, I think we all agree it could have been much worse."

Marissa's eyes widened. Someone snickered.

A tiny, balled-up piece of paper rolled across my desk. I looked around, irrationally hoping Ralston might have managed to lob something through a window. Or maybe it was from Rod? I felt a flutter in my stomach as I unfurled it. Smiley faces peeked out among vines of dainty cursive, reading: "S.M.I.L.E. Brown Bag Lunch today. Be there or be sad! ~ Marissa ☺" Nothing like a smiley face to accompany a threat of sorrow. I guess Marissa was trying a new approach. Either that or her science project involved cultivating multiple personality disorder.

"Also, please—Sophie, am I boring you?" Ms. Gant interrupted herself.

My face burned. I shook my head.

"I'm glad to hear that. As I was saying, as you arrive at your final conclusions, you need to question your underlying assumptions. What variables haven't you considered yet?" Ms. Gant threaded her way through the rows of desks as she continued her lecture. "Let's take for example a project from a few years back entitled 'What's My Dog's Favorite Color?'"

"Dude, that's, like, one step above 'Where Does My Dog Like to Take Dumps?'" Trent's friend Matt called out. His face lit up. "Hey, can I change my project?"

"Don't dogs see in black and white?" Rod interrupted.

Marissa's soprano chimed in behind me. "Actually the canine visual spectrum ranges from blue to bright yellow."

Rod coughed to cover his fake gag. He and I traded a look.

"Raise your hands, please," Ms. Gant said. "But you are all touching on a critical issue. First, the experiment operates under the assumption that dogs perceive as we do. It privileges our way of seeing over all else. But that wasn't the real fatal flaw in this experiment."

"No kidding," said Matt.

Ms. Gant turned to the whiteboard. She drew two overlapping circles. She labeled one Things My Dog Likes and the other The Color Yellow. She tapped the circles. "My dog likes squeaky toys," she said. "Some squeaky toys are yellow. Does that mean my dog likes all yellow things? Of course not. So what went wrong?"

Marissa raised her hand and grunted her usual *oo, oo!* As I looked at her, her eyes shining, leaning out of her seat as she waved her hand, I almost felt sorry for her. How were she and the rest of S.M.I.L.E. going to feel when they realized a fugitive had been using them all along?

Ms. Gant ignored Marissa and answered herself. "The student made an assumption. He didn't consider other possible reasons for his dog's attraction to a color and, as a result, he reached the wrong conclusions. Sometimes we only see evidence that confirms our opinions."

Ms. Gant's words settled over me like stones. The red circles she had drawn on the board blurred and crossed together, reminding me of yin/yang symbols. I don't know how I hadn't seen it before, but my entire friendship with Grace had been based upon one wrong conclusion after another. Grace spent time with me. That did not mean Grace really cared. I thought of Grace as my best friend. That didn't mean she felt the same way about me. I drew one circle in my notebook and labeled it Young. On the other side of the page, separated by the harsh red margin line, I drew another and labeled it Yang.

"So check your conclusions," Ms. Gant said. "Could the facts suggest other possibilities? Are there leaps in your logic? You can trust instincts when you first develop your hypotheses. But remember to be open to change if you find contrary evidence. Until several different avenues of evidence support it, you know nothing for sure. Always question your assumptions."

I reached for the place my yin pendant used to hang as Ms. Gant's words echoed in my head. *Always question your assumptions.*

It was about time I started to.

I stood outside Agford's office, my heart racing. One more meeting. That's all I had to survive. Ralston would get in touch. She had to get in touch. I took a deep breath and turned the knob.

Agford's perfume overpowered me as soon as I stepped inside. I wouldn't have been surprised to discover she'd dumped an entire bucket of it onto the nubby carpet. Either she was running a chemical-warfare campaign or *eau de Lysol* was simply at its strongest in the morning. I steeled myself and prepared to look into the twin cold, dark abysses of Deborah Bain's eyes.

But Agford was hunched over some papers on her desk, her hand resting over her mouth. When she finally raised her head to look at me, I nearly fell over.

Charlotte Agford was crying.

"Excuse me," she said in a strangled voice. She dabbed at her mascara-smeared eyes with a crumpled tissue and turned away. "Please," she said, still facing the wall. Her shoulders convulsed as she took a deep breath. "Make yourself comfortable."

I shouldn't have been so surprised. It was like advancing through levels in a video game. I'd survived the various assaults of fake sweetness, bullying, humiliation. Heartwrenching sobs were simply next. "Maybe I should come back later."

"No, Sophie. I want to talk with you."

The purple beanbag waited for me like a set trap. My eyes flitted to the door. I felt an urge to run. It was too late for that. I made my way over to the beanbag. It sighed as it closed around me.

"You were right. This is definitely not a game. It's time we stopped pretending it is." Her chair creaked as she swiveled around to face me.

I fought to keep my face still—to show not even a flicker of emotion. If there was one thing I didn't need to worry about, it was that Dr. Charlotte Agford was about to tell me the truth.

"You deserve an apology." Agford laid her hands flat on the desk in front of her. Her French-manicured nails gleamed. Her eyes were literal dark pools now—muddy messes of tears and smeared mascara. "I overreacted to your snooping, and though it's no excuse, you need an explanation."

I did not need an explanation. What I needed was for Dr. Agford to be miraculously struck by a devastating case of laryngitis until Ralston got in touch. Grandpa was right. Words could be more dangerous than missiles.

"Oh, that's not necessary, Dr. A," I said. "Why don't I—"

"I should have told you from the very start, Sophie. But fear is a powerful emotion. Almost as powerful as my grief."

I blinked. That wasn't a word I expected.

Agford looked down at her lap. Her lips quivered as she formed her next words. "Before I moved here from Texas two years ago . . . my name was Dr. Cassie Ogden."

A wave of unease rippled through me. I repeated the name in my head. I hadn't misheard her.

"I was a single mom to a beautiful seventeen-year-old daughter," Agford said, her eyes growing faraway. The slightest hint of a Texas drawl crept into her voice. "Her name was Lila. She was bound for UT Austin the next fall. She was a cheerleader. A candy striper at the hospital. A varsity-swim-team star at Tilmore High."

I stiffened. Agford could not be saying what I thought she was saying.

"She was so full of *life*." A single tear escaped and ran down Agford's caked-on foundation. "Then, like that, she was taken from me. Electrocuted in a pool at the swim-meet division championship. I was there, in the stands." Agford hiccupped a sob and quickly stifled it.

I tried to keep my head clear, my breath even. Agford was lying. *Deborah Bain* was lying. Grieving mothers don't change their names. They don't get plastic surgery and move to new towns. The FBI doesn't hunt them down.

"To lose a daughter . . . my only daughter . . ." Agford dabbed at her eyes. "I thought nothing could be worse. My world went black. Every day—every minute—I faced another reminder of her. The playground where she chipped her front tooth. The gym where she had cheer practice. The pizza parlor where we celebrated her tenth birthday. The peppermint Tic Tacs in the grocery checkout line she always begged me to buy."

Agford looked at me with tear-filled eyes. I turned away and stared at the flaking paint on her metal desk. She sounded so . . . convincing.

"But there *was* something worse, Sophie." Agford looked down and collected herself. Maybe it was the sickly glow of the office fluorescent lights, but I pictured Agford's kitchen the day I had first sneaked in. The single dish in the sink. The half-empty coffee mug. The twinge of sadness I'd felt as I imagined her eating toast alone. Was there even a chance she was telling the truth?

"Lila hadn't been dead a day before they swooped down like vultures. News vans with cameras on cranes camped outside the house twenty-four hours a day." Agford's voice grew louder as she continued. "Reporters shoved microphones in my face if I dared open the front door. The phone rang until I ripped its cord out of the wall. Lila's picture in the paper, on every TV channel, staring back. My private tragedy turned into entertainment." She thumped her fist on the desk.

I shuddered as I remembered the photos of the Tilmore Eight. The hollow faces of their grief-stricken family members. Grace and I would have recognized Agford if she'd been among them. Wouldn't we have?

Dr. Agford rose and stood at her office window. Shouts from PE class mingled with the sound of a distant lawn mower. I fixed my gaze on her stupid rainbow Koosh balls and Rubik's Cubes and tried to focus my thoughts. Agford was telling a story that I could check online in seconds. The thought terrified me. Would a woman who's lying take such a reckless risk?

"The story was everywhere. People love a good tragedy, as long as it's not their own," Agford said, her voice tinged with anger. "Lila wasn't just taken from me once. She was taken from me *every* day. She wasn't Lila anymore. Just one of the Tilmore Eight. And me? I would never be anything but a Tilmore Eight mother."

My own heartbeat dulled the sound of Agford's voice as she went on to describe how the media frenzy only grew worse once authorities realized the electrocution wasn't an unlucky accident but the result of Deborah Bain and her brother's money-funneling scheme. People she'd once considered dear friends sold the tabloids "up close and personal" accounts of her life. So-called journalists speculated about her mental state, especially after her public outburst at a photographer. She explained how, just when it seemed the media spotlight might shift away, a new twist in the investigation—Deborah Bain's apparent suicide by fire, the arrest of Bain's brother for manslaughter—would come along, and the spotlight would swivel back.

"I tried moving in with my mother in Kansas," Dr. Agford said. "The circus showed up on her lawn three days later, when the news came out that Daniel Slater had received a light sentence. It didn't stop. Sophie, I felt like it would *never* stop." Agford's voice caught as she turned back to me. "Starting over with a new identity was the only way I thought I could put an end to the madness and piece my life back together," she said, struggling to steady her trembling voice. "When you started poking around, it felt like my world was crumbling," she continued. "I could see the headlines already. The news crews descending. I panicked."

I remembered the sad, defeated look the night she came for her wig. The lonely feeling in her house. The tacky jewelry and loud holiday decor had always seemed strange for a fugitive. My pinpricks of doubt widened, and I felt as though I'd sprung a hundred tiny leaks. I was sinking through the beanbag chair, through the floor, through the building's very foundation.

Then I caught myself. How could she almost make me forget? Agford could spin stories about peppermint Tic Tacs and paparazzi all day long, and it wouldn't explain why the FBI was tailing her. She could never account for that gaping hole, because she didn't even know she had to cover it. Even if *she* knew the feds were on to her, there's no way she could know *we* did. Ralston had only revealed herself to us because she'd messed up so royally. We'd been with her in public once, last week. If Agford had seen us, I'd have gotten the sob story then, not now. All I had to do was stay calm, watch the show, and act like I believed it.

Agford bit her lip. "It's probably hard for a kid to understand that kind of panic. But look at me." She gestured to herself. "Look at *this*, and maybe you'll understand how crazy it made me. Can you imagine a woman wanting to hide so badly that she changes everything about herself? Bye-bye, brown hair. Sayonara, snub nose! And, well . . ." She let out a little snort-laugh and pointed to her chest. "While they were at it, might as well, huh?" She slumped back into her chair. "That's how much I never wanted to be found again, Sophie. And, you know? It helps that I can look in the mirror without seeing Lila staring back at me anymore. I used to love it that people said we looked alike. And after—it was too much to bear." She closed her eyes and bowed her head.

I resisted an urge to burst into applause. Her performance

was Oscar-worthy—well, at least Daytime Emmy–worthy. Standing before an audience of purple stress balls and other stupid trinkets, in her bright orange cowl-neck sweater and ugly turquoise brooch with the fake A, she might have even seemed funny. But it wasn't funny when I thought about the truth. When I thought about the horror she was trying to hide.

"I know that doesn't excuse my behavior, Sophie," Agford continued. "I'm ashamed. The study halls, meeting with your parents, the assembly . . ." She held up her hands. "And, of course, these sessions. I'll admit it. It was all me trying to hang on to my new life. I hope you can find some way to forgive me?"

I put my hand to my mouth. "Oh, Dr. A." I sniffled. Twice. "I can't believe how awful I've been." Forget tai chi. I needed drama classes.

Agford passed me a box of tissues. It reminded me of the day she comforted my mother in Mr. Katz's office. She had them at the ready so quickly. Like she'd been waiting for that moment and knew she had won.

"I'm just so sorry." I blew my nose to hide my face and—hopefully—my lie. "When you said something about 'people finding us,' on the phone, I just got so carried away." I couldn't resist. For once I really had the upper hand.

Agford cocked her head. "I'm not sure I follow, Sophie."

I reminded her of her phone call. "See, even now, it's that 'us' that's so confusing," I added. Maybe Grandpa was right about silence being the most powerful defense, but it felt so good to make Agford squirm.

I could see her mind working. She shook her head. "I don't know, Sophie. I must have been talking to someone back in Texas. . . ." She brightened. "'Finding us,' I said? Do you think it might have been *fining* us? My ex-husband and I had a little trouble with some tax returns we'd filed years ago. He called me from Texas recently, worried the IRS might fine us. I'm not sure if we talked that night though." She shook her head. "Oh my goodness. So *that's* what started all of this?"

I had to hand it to her. She was good. Very good. So good that I almost felt relieved. Anyone could have been sucked in by her lies. If Sun Tzu was right about all warfare being deception, then I'd been up against a five-star general.

"I know, Dr. Ogden. I'm so, so sorry." I dabbed at my eyes and tried to make my voice quaver. "Maybe there's some way this all doesn't have to get out?"

"I appreciate that, Sophie," Agford said. "But I'm afraid that might not be possible anymore. Not with Louise Ralston involved."

A thousand volts shot through me. It was as if I'd landed back in my dream, and the water in the basement had reached the exposed wiring.

"Sophie? Are you okay? You look so pale."

I nodded. "I was just about to ask you about her." My voice came out as a rasp as I forced the lie past the lump in my throat.

"When I saw Louise in town this morning, I was very concerned. She's been in touch with you, hasn't she? Louise Ralston is not well, Sophie. Not well at all." Agford rubbed her neck worriedly. "I've called the police. They're tracking her down."

"Tracking her down?" I swallowed hard.

"Oh, sweetie, you must be so confused," Agford said when she saw my expression. The term of endearment felt naked without her usual cluck of the tongue. Her voice cracked with emotion. Sincerity, even. "Louise's daughter, Sara, was a junior with Lila. She was"—Agford looked down at her desk—"one of the Tilmore Eight."

I felt short of breath. Ralston had mentioned a daughter. I could hear her drawl as clearly as if she were sitting next to me: *What was it my daughter always used to say? "I've got your back."* She said she hadn't been around kids in a while. I'd assumed her daughter was grown.

"She told me she was FBI."

Agford nodded. "Louise works for the FBI, all right. At least she did. As a software programmer. I suppose she flashed you her ID? Or have they taken it away?"

I pictured Ralston flopping her badge down on the table at the Seashell. The way her blazer gapped and revealed the strap of a shoulder holster for her gun. Ralston had an FBI email account. A business card. A team of agents that reported to her. Didn't she?

"Ralston lost her mind after Sara passed away," Agford said. "Even after Ms. Bain died and her brother was found guilty of manslaughter, she wouldn't accept it. She kept imagining a new culprit was to blame for Sara's death. At one point she went after the school librarian. The librarian! Could there be a more noble soul?" Agford paused and shook her head. "In some ways I can't blame her. We all deal with tragedy in different ways. The media attention was unbearable. I had to escape, start fresh. Other parents spoke out about school mismanagement. Louise, she couldn't let it go. It's common in grief. The denial is so great, it manifests itself in delusions. Don't I know it," she said softly. "I had to learn to forgive. Deborah Bain and her brother were two people looking for a shortcut in life. They hadn't intended to take our girls."

Agford's—Ogden's?—eyes brimmed with tears. Her eyes looked so much lighter, softer—warm, even. Were they even the same color as the ones in Bain's picture? It was hard to believe I'd ever been so sure. It was like Ms. Gant had said. Maybe I'd only seen the evidence that confirmed my opinion.

"I don't understand why she's after *you*, though. How did she find you?"

"I don't know, Sophie. Maybe it had something to do with your nine-one-one call? Her job was to design software for monitoring parolees. They thought she was well again. Maybe she was back at work. Maybe she was using the system to track her imaginary culprits. Daniel Slater was released recently. That might've triggered something. If there's one thing I know, mental illness is not rational. I didn't even work at a school then, let alone Tilmore. I had a private therapy practice in Texas. I took this job because I wanted to try to make something of my life, counseling kids closer to Lila's age. I thought it would bring me some peace of mind." Agford dabbed at her smeared eye makeup one last time before throwing out the balled-up tissue. "I was right, for the most part. The thing is, though—I see Lila everywhere." Dr. Ogden paused and looked at me. Her voice grew even quieter. "I told you that you reminded me

268

of myself when I was younger, Sophie. That wasn't true. You remind me of *her*. The blue eyes. The freckles. It's like, when I bought that house across the street from you, part of me knew I'd be moving closer to her."

Agford's bookshelf blurred in front of me as the weight of what Grace and I had done began to settle over me. Agford had lost her daughter. She'd wanted a new start. Some peace. We'd taken that away. All that time I'd thought Agford's vacant expression showed how little she cared. But maybe her eyes weren't lifeless from not caring. Maybe they looked so dead because she had cared too much.

Dr. Agford reached out across the desk toward me. I felt a pang as I remembered all the times we'd made fun of "Dr. Awk-topus" and her tentacle touches. "I'm sorry, Soph. I know it's hard to wrap your head around." She thought for a moment, then swiveled toward her computer. "Let me see here. Maybe . . ." Her nails click-clacked across the keyboard. She scanned the screen. "Ah, here we go. This might help?"

Agford's printer buzzed and spat out two sheets of paper. My fingers, damp with sweat, smeared the black print as I took them from her outstretched hand.

It was an article from the *Austin American-Statesman*. Though it was brief and direct, I had to read it three times before the words began to sink in. Dated only a few months after the articles we had found, it reported that a woman by the name of Louise P. Ralston, a software developer in the FBI's Austin field office, had been placed on administrative leave for verbally threatening a neighbor and bearing an unlicensed concealed firearm. No charges had been filed. One sentence echoed in my head like a musical round, looping and doubling back over itself: "This is the second time that Ralston, who lost her daughter in the tragic pool electrocution in Tilmore, believed a neighbor was responsible for her daughter's death. This is the second time that Ralston . . ."

It all seemed obvious now. It was like doing a math problem, arriving at an answer like 532.9898, then redoing it and discovering the solution to be a very math-textbook-friendly 10. I had thought it was weird when Ralston admitted to the code in the Seashell. What kind of adult spies on kids and sends codes? What kind of *FBI agent* spies on kids and sends codes? An FBI agent who isn't an agent at all. A woman who, as Agford had said, is not well.

Other facts clicked so easily into place. Ralston's vacation message on her email? Of course she was "on vacation." She was on vacation so she could run around the country hunting fictional criminals. The oaf lurking around

Agford's house was probably a private detective Ralston had hired, which explained why he seemed so incompetent. Even Ralston's software-engineering job made sense. She'd looked proud when she'd mentioned that our 911 call had triggered an anomaly in the "bureau's system." Meanwhile, Ogden had been on her list of "suspects" she'd been tracking the whole time. Our call just put her over the edge.

Then there was the most incriminating detail of all: Ralston's hemming and hawing about how long it might take to wrap up the case made perfect sense according to Cassie Ogden's story. Ralston hadn't been able to make a quick arrest because *there hadn't been an arrest to make.*

Just two weeks earlier, I'd sat in the same beanbag chair as Agford lectured me on perception. Kids don't see reality, she'd told me, holding up a picture of a frightened woman she claimed most kids thought was angry. I'd thought it was all part of Agford's mission to make me doubt myself. But she'd been right all along. I hadn't seen reality. I'd accepted Ralston's story at face value. I hadn't seen my friendship with Grace for what it was. I'd been stupid enough to imagine myself locked in a battle of wits with my school counselor, and now I'd delivered her into the hands of a madwoman.

"I'm so sorry," I croaked. What else was there to say?

This time it was at least for real.

Dr. Agford held up her hand. "Sophie, the apology is mine to make. If I'd been honest to begin with, we wouldn't be here now."

"But now it'll start over. The Tilmore Eight . . . ," I said. "All because of us."

"It might." She nodded. "I've asked the police to be discreet. Mr. Katz has known the truth from the start. He needed references before hiring me, of course." She patted her hair absentmindedly. I thought of the stolen wig and felt my cheeks flush. We'd been awful. Truly awful.

"Either way I have to think about whether it's time to stop living in secret, Sophie," Agford continued. "You have no responsibility to hide my past. You understand that, right?"

I nodded, but I didn't understand at all. If it hadn't been for Grace and me, Cassie Ogden would still have her peaceful new start away from the Tilmore Eight media circus. Louise Ralston would be sitting at her desk in Texas, coding software. "But no one else knows. Agent—I mean, *Ms.* Ralston—said it was dangerous to tell our parents."

Dr. Ogden's eyebrows arched. "So *have* you told your parents?"

I shook my head.

"I see," she replied, tucking her lips over her teeth. She didn't have to say what she thought. I knew it myself. We should have known Ralston was crazy from the start. No reasonable adult demands secrecy.

"When was the last time you were in touch with Ms. Ralston?"

I felt like pulling the beanbag over myself and hiding. "Last night I told the guy she has working for her—I guess he's a private detective—that we wanted to meet with her, so . . ."

"She's hired someone to help? Oh dear. This has gone even further than I thought. But don't you worry, Soph. If and when she contacts you, let me know immediately. Try to set up a meeting. We'll tell the police." She scrawled her home phone number on an apple-shaped pad that read A+ Teacher. "Now what's the best number to reach your parents?" she asked.

"Their cells," I said, cringing. "They're off the coast at AmStar's missile test station. They will be until early tomorrow."

"That's right. Tonight's the big launch, isn't it?" Agford asked.

I hesitated. "You couldn't, by any chance . . . hold off on calling, could you?"

"Now, Sophie, that wouldn't be responsible. I know the launch is important to them. But they need to be informed."

Outside, Coach Knight blew sharply on his whistle. Dr. Ogden's eyes darted to the clock on the wall. "You'd better get to your next class," she said. "Listen. The police will find her before she does anything rash, I'm confident of that. Don't you worry."

I heaved myself up from the beanbag nest. My legs felt like rubber as I wobbled to the door.

"Oh, and Sophie?"

"Yes?"

"The things you have of mine? There's a picture of my daughter. Her cheer-team photo. She'd been so proud of it. . . ."

"Yes," I said, burning with shame. Of course that was what the newspaper had been. "I can bring them by after school. Um, Dr. Ag—Ogden?"

"Please, call me Dr. A. That's who I am now." She managed a small smile.

"Dr. A, I also . . ." I almost couldn't bring myself to form the words. "I also have a yearbook from Tilmore High, and I think it might be . . ."

The woman formerly known as Cassie Ogden drew in a sharp breath. "It's Lila's." She brought her hand to her mouth.

"If you could bring that too, please."

As I opened the door and turned to leave, I took one last look at Cassie Ogden. Her smile was faint, and—for the first time—I believed it.

Chapter Twenty-four

Over and Out— Forever

I sleepwalked through the remainder of my morning. In pre-algebra, as Mr. Hawkins's lazy eye lolled around in his head during his lecture on graphing equations, I closed my own eyes and kept them shut. I had enough confusion without wondering if Mr. Hawkins was really looking at me or not.

When the lunch bell rang, I made a beeline to the outdoor patio to find Trista.

"Sophie! I'm so glad you decided to join us," Marissa chirped. My head yanked up just as she came at me with a right jab—but she wasn't landing a punch, she was slapping a large yellow happy-face sticker on my shoulder. She wore three of the same. The captions read: "Look on the Bright Side! S.M.I.L.E.!" Then, in smaller print: "Society for Making

Improvements in Lives Everywhere.™"

"Cute, isn't it?" Marissa grinned. "C'mon, we're sitting in our usual spot." She tugged at my sleeve and pointed to S.M.I.L.E.. They waved aggressively. I considered telling her I would rather eat a plate of spiders for lunch than sit anywhere within a twenty-foot radius of her and her brigade. I couldn't believe I'd felt sorry for them.

"I'm giving Dr. Agford back her stuff, okay?" I said. "So you can stop trying to get it."

Marissa pretended to be offended. "Sophie, this is an antidepression outreach. You of all people should open yourself to the possibility for healing."

"Hey," a voice interrupted. "Turn that *frown* upside *down*!" Trista flashed an exaggerated grin as she sidled up to us and clapped her hand down heavily on Marissa's shoulder. "Look on the *bright* side!" she yelled so loudly, I swore it rattled the various cause ribbons pinned to Marissa's sweater.

I smiled at Marissa. "Trista's helping me with my science-fair project at lunch. I'm sure S.M.I.L.E. will be better off without me," I said. As Marissa walked away in a huff, I turned to Trista. IT IS WHAT IT IS, the letters on her T-shirt announced.

Trista's face fell when she saw my glum expression. "Let

me guess. You and Grace haven't come to your senses yet."

"Nope," I said.

"And I just saw Agford shimmying past the art room, so you haven't gone to the police either?" Trista asked.

"Remember how you said there's always more than one explanation for something?"

Trista squinted at me. "Yeah . . ."

I glanced around the lunch crowd. S.M.I.L.E. was in earshot, fluttering through on their sticker rampage. "Come with me. We're going to need your network login."

"All that to avoid the media?" Trista said—too loudly—as we sat down in the computer lab. Trista had kept unusually silent as I'd told the whole story, but now she shook her head. "I don't know, Sophie."

Trista's fingers flew across the keyboard. A row of smiling teens materialized on the screen, shrinking under bold, black letters: **REMEMBERING THE TILMORE EIGHT**. Trista pointed to a pale girl with shoulder-length brown hair and a toothy smile. I shivered when I read the caption: "Lila Ogden."

"Anyone can get a name right." Trista shrugged, but her eyes flicked back and forth as she scrolled and clicked, scrolled and clicked. Pictures of the families and the victims filled the screen like a collage. Two parents making their way out of a cemetery and past a throng of photographers. Teenagers holding candlelight vigils. A man sitting on a curb, head in hands.

"Can she get two names right?" I pointed to a picture that was unmistakably of Louise Ralston, though her face was even more pinched and hollow than it had been when I'd seen her. "Louise Ralston, mother of Tilmore Eight Victim Sara Frank."

"Must be the father's last name," Trista said. "And then there's this." She tapped the display.

My eyes widened. Pictured on the screen was a brown-haired woman whose puffy perm appeared shellacked with hairspray. It was different from Agford's, for sure, but it was so eerily reminiscent, I felt like I could smell *eau de Lysol* through the screen. Cassie Ogden.

"Oh man, Sophie," Trista finally said. She leaned back in her chair and let out a long breath. "Well, in keeping with today's theme"—she pointed to the bright yellow smiley face on my shoulder—"on the bright side, our school counselor is not a fugitive."

Neither of us laughed.

"So you're returning her stuff after school?"

I nodded.

Trista patted my shoulder awkwardly. "Well, if it'd take

your mind off it, maybe after . . . you want to hang out?"
She shrugged as if she wasn't really sure what that would
involve, exactly. "I was going to work on my solar panel
after school, but I could use some help with it," she lied.

I was genuinely touched. A few days ago, nothing short
of a tsunami could have come between Trista and her solar
panel. I suppose she wasn't really offering to abandon it
altogether, but still. "Thanks. But it's my mess, right?" I
smiled.

"True," Trista said. She wasn't joking.

"I *am* worried about Ralston, though," I said.

Trista picked up her lunch bag. "Don't worry. If the
police are on it, they probably found her already. It'll be a
done deal by the end of school today."

For Trista, the world was simple. There were problems,
and there were solutions. This problem was solved. I sure
hoped she was right. I pictured the woman I knew as Agford,
two years ago, tucking away her daughter's yearbook for
that time when she might be ready to look at a picture of
Lila again. We'd practically led Ralston right to her—maybe
even given her the permission she needed to justify doing
the worst. If anything happened, I would never forgive
myself.

When I came home that afternoon, I went straight to my room, wrenched open the poor red elephant's head, and took out his new innards. I'd made up my mind. If I was going to have to face Dr. Agford again and hand over her cherished possessions, I was dragging Grace along with me to apologize. Some dark part of me actually looked forward to telling her. Ms. FBI Know-It-All couldn't even tell the difference between a grief-stricken software programmer and a real agent.

I had rehearsed what I was going to say to Grace during my bike ride home. By the time I actually stood at her door, I'd worked myself into such a state that when Mrs. Dr. Yang opened up, all I could do was stutter.

It didn't help that Mrs. Dr. Yang didn't greet me with her usual smile. In fact, she'd even managed to twist her eyebrows into a frown. "Grace can't see you today." She folded her arms across her chest.

My insides hollowed. Had Grace told her everything?

"She's in trouble with a capital T," she said, raising her voice. I let out a breath I hadn't realized I was holding as she told me about Grace's paper on internet addiction. "I let her go to the library for an hour to do research." She softened. "But I'm sorry, Sophie, no friends. She'll be so disappointed to miss you."

"That's all right." My throat tightened. Grace hadn't even been upset enough about the breakup of our friendship to tell her mom? I would have even told *my* mom had she been home, and she wasn't much help when it came to serious things like that. I looked at Agford's, then back at Mrs. Dr. Yang. "Could you let her know I have something really important to tell her?"

Mrs. Dr. Yang's gaze fell to the yearbook, wig, and papers clutched in my hands.

I gave them a nervous pat. "It's for my relationship chi?" I offered. "You know."

Mrs. Dr. Yang didn't chuckle like she usually would. She looked as though she was considering bringing me into the clinic for evaluation. "I'm not really sure I do, Sophie."

"I'd better get going!" I called out, already halfway down the steps.

Mrs. Dr. Yang stared after me, mouth open, as I tromped across the street.

Figuring a quick drop-off might make it easier for both of us, I handed Dr. Agford's things back to her as soon as she opened the door. Her hands trembled as she took the yearbook. She fought to keep her composure. Though she'd touched up her foundation, her eyes remained puffy and red.

"Thank you, Sophie," she said quietly. "We can let bygones be bygones, hmm?" She tilted her head. A day ago her tone would have made me shudder. Now I realized how easy it was to mistake her awkwardness for creepiness. From her story I gathered that working at Luna Vista was the first time she'd counseled kids. She *was* fake. Just not the kind of fake we thought she'd been.

"I can, if you can," I said.

"If you can forgive that assembly, I can forgive anything." Dr. Agford looked genuinely embarrassed. "Oh, I almost forgot," Dr. Agford said before she disappeared into the house.

She reemerged in the doorway, holding out my walkie-talkie. "I was afraid your parents might give it back to you," she explained guiltily.

As I thanked Dr. Agford, I looked up at her eyes and saw my own reflection in them. All this time she'd wanted to look out for me, the girl across the street who reminded her of the daughter she would never see again. To think how I'd repaid her.

She smiled warmly as she said good-bye and shut the door.

I looked down at the walkie-talkie. A few days ago, it had been my only lifeline. Now it was just a useless piece of plastic. I was about to dump it into Agford's trash bin on the street when, on a whim, I clicked it on and raised it to my lips. Hidden Dragon should announce her retirement, once and for all.

"Breaker, breaker, this is Hidden Dragon," I said. "Over and out. Forever."

I gazed up at Grace's and my houses side by side and listened to the lonely hiss of static. Behind them the bold colors of the fall leaves burned against the bright blue sky. Anyone else would have called it a beautiful day.

My walkie-talkie crackled, startling me.

"Sophie?" came Grace's hesitant voice. It sounded as though she were trapped in a glass jar. "Is that you?"

Chapter Twenty-five

The Nightmare Begins

The murmur and clatter of the after-school crowd washed over me as I entered the Seashell. If it had been any other day, I would have looked for Rod. Instead I made my way directly to Grace, who was sipping a Diet Coke at our usual corner booth.

She crossed her arms as I made my way to her. I was surprised to see she wore her hair down. It hung over her uncharacteristically plain long-sleeved blue T-shirt.

"Hey," I said.

"Hey."

"Listen—" I didn't even know where to begin.

"I'm not going to say I'm sorry," she announced.

"Who said you had to say you were sorry? I'm not even the one who asked to meet down here—wait, why was your walkie-talkie even on?"

Grace shrugged and nodded toward the server. "She was all, 'Your backpack's trying to talk to you,' and I thought she was crazy until I realized I'd left the walkie-talkie in my bag. It must have been on standby." She cast a glance at the groups of Luna Vista middle schoolers clustered around the other booths. "I don't know. I guess I came to find you."

"Really?" I said. I tried to act casual. I hadn't dared hope that was why she'd come. My heart soared. I felt light—elated almost. "Aw, Grace—"

"I figured you needed my help," she interrupted flatly. She shrugged again and tightened her arms around her chest.

Anger uncoiled in me like a spring. "Right," I scoffed. "I couldn't possibly handle anything without you."

"That's not what I meant," Grace said quietly. The chatter in the café subsided for a moment. It felt like a wave pulling back to gather power before it crashed to the shore.

"Well, I don't need your help," I said. "I took care of it."

Grace pressed her lips together tightly. "Yeah? I saw Agford drive by half an hour ago, so if it's all over, you might want to tell her about it."

"Oh, she knows."

"She knows? Then, why . . . ?"

"She's not Deborah Bain," I said.

Grace sputtered out Diet Coke all over her shirt. It fizzed and settled into a stain as she sat, her mouth agape. I wasn't even sure she could hear me as I ran down all the matching details—Ralston's daughter, her software programming, and the alert the "bureau's system" had triggered. "Even Agford's phone call," I added. "Think about it. She must have said, 'If they *fine* us, we'll take care of it.' Not *find*. Agford said she was talking to her ex-husband about IRS fines for back taxes."

Grace looked pale. She rested her forehead in both hands. "It's like the beets all over again," she said. "We should have seen it. But it made sense at the time, didn't it?" she asked.

"It made sense at the time," I repeated.

Grace ran her fingers through her hair. The fluorescent polish was flaking off, and she hadn't bothered to retouch her nails. The night before, I had imagined her at home, carefree, flipping through magazines. But her tired eyes told a different story. She'd lied about the library and come to the Seashell. She'd been looking for me. That meant she cared.

Or did it? Ms. Gant would probably call that an assumption. Maybe Grace was just worried that I'd rat her out to her parents now that we weren't friends. I looked out the window onto the square. The wind had kicked up, setting the entire landscape in motion. Pepper trees swayed. Brown hills rippled in the distance. Colors and textures melted together, and I couldn't see where one thing ended and another began. That's how it had been all along, hadn't it? Everything had jumbled together in my "tender preteen brain," as Agford had called it. Beet juice was blood. A knife meant murder. A school counselor was a fugitive.

A victim was a criminal.

Grace bit her lip. "So all along . . ." She closed her eyes and let out a long breath. When she opened them again, they glistened with tears. "Oh my God, Sophie, I'm so sorry. You were right. This is all my fault."

Grace reached her hand out to me across the table. I couldn't remember ever seeing her cry. My throat tightened. "No, Grace," I said. "*I'm* sorry. We did this together." I put my hand over hers.

Grace swallowed hard. "I didn't mean what I said yesterday. I wish I could take it all back."

"Me, too," I said. My voice shook. "Every word."

Grace looked down at the table. "I *am* a little superficial though, aren't I?"

"Because you like clothes?" I made a face. "C'mon! I was grasping at straws."

Grace looked relieved. "And I never thought you were some shy little mouse."

"I don't know," I said. "Maybe I was. But I don't feel that way now."

A server noisily cleared the booth behind us. I looked around the Seashell. The stainless-steel napkin holders at each table, the Formica counter by the register. All the usual kids who came after school were clustered together with the same people they always sat with, at the same booths they always sat at. But it all did feel different somehow.

"I could use a Sun Tzu quote around now," Grace said, smiling weakly. "Does he have any advice on apologies?"

"He wasn't so big on friendship." I smiled back. "That's where he and I differ."

"You're the opposite of boring, Sophie Young, you know that?" Grace squeezed my hand. Outside in the square, the trees seemed to settle into place as the wind died down. I wasn't assuming Grace had meant what she said. I felt it. I *knew* it.

"Thanks."

"And if you really want a babbling fountain in your northwest *gua*, go for it," she added with a laugh.

"I think I can do without one," I said. "Besides, you were right. It'd get old fast if you were dancing jigs and quoting

Saint Patrick all the time. I never thought of it like that. Why don't we pretend it all never—"

A shadow fell over our table. "There y'all are" came a familiar drawl.

My heart nearly burst through my chest. Louise Ralston leaned over our table, her blazer gaping open to reveal the shiny metal of her gun in its holster. "I've been looking all over for you two," she said as she pushed her sunglasses down her nose to peer at us.

Grace looked horrified. I slammed my foot down on hers in warning. She disguised her grimace with a smile.

"Agent Ralston! What a relief to see you." I beamed, fumbling in my pocket for the A+ Teacher notebook paper, where Dr. Agford had scrawled her number. I darted a look toward the restrooms. Did they have a phone? Would it be too obvious if I excused myself right away?

"Sorry for the delay, ladies," Ralston said as she tugged at her frayed blazer cuff and slid in next to Grace. The dried mustard stain was still there. The FBI wouldn't let agents run around dressed so sloppily. Why hadn't I ever thought of that? "I had some business in Texas to tend to, but I came back as soon as I got your email." She glanced over her shoulder and lowered her voice. "I'm not pleased you ignored my warning, but I can't lie. Y'all may have wrapped this up."

I'd once thought the bags under Ralston's eyes and her sloped shoulders indicated she was working too hard on a dangerous operation. Now I realized they could just as easily have been signs of a woman racked with insomnia and lost in her delusions. Dread crept through me. I knew there was no good reason for her to go through the charade of collecting "evidence" against Dr. Agford. What if she was planning something so awful for Agford that, even in her fantasy, she felt she needed justification?

"You really think the case is closed?" Grace asked.

I weaved through the twisted maze of my thoughts to assemble a plan. What we needed was time. As long as Ralston didn't realize we didn't believe her, we could buy as much time as we needed.

"Depends on the evidence," said Ralston. Her blue eyes twinkled. "If it's not stolen, I think so."

I made a show of looking around for eavesdroppers. "The evidence is secure," I whispered. I felt as though I were playing make-believe with a six-year-old. "We'll email the exact drop location as soon as we can, but it's going to take some time."

"My mom said I had to be back by four thirty. She doesn't mess around," Grace said, following my lead. It felt like we were on the night patrols again, tiptoeing and maneuvering, communicating wordlessly as we stalked our pretend prey. Only, I was in charge. And this time it was for real.

"And I'm late for study hall," I explained. I slid from the booth, my hand already diving into my pocket again to retrieve Dr. Agford's phone number.

"I understand," Ralston said. "I've got my handheld." She patted her jacket pocket. "I'll get your email right away." Ralston darted a glance around the Seashell as she stood to leave. "We shouldn't meet in public like this anyway." She turned back to us as she reached the door. "And Young and Yang?" Her laugh lines creased as she gave us a tired smile. "Thanks to you, this nightmare's just about over."

"More like the nightmare's just begun," I murmured as Ralston walked across the parking lot to her blue sedan.

"You can say that again." Grace cast a dark look Ralston's way and wheeled her vintage ten-speed from the rack.

"We should use the phone at the Preppy Plus," I suggested. "It's faster. Unless your parents gave your cell back?"

"Are you kidding?" Grace flung one long leg astride her bike. She glanced worriedly up Luna Vista Drive. "Soph, I was serious back there. If I'm not back in five minutes . . ."

"Don't worry about it," I said. I didn't sound bitter. More surprising, I didn't even *feel* bitter.

"I have to finish my paper tonight?" Grace's statement tilted into a question.

"It's okay," I repeated.

Grace fiddled with her hair and looked away. "Oh, you're right, Sophie. Forget about it. Let's go—"

I held up one hand. "I've got this."

Grace squinted at me, mouth half open. "You sure?"

"I'm sure," I said, starting toward the Preppy Plus.

"Hey," Grace called out.

I turned back. She held up her walkie-talkie uncertainly. "Radio me, okay?" she said. The wind rose up, tossing her hair against her face. She looked as though she wanted to say something else. She'd already said it all.

"Of course," I said. "Of course I will."

Chapter Twenty-six

Initial Breakthrough

"Hello?" Dr. Agford sounded breathless as she picked up the phone.

"Louise Ralston just found us at the Seashell," I murmured into the receiver as I stared at a sea of ample-sized pastel polo shirts on display at the Preppy Plus Boutique. My hands were cool and clammy. It felt strange to be calling Agford for help.

Mrs. Maxwell stopped fumbling with hangers outside the fitting room and cocked her head to listen. I lowered my voice to a whisper. "To buy time I told her we'd email information about the evidence drop." A long pause followed. "Are you still there?"

"That's perfect, Sophie," Dr. Agford said at last. "I'll call the police. I'm just thinking . . . If they can't locate Louise immediately, we could use a backup plan. I'll need your help."

My stomach churned with worry as I pictured the glint of Ralston's gun in its hidden holster. If Dr. Agford had told me that dancing naked past Rod's house would help arrest Ralston, I would have done it. "No problem, Grandpa!" I hollered into the phone as Mrs. Maxwell waddled next to me under the pretense of having important business at the cash register.

"Smart thinking," Dr. Agford said. "Just answer 'yes' or 'no.' Can you email Ralston a meeting time and place for late tonight? Say, eleven p.m. somewhere at school?"

"Yes," I said, my hands trembling. Even if I could have spoken freely, I wouldn't have dared point out that, thanks to her intervention, I had no access to a computer. I'd have to break the password on my dad's laptop. It was probably either "LedZeppelin" or "LedZeppelinIV," his favorite album. At least I hoped it was.

"Good. Say you'll meet by the lockers in the central courtyard. It's private enough that she won't be suspicious. Then tell her the evidence is in your locker, and you'll meet her there. If she replies and asks for the combination, don't respond. We can't have her going down there earlier."

"Sure, Grandpa," I said, eyeing Mrs. Maxwell as she turned down the god-awful xylophone version of Christina

Aguilera's "Genie in a Bottle" that piped through the Preppy Plus's loudspeakers. "I'd better go."

A woman emerged from the fitting room. I was startled before I realized it was just another Preppy Plus regular—a middle-aged woman with a bright red face and an armful of salmon-hued beach cover-ups. If there was one thing in the world I could safely assume, it was that this woman should (a) not wear salmon-colored tunics and (b) not spend any more time at the beach.

"I'll call your house as soon as the police have her," Dr. Agford said. "Blind copy my school account on the email. And Sophie?"

"Yes?" I braced myself for another request.

"I don't want to alarm you, but I couldn't reach your parents yet. Could be the cell service at the launch station, or they might be too busy to pick up. The police are trying to reach them on a landline. In the meantime, when you get home, lock the doors. Stay there with your grandfather. Don't answer if anyone knocks." Dr. Agford's voice was steady, but I could hear the edge of fear behind it. "It's best to play it safe," she added.

A chill came over me. It was the same feeling I'd had at my first therapy session with Agford. I had to remind myself that Dr. Agford wasn't the one I needed to worry about anymore. "I will, Grandpa," I replied, my throat closing around the words.

I clicked off the handset and handed it back to Mrs. Maxwell. She stared at the rivulets of perspiration running down the phone, then back at me. "Everything okay, sweetie?"

"You bet, Mrs. Maxwell." I forced a grin. "Everything is just fine."

When I came through my front door, Jake was drinking Coke out of a clear plastic cup. I could hear Grandpa upstairs shouting at the television. "Buy a vowel, nitwit!"

I frowned at Jake. "Did you find that on the counter, by any chance?"

"That's for me to know and you to find ou—" Jake hesitated, puzzled. He squinted into the bottom of the cup and shook it. It rattled. "What the—"

"It's my baby teeth," I clarified. "I'm testing the effects of soda for the science fair."

Jake dropped the cup and ran from the room, retching. If I'd have known dropping teeth into drinks could so effectively remove Jake from my presence, I would have made it a more regular practice.

"You doing your homework down there, Sophie?"

Grandpa yelled. I wondered if I should tell him about Ralston. A sudden vision of him suiting up into paramilitary gear and hauling out some secret stash of Korean War–era rifles stopped me. At the very least, he'd probably have tried to round up his VFW buddies for a Ralston search posse. Better to wait.

"Yep!" I called back. I refilled the Coke cup, so it wasn't technically a lie.

"It's 'Can a leopard change its spots!' C'mon, nimrods!" he shouted, his attention already back on the TV.

I padded over to the kitchen counter and flipped open my dad's laptop. I logged in on my third try (LedZeppelin4, not IV), and soon I was staring at the blank Compose Mail screen on Luna Vista Middle School's web-mail page. I pulled out Ralston's business card, took a deep breath, and typed:

To: lr154@fbi-gov.us

Cc:

Bcc: CAgford@lunavistausd.k12.ca.us

From: SYoung@lunavistausd.k12.ca.us

We'll meet you in the central outdoor courtyard at

LVMS, by the lockers, 11 p.m. tonight. Please confirm.

—Young & Yang

Ralston's confirmation reply came even before I'd shut the web-mail window, robbing me of any hope the police had picked her up already. I looked at the microwave clock. "Everything is just fine," I repeated like a mantra.

I walked to the front door, checked the dead bolt, and peered at Dr. Agford's house. "Agent" Stone's white pickup truck was parked a little way up the street, right where it had been the previous night. Ralston must have dispatched him to track Dr. Agford while she waited. I shuddered and shuffled back to my room to radio Grace.

"You there, Grace? Frequency ten?" I said.

The speaker screeched with feedback. I heard voices rise and fall amid static and fumbling.

"Grace?" I repeated.

"Hey." I heard muffled Mandarin in the background. "Sophie?"

I managed to tell her about the police trap set for Ralston at school before a clicking broke onto the line. It sounded like the clucking of a tongue.

It *was* the clucking of a tongue. I could practically see Mrs. Dr. Yang's eyebrows trying to twitch as her voice cut in and out. "Sophie! I — old you! — trouble!"

"Mom." Grace groaned in the background. "Like this. Hold *down* the button. Sophie, I'm so sorry." The line cut to static. At least Grace knew I'd scheduled the "drop" at school and the police were on it.

I closed my eyes and took a deep breath. Not only did I have the science fair Monday, but thanks to Grandpa's storyfests and my distraction during study hall, I was a week behind on *To Kill a Mockingbird* reading and had to teach myself how to graph polynomials before Friday. It was all over, I told myself. *Everything would be fine.* Dr. Agford would call any minute to confirm the police had Ralston. Time to get back to real life.

I looked around my room. Clothes spilled from the closet, cluttering my relationship *gua.* A pile of binders, books, and papers towered like one of Grace's magazine stacks in the corner. Apart from Mrs. Dr. Yang's red elephant, I'd done nothing constructive for my chi since way before the night we'd first spied on Agford. I put my iPod on my mellow playlist and hummed along as I tossed out old vocab lists and review sheets. It felt good to reorder my bookshelf and scrub out the sticky ring a Coke had left on my nightstand.

I'd just rescued my jeans from the dust bunnies near my closet door and given them a good shake when something clattered to the hardwood floor. I looked down and frowned. It was a pen. A heavy silver kind, like the ones Mr. Katz wore clipped in his shirt pocket. It wasn't until I saw the fancy curlicue decoration on the cap that I recognized it. Agford's pen—the one I'd accidentally pocketed during my cleaning frenzy on that first mission. I guess she hadn't missed it. It was a really nice pen, I thought as I tested it out on a blank page in my science notebook. It slid across the paper so smoothly that it practically propelled itself. Was it awful that I wanted to use it for writing up my science notes, just for one night? I'd give it back to her tomorrow, for sure.

I retrieved the plastic cups where my baby teeth soaked, then propped up my crisp white poster board and squinted at it, envisioning where I'd put the charts. There'd be no repeat of the volcano disaster. I lined up my coloring pencils, markers, ruler, and high-powered magnifying glass, and set to work.

"HYPOTHESIS," I wrote in big blue block letters across the left panel of my poster board, relishing the smell of fresh ink. How should I phrase it? "Sugary sodas cause tooth decay?" No, that didn't account for the orange juice. "Sugar in drinks causes tooth decay," I wrote, my pen squeaking across the white foam board. There. Nice and basic. I skipped lines and added "FACTS" and "CONCLUSIONS."

Hypothesis. Facts. Conclusion. Step One. Step Two. Step Three. Why couldn't everything be so simple?

Hours passed. Dr. Agford's sleek pen filled the clean sheets of my notebook as I jotted down each new discovery. Dinner came and went. Dr. Agford still hadn't called, but I wasn't worried yet. They knew where to find Ralston at eleven, I told myself. Grandpa went to bed early, his VFW beers having taken their toll. I almost asked Jake if he wanted to finish the nightmarish ocean puzzle with me. It would have been the perfect distraction. I wasn't ready to tell him everything, though. Besides, he sneaked out late, claiming he had to work on an "important group project." Perhaps, in some circles, making out with his girlfriend counted as an important group project.

I pulled out my magnifying glass and returned to inspecting the baby teeth, peering at each nook and cranny and noting changes. It seemed strange that the glass could make reality clearer by exaggerating. When Grace and I exaggerated, we'd made reality about as muddy as it could get.

I put down the magnifying glass and looked up at the

clock. Ten thirty. Thirty minutes, and the police would have Ralston. It would be over. A draft rustled the pages of my notebook. I looked down.

My heart jumped.

The magnifying glass lay propped against Dr. Agford's silver pen. It rested just over the end of the pen, enlarging the curves of the fancy curlicue etched there.

But it wasn't just a fancy curlicue. Those were letters. Spindly, curly, and hard to read—but definitely letters. Initials, maybe? Agford loved that brooch with the A, after all. I could imagine her monogramming a nice pen. I felt my skin crawl as I made out the sweeping arc of the first letter. It looked a little bit too much like—it was a D. No doubt about it. And next to it was . . . No. It couldn't be.

Hands trembling, I leaned closer and lifted the magnifier until the curvy shapes filled the whole glass:

$\mathcal{DSB}$

Three letters.

DSB.

I wouldn't need vowels to solve this puzzle.

Chapter Twenty-seven

The Art of War

I flung open the blinds of my front window. The house across the street was dark. I took a deep breath. No jumping to conclusions. Not yet.

I reached for a black marker and flipped over my white poster board. HYPOTHESIS: I wrote in my shaking hand. CHARLOTTE AGFORD IS DEBORAH S. BAIN.

Eight teens were dead. Eight families' lives destroyed. One of them Ralston's. And the woman responsible? If I was right, she was on her way to Luna Vista Middle School that very moment. She'd used me to get Ralston alone. All she had to do was find her, and she could silence the truth. But if I was wrong . . .

I couldn't get it wrong. Not this time. I raised my pen and tried to lay it all down in black and white:

FACT: CHARLOTTE AGFORD OWNS A PEN WITH THE INITIALS DSB.

FACT: DEBORAH SLATER BAIN'S INITIALS ARE DSB.

FACT: A WOMAN WHO WORKS FOR THE FBI THINKS CHARLOTTE AGFORD IS DEBORAH BAIN.

FACT: DEBORAH BAIN HIRED DANIEL SLATER FOR THE POOL WORK AT TILMORE HIGH.

FACT: CHARLOTTE AGFORD WAS TALKING TO SOMEONE NAMED "DANNY" ON THE PHONE.

FACT: DEBORAH BAIN'S BODY WAS NEVER FOUND.

FACT: CHARLOTTE AGFORD MOVED HERE ABOUT A MONTH AFTER DEBORAH BAIN'S DEATH.

I stared at my shaky black scrawl, heart pounding. That morning, in Charlotte Agford's office, I'd made my biggest assumption to date. It had been reasonable to see smears of red and think it was blood. It had been reasonable to assume a woman with an FBI badge and email address was really the FBI. It had even been relatively reasonable to think a woman doing everything in her power to hide might be a fugitive. But it hadn't been reasonable to assume Charlotte Agford was telling the truth. Especially when that truth accounted for the exact evidence we had collected so far. *Wheel of Fortune* and Grandpa had it right: A leopard cannot change its spots.

Charlotte Agford had changed her name and gotten plastic surgery. She wore a wig and had lied to everyone about who she was. These could be the actions of a mother desperate to avoid the Tilmore Eight media spotlight and start a new life. Or . . .

FACT: CHARLOTTE AGFORD'S ACTIONS COULD BE EXACTLY THE SAME IF SHE WERE A FUGITIVE.

I stepped back and looked at the board, dizzy from the marker fumes. Trista had been right from the start. There was always another explanation. What were the chances that "Cassie Ogden" just happened to have an ex-husband named Danny, as in Daniel Slater? I'd always hated the way a bad movie's sound track swells at emotional moments to distract from the terrible acting and story line. How hadn't I recognized Agford pulling the same trick? She had surrounded me with a symphony of sighs and sniffles. She'd hoped all her lectures on how preteen brains can't perceive reality would finally pay off. And she'd gotten her wish. Until now.

I reached out my pen and made my final note:

CONCLUSION: CHARLOTTE AGFORD IS DEBORAH BAIN.

And she was on her way to Luna Vista Middle School to silence Louise Ralston forever.

There it was. Hypothesis, facts, conclusion. Three easy steps.

But the next part wasn't easy at all. I whirled back to the clock. Ten forty-five. There might still be time to stop her.

I swung open my door and tiptoed to the cordless phone in the kitchen. Grandpa's whistling snores drifted from his bedroom down the hall. My fingers shook as I dialed the police.

"This is Sophie Young," I said in a surprisingly steady voice. "I'd like to report an emergency at Luna Vista Middle School."

"Sophie Young?"

I recognized the gruff voice immediately. It was Officer Grady.

"Sure you don't want to remain *anonymous*?" he asked. I could practically hear his smirk.

I paused to gather my thoughts. I wanted to list the facts clearly and calmly. Instead I rambled like a maniac about fugitives and FBI software programmers, yearbooks and plastic surgery, monogrammed pens and wigs. "Don't you see?" I said, breathless. "She thinks Ralston's the only person who knows the truth, Officer. You've got to get down there before she does something!"

Officer Grady didn't try to hide his irritation. "You've been watching too many movies, Miss Young," he said.

"Did Charlotte Agford call you today? To try to reach my parents at the missile station?"

Officer Grady sighed. "Not that I'm aware of. Miss Young, I think—"

"If I were wrong, she would've called! Will *you* call them? They're at the AmStar test station off the coast. I'll never be able to get through. Not right before the launch. But if the police called . . ."

Officer Grady hesitated. My hopes soared. After all, what kid wants the police to call their parents? But he just cleared his throat. "Get some rest now, Miss Young," he said.

A dial tone hummed in my ear.

I looked down at my clothes. Dark blue sweats and a hoodie. That was as spy-stylish as it was going to get tonight. I slunk back to my room and snatched my walkie-talkie from the desk. Grace's mom had surely confiscated hers. It was worth a try, though. "Grace!" I whispered. "Agent Yang, are you there?"

Static hissed like ocean waves.

I stared at Kai Li, smiling uselessly out at me from his two-dimensional poster prison. My wind chimes swayed gently. I had to think. What next? I'd call Trista. The police wouldn't be able to ignore Trista Bottoms. I'd call Trista; then I'd go get Grace.

My heart sank as Trista's phone rang and rang. I left a garbled message I wasn't sure even Trista would be able to decode.

I clipped my walkie-talkie onto my sweats and ripped open my desk drawer. I grabbed the pepper spray Grace had given me the morning after our meeting with Ralston and, careful to dodge my wind chimes, dashed toward my closet. The trusty black rope waited hidden in the back, coiled and ready to strike. I pulled it out and lashed it to the bed frame, yanking it tight to check for safety before I snaked the free end down the side of the house. All systems go. No time for equipment and frequency checks tonight.

I pulled on my knit black gloves, grabbed the rope, and fell back into the night, free-falling for only a second before the rope held fast. I shimmied down and leaped over the roses to the lawn, my legs bending to break my fall as I landed with a quiet thud. I'd cleared the bushes by at least a foot.

Easy. Just like in the movies.

I sprinted across the dew-soaked grass to Grace's patio door and pounded against the glass. Lucky's green eyes glared out at me from the darkness. I thumped again. He disappeared with a flick of his tail.

Panic bolted through me. Where was she? I pressed my face against the glass. Her bed looked empty, but it was too dark to tell for sure. I tried to tug the door open. No luck.

Time was running out. It might be too late. If Ralston was early . . . if Bain was waiting already . . . Please, Agent Ralston, I thought. Please have brought Stone with you. But she wouldn't bring backup when she was meeting a couple of kids at school, would she?

My reflection stared back at me from Grace's patio door. With the darkness nearly eclipsing my tiny frame, my pale face looked as though it were detached from my body, free-floating. I closed my eyes and listened to the wind rustling through the trees. Sun Tzu never wrote about a general entering battle alone.

I took in a long breath. *Gather energy like bending a thousand cross-bows,* I imagined he might have said. I exhaled. *And you will discover in yourself the force of an entire army.*

I launched myself down the hill. Seconds later I was on my bike, zipping down Luna Vista Drive.

I pedaled as if my life depended on it. Tonight someone's did.

Chapter Twenty-eight

Amazing Grace

On any other night, I would have marveled at the clear sky. With no marine fog blanketing Luna Vista, the Orion constellation blazed above me, his sword and belt shimmering as the wind whipped my cheeks and fanned back my hair.

I stopped half a block away from school, stashed my bike in the bushes, and peered out. Neither the blue sedan nor Agford's—well, Deborah Bain's—convertible was in the parking lot.

I crept down the sidewalk, tiptoeing once I reached the main building. The outdoor campus was easy to enter, but that only meant it was even more likely that Agford lurked somewhere in the shadows. I pressed myself up against the science building, listened for a moment, then inched my way toward the central courtyard.

Dead leaves skittered over the concrete as the wind gusted. I kept my breath slow and steady. An electric hum startled me. A refrigerator in the cafeteria kicking into higher gear maybe? Ralston was nowhere. What if I was already too late?

As I rounded the corner into the courtyard, something scraped against the concrete in front of me. I stopped short. A large, black shadow flickered by the lockers.

I sighed in relief. Who'd have thought the bulky frame of Agent Stone could have been so reassuring? So what if he was some fly-by-night private investigator? Dressed all in black, he stood by a bank of lockers, sucking in his bulging gut as he tried to flatten himself against the wall.

"Pssst!" I hissed across the courtyard. "Bain knows! Get Ralston and clear out of here!"

Stone's monobrow lifted in surprise. With surprising agility he jumped up and broke into a run. But wait—why was he—

Searing pain split down my side as Stone tackled me, sending me sprawling to the concrete. My walkie-talkie skidded into the darkness. I groaned in agony as he pressed his knee against my back and wrenched my arms behind me.

"One word and it's over," he whispered, his coffee and cigarette breath pouring over me. He tightened his grasp and yanked me to my feet. If this was how the FBI saved people, I couldn't wait to see what they'd do to criminals like Bain.

"I think there's been a mistake," I croaked. It hurt to breathe, let alone talk.

A woman's voice echoed from somewhere in the darkness. "You're right, Sophie. There *has* been a mistake." My veins turned to ice. I'd know that voice anywhere.

Charlotte Agford glided from the shadows into the hazy fluorescent glow of the courtyard light as though she were stepping onstage. Her auburn wig was surprisingly intact despite the wind, and she wore a striped Oxford shirt tucked into her ironed mom jeans. Her lips stretched into a gruesome smile while her eyes remained black and empty. How had I ever seen even a glimmer of warmth behind them?

"I see you've met my brother," she said.

Her *brother*? I felt like my head was collapsing in upon itself as firework bursts of images exploded through it. Ralston. The blue sedan. The white truck. The heavyset man lumbering through the yard. For me, he'd always been one of Ralston's men. First the FBI, then a PI she'd hired. I'd never even considered another possibility.

Bain stepped closer. "Danny, dear, everyone likes a firm handshake, but that's a bit much." She snorted.

Danny. Danny, as in "I'll rip their throats out, Danny." I pictured the grainy newsprint image of Daniel Slater and his bulging beer belly as he hid his face and pushed through the throng of reporters. Daniel Slater's fingers—the same fumbling fingers that miswired the pool circuitry at Tilmore High School—dug into my arms. My own fingers grew numb, and my legs buckled. It was no wonder he had looked surprised the night before. His enemy had walked up and surrendered. No one had needed to spin a story to twist my assumptions. I'd done it all by myself.

Sun Tzu said that victory is certain only when you make no mistakes. I was going to prove the old philosopher wrong for once.

"I don't want to cause any trouble for you, Doctor," I said meekly, stalling. There was a slim chance Ralston had seen us already and radioed the cops. I scanned the courtyard. Daniel Slater tipped the scales at well over two hundred pounds. He was at least a foot and a half taller than I was. Even if I broke free, could I outrun them both?

Deborah Bain answered the question for me. She reached behind her creased mom jeans and pulled out a gun. Her wrist dipped with the heft of it as the steel glimmered in the night.

She clucked her tongue and tilted her head as she stepped

314

in front of me. "Shame on you, Sophie. Lying? At your age? You should know better. If you didn't want to cause any trouble, you'd have stayed home, just like I told you." Bain waved her gun as if she were wagging her finger at me. "Now let me see. If you're here . . . I suppose that means your parents didn't believe you? And neither did the police? Shocking. Where *do* our taxes go?"

Danny let out a snort. Ah, there was the family resemblance.

"But I can tell you one thing, *sweetie.*" She hissed the word. "You're certainly not going to cause trouble anymore."

I stiffened. Breathe, I told myself. I had to stay loose. Strength wouldn't win this battle. I had to watch and wait for the enemy to make her own mistakes.

"You want me to take care of her?" Danny asked, wrenching my arms back even more. I cried out.

Bain shook her head. "We need her as a hostage." She turned and raised her voice, addressing the darkness. "Isn't that right, Louise? Come on out, now. You don't want this nice girl to get hurt, do ya?" Her voice reverberated against the lockers. She didn't bother hiding her own Texas twang anymore. "That's strange," Bain said, wheeling back to me. "I guess she's late for her big night."

I closed my eyes and breathed as if I were sliding into my Embrace Tiger opening stance.

Bain must have sensed me gathering myself. Her eyes flitted around the courtyard.

"Careful, Dan," she said. "Wherever there's Young, there's Yang." She peered into the shadows by the lockers before sidling over to me. Her toxic perfume engulfed me as she leaned close. "Or maybe not," she said, studying my expression. "What? Did Grace have to stay home and do her hair?"

I glared back.

"Oh! Look at that, Dan." Bain smiled with all her teeth. "I nailed it!"

"Bravo," grunted Danny.

"It's *brava*, Dan-Dan," Bain said in a tone that reminded me more than a little of Marissa Pritchard. "The feminine ending for ladies: brav*a*. Right, Soph?"

I didn't answer. Every move could give the enemy an opening. Engage only when necessary. I felt the hard cylinder of Grace's pepper spray in my pocket. If I could just get my one hand free . . .

Deborah Bain sighed. "If you had always been this quiet, Sophie, we wouldn't be standing here now." She spoke with her hands, waving the gun around carelessly. "You have to

 316

know this isn't easy for me. I never wanted anyone to get hurt."

The wind howled through the archway behind us, sweeping a pile of leaves against the lockers. I shuddered.

"But, you see, Louise is probably off to get the police now. There's not much time." She pouted. "You almost won, Sophie Young. I'll admit it. Right, *Agent Stone*?" she mocked.

Danny's laugh burst from him like an explosion.

"Until you ran up to Danny here and spouted all that business about airtight evidence and needing to find Ralston, I hadn't realized just how far you two had gotten." She slipped into her fake Charlotte Agford soprano: "I'm just so proud of you, Sophie." Her ensuing giggle came out as a series of snorts. "Drag her over here, Danny. Tie her up quick. She's small but feisty."

"Freeze!" screamed a voice from the outdoor hallway opposite us. Slater jerked up at the shout. My heart stopped. It wasn't Agent Ralston. It wasn't the police either.

It was Grace.

"No!" I shrieked as Deborah Bain swung around and pointed her gun into the darkness. It wasn't supposed to happen like this.

317

Bain jogged toward Grace's voice, gun raised. Any second she could pull the trigger. I had to—

There wasn't time to think. When I felt Daniel Slater's weight shift, I hoisted my knee up and rammed my foot down over his with the full force of my gathered chi. While he cried out and loosened his grip, I flung myself into Golden Rooster Stands on One Leg and delivered a swift donkey kick square into his crotch. He crumpled, groaning. I grabbed my pepper spray, windmilled into Strike Tiger's Ears, then pulled the trigger right into his eyes. Slater screamed. His hands flew to his face as he stumbled backward.

I ran toward the archway, then stopped cold. Bain crouched, the white stripes of her Oxford blouse eerily aglow. Was she leaning over Grace's body? But she hadn't even fired her gun!

I gasped. Grace had disappeared. Deborah Bain swung back toward me, gun in one hand and—in the other—my walkie-talkie.

She roared in frustration and hurled the little black box down the concrete hallway.

In the last instant before Bain launched herself at me, gun aimed, I saw a flash of pink by the French room and understood it all before it even happened. Grace must have seen my walkie-talkie in the hall and realized she could lure Agford in by radioing. But where had she hidden herself in the meantime?

Grace rippled into view now, like a mirage in neon-pink pajamas. She flung her leg out into a perfect imitation of Snake Creeps Down and . . . *voilà!*

Deborah Bain went flying, eyes wide and arms flailing, as her gun broke free from her grasp and clattered to the concrete.

"Run!" Grace shrieked as she burst out of the darkness and into the courtyard, Bain's gun in hand. Her footfalls were heavy. I looked down. Her pink pajamas were tucked into—cowboy boots? She'd obviously had no time to plan her rescue outfit.

"That way!" I pointed to the archway opposite the main entrance. It led past the sixth-grade classrooms and, eventually, to the soccer field. If we could just get to the bluffs trail that led to the beach, we might be able to escape. I doubted Bain knew the path was there. Besides, it was hard enough to find in the daylight, let alone at night.

"Get them!" Deborah Bain's scream followed us.

But we were already gone.

We sprinted down the hall as far as we could before needing to catch our breath. We listened for footsteps. It was eerily quiet. Where were they?

"I can't believe it worked!" Grace said, panting and leaning on my shoulder.

"Well, you *are* Amazing Grace." I wheezed, trying to ignore the pain that stabbed across my ribs with each breath. "Speaking of which, how did you know to come?"

"You radioed me that you set up the Ralston meeting for eleven at school, remember? I put it together." In between gasps for breath, Grace explained that she'd heard me radio around ten forty-five but couldn't find her walkie-talkie because her mom had confiscated it. We figured out that I must have been pounding on her glass door while she was off looking for it. By the time she radioed back, I'd been on my bike and hadn't heard her above the wind. "I ran to your house to check on you, saw the rope, and well . . . here I am." She grinned. "I never did do well on the sidelines."

"That's for sure." I glanced worriedly behind us. Still no sign of them. "They must have thought we ran out the front," I said.

"Never a good idea to jump to conclusions, is it?"

"Guess not." I smiled back. "Now, c'mon." I grabbed her arm. We ran past the sixth-grade buildings and flung open the chain-link gate to the field.

"Wait—" Grace looked down at the gun in her hand and back at me, uncertain.

I shook my head. "We're safer without it."

Grace nodded, then whirled toward a white banner flapping above a series of irrigation ditches, where a new sprinkler system was being installed. PARDON OUR DUST, it read. WE'RE BUILDING FUTURES. She reached her arm back and, with all her force, hurled the gun over the banner and—I hoped—into one of the ditches. But as she turned to run, her boot caught something in the dark. She stifled a cry, but it was too late. A wild clanging rang out as a pyramid of stacked pipes cascaded to the ground.

We looked at each other in panic.

"Go ahead!" I cried, waving Grace toward the bluffs. Even in her cowboy boots, with her long legs she stood a much better chance of getting away. "The beach trail!"

Grace stopped short. Her eyes went wide. "The beach?" she said.

"It's our best chance."

Grace trembled. She rooted herself in place.

The pounding surf raged below. The closest I'd ever seen Grace go to the beach was the top of the bluffs. She'd gone once for moral support when I wanted to see Rod surf. She'd gone again to see Agford's evidence stash. Even then, she'd turned her back to the ocean, and that was a windless day. I grabbed her arm and tugged. It was stiff, like laundry dried on the line.

My heart leaped as the gate smashed open behind us. A figure spilled out behind Grace's frozen silhouette.

Relief replaced my shock as the figure moved into the dull orange glow of the field light. Maybe Louise Ralston wasn't a real FBI agent. Maybe she had a lot to answer for. But she had stayed for us when she could have easily escaped and saved herself. She stood like a protective seawall, the wind slapping her brown hair against her face. "They're coming! Go!" she cried. "I've got your backs, remember?" Her watery blue eyes shone in the darkness. They pleaded with us—not just to flee, but also to forgive.

Just then Bain burst onto the field behind her. Louise Ralston reached into her blazer and pulled her gun from its shoulder holster. "It's over, Debbie," she said, wheeling around to aim at her chest.

But it wasn't over. Danny Slater had been only steps behind Bain. Still half blinded, he charged through the gate and lunged toward Ralston. Ralston turned to shoot but fell to the ground, gun glinting in the air as it spun and then landed in the grass with a thud. The irrigation ditch! She must have lost her footing. All three of them scrambled toward the gun. I turned and grasped Grace's hand. There was no way we were waiting to find out how this would end.

"Run, ladies!" The wind carried Ralston's shout.

"You can do this," I coaxed Grace. "You have to do this."

Grace lurched forward unsteadily, then broke into a run. I sprinted as far and as fast as my short legs would allow, pumping my arms as I scanned the cliff edges for the scraggly bush that marked the beach trailhead.

The night air burned my throat. In the moonlight our slender shadows stretched across the field to guide the way. Grace's footfalls pounded behind me. "These stupid boots!" she cried.

I looked back. Grace waved me onward. Bain and Slater were several hundred yards across the field, still by the gate, but their shadows bore down on us. Where had Ralston gone?

A gunshot split the night. I hoped it was Ralston's, but I wasn't about to turn around to check. "We're almost there!" I screamed above the wind and surf. We launched ourselves toward the trailhead, my sleeve ripping as I scraped past a bush to the steep path below.

Sand flying and lungs bursting, Grace and I barreled down the cliff trail as the roar of the waves deafened us. The wind thrashed our hair against our cheeks as we tripped over stones and scrub brush.

Another gunshot rang out above us, this time closer. I

tripped and landed on damp, tightly packed sand. Pain shot through my shoulder. I didn't even dare move my arm to wipe the sand from my eyes. Now it was Grace who pulled me up and shoved me forward. "Keep going!"

I sprinted for cover behind a boulder near the shore, reaching it as my lungs nearly gave out. Grace caught up and crouched with me, flinching as waves crashed at our feet. She carried her cowboy boots in one hand. We huddled together, breathless and near tears, as the waves pounded and pulled away, pounded and pulled away again.

"If we don't make it out of here alive . . ." She clapped me on the shoulder.

I winced.

"Oh, sorry." She clapped me on the opposite shoulder and held her hand there. "I just want to say, for the record . . ." She smiled. "From day one I wanted to be your friend."

"And still?" I asked.

"And still. I always will. You never really doubted me, did you?"

I had. But as we crouched there in the blackness, waves crashing down around us, I finally understood. I guess I'd needed to strip away every last layer of assumptions to see it: I never would have doubted Grace if I had trusted myself.

Yang needs yin, and yin needs yang. We were two opposites with just enough of the other to balance everything out. And no matter what, Grace Yang had proved that she would—as Ralston and her daughter would say—always have my back.

I looked Grace in the eye. Another swell crashed down. "Maybe for just a second," I confessed. "But never again."

We heard a cry behind us. A figure—or two?—emerged from the brush at the base of the trail. No way the rock we were hiding behind was going to provide enough cover.

"Over there!" I gestured to the jumble of shadowy large boulders that jutted into the surf at the far end of the beach. I ran. Sprinting on sand in wet sweatpants felt like the labored running in dreams. No matter how hard I tried, I just couldn't go faster.

"Don't worry, the water's not deee-eep!" I yelled back as my voice warbled with each of my footfalls. It wasn't an outright lie. It wouldn't help Grace to know that a big breaker could rise up and sweep us into the rip current at any second.

I dove for cover behind the cluster of craggy rocks. The high tide washed over me as I clung to them. I sputtered and looked around to reassure Grace. The waves tugging at my clothes even frightened me, and I knew how to swim.

That was when I realized Grace wasn't there.

I peeked over the tallest boulder, making sure I could see without being seen. There was Deborah Bain, holding Grace in a headlock. They were knee-deep in the swirling, surging surf.

"Scared? Serves you right," Bain hissed before dunking Grace face-first into the avalanche of waves hurtling in to shore. Grace came up for air and screamed, only to have Bain dunk her again.

I had to think fast. If Bain had a gun, I couldn't see it. Daniel Slater was out there somewhere. I prayed he was still blind enough from pepper spray that he couldn't find the beach trail.

I pulled off my blue hoodie and wrapped it around a fat piece of driftwood, tying the empty sleeves around it. Maybe it would look like I just had my arms crossed? I raised up the wood, lodging it between the boulders to prop it up. Thank God I was so small. It could actually look like my tiny frame.

I shouted to Bain from behind the boulders. "You really think you're going to get away with this?"

Agford's head shot up, sending her lopsided wig farther off-kilter. She squinted at the silhouetted driftwood figure atop the rocks.

"No matter what you do, I'm still here to tell the truth," I yelled, hoping she couldn't hear my sharp intake of breath as I pushed forward into the icy waves. If I could just swim until I was across from them, maybe I could angle in and sneak up behind Bain while she screamed at the scarecrow version of me. I dog-paddled far enough out that I could dive underwater—but not so far that I couldn't stand if I needed to. The rip current was strong. It could pull me out to sea in no time.

"You know I can never let that happen, *Soph*," Bain yelled. I treaded water and glanced back to check my makeshift dummy. In the dark, silhouetted against the moon, it could look like me, I supposed.

Grace surfaced, sputtering from another dunk into a wave breaking on shore. "Sophie, just run! It's too late! Save yourself," she cried.

I sucked in a breath and slipped under a wave, fighting to swim parallel to the shore as the current dragged against me. How far was far enough?

I held my breath until I couldn't hold it any longer. As I gasped to the surface, a heavy object knocked against my forehead, stunning me. A rock? A gun? I looked down. One of Grace's cowboy boots spun in the surf. She must've dropped it when we ran. Its heel had gashed my forehead.

The salty water stung.

I shivered as I treaded the frigid water. I'd paced my swim well. Bain stood not more than fifteen feet in front of me, still turned toward my makeshift figure on the rock. Grace struggled in her grasp as the surf rushed against their feet.

"Give it up, Sophie," Bain yelled. "Danny's going to be here any second. He has the gun. It's over."

I grasped the boot and dove with the next wave. As it launched me toward shore, I didn't even feel like I was Sophie Young. I was Sun Tzu himself, coming to the rescue. As soon as I could stand, I heaved myself out of the water just behind them, teeth chattering. The tide slurped against my clothes. I cringed, praying Bain hadn't heard me, then edged closer. I tightened my grip on the end of the boot and—once I was right behind her—raised my arm. She could turn around any second. . . .

Bam!

I slammed the heel of Grace's cowboy boot directly into the back of Deborah Bain's skull. She let out a bloodcurdling yell and crumpled to the sand in front of me. Her wig tumbled into the surf and swirled away as if disappearing down a drain. Grace cried out as she kicked herself free and shot toward my figure on the rocks. The waves roared.

"Grace! I'm right here!" I tried to run to her, but my frozen legs wouldn't cooperate. The wind howled against my soaked clothes. I couldn't even feel the cold anymore.

Grace turned back. I stumbled forward. She grasped me in a tight hug and let out a single sob. The sound of our chattering teeth almost drowned out the waves. After a long second, Grace leaned back and gave me a weak smile.

"N-now *that's* what I call Dragon Emerges from Water," she said.

I smiled back. "It's always been my best move," I said.

Grace pulled me toward Bain's unconscious form on the tide line and pointed. "F-f-first Rule of C-conduct." She gestured for me to help drag Bain higher up on the sand. "The F-F-BI never k-kills a suspect unless necessary." She checked Agford's pulse. "She's alive."

We jumped at the screech of a bullhorn. "THIS IS LVPD! DROP YOUR WEAPONS! YOU ARE SURROUNDED! I repeat, YOU ARE SURROUNDED!" it blared.

We squinted into the glare of bobbing floodlights. A line of black shadows scuttled down the trail and across the beach. Nightsticks swinging in their belts, radios rattling, the officers sprinted toward us with weapons raised.

We lifted our hands in surrender.

Officer Grady approached, panting. He looked down

at Deborah Bain's slumped form and back at us. "How on earth . . . ?"

Grace and I exchanged a look.

I turned back to Officer Grady. I folded my arms.

"You're welcome," I said.

Chapter Twenty-nine

Happy Family

Back up atop the bluffs, officers wrapped us in blankets and led us across the field to the front parking lot. They ushered us past Daniel Slater, who lay facedown on the ground while an officer perched over him, knee digging into his back. Slater grunted in pain as the cop wrenched his arms back and cuffed them.

The reds and blues of the police cruisers washed over us as a booming voice rang out.

"I told you they'd kick butt!" Trista waved at us through the half-open backseat window of a police car as its lights flickered across her face. "Didn't I?" She turned her head to the officer standing outside the cruiser. "Just like I told you to get down to school."

"You told us," the officer said. "You told us."

Trista looked smug. "Now are you going to let me go

give them a hug, or do I have to disassemble this door?"

The officer reluctantly opened up, and Trista spilled forward. "Finally got your voice mail," she said. "If these jokers had let me, I'd have saved you myself." She wrapped Grace and me in an awkward bear hug that crushed my already bruised ribs and shoulder. I heard a muffled groan. I thought it was my own until Trista pulled away to reveal its true source.

Deborah Bain, cuffed and held upright by two burly officers, groaned again. She stared at us, dazed. Something else lingered in her dead eyes now. It took me a moment to realize it was defeat. The waves had washed away her makeup. Her hair—if you could call it that—was plastered to her head in matted brown clumps, and her striped blouse was untucked and soaked. If it hadn't been for the single sharp crease running down each leg of her high-waisted jeans, I wouldn't have been able to say for sure it was her.

"In you go," one of the officers barked as he shoved her into the waiting car. She didn't break her gaze; her lips moved soundlessly like a fish caught on a hook. For once, Deborah Bain had nothing to say.

"What about this one?" a female officer behind me asked. I turned to look.

Louise Ralston stood flanked on either side by officers.

"Cuff 'er and book 'er," Officer Grady snapped.

"Wait!" I shouted. "Ralston's FBI!" I added, though I knew it wasn't exactly true. They couldn't just take her like that. "If it weren't for her, you'd have never—"

"It's all right, Sophie," Ralston interrupted. Even in the harsh glare of the floodlights, her blue eyes looked soft. She smiled. "This will all be cleared up."

"But—"

"I promise." Her slumped shoulders swayed as the officers handcuffed her. She still smiled. "Now I know y'all have no good reason to take my word. But I swear. This time it's the whole truth and nothing but the truth."

The police radios blared louder as one of the officers opened his cruiser door and helped Louise Ralston inside.

At three p.m. the next day, I woke up with a start. Only when the room finally came into focus did I realize the two figures hovering over me were my parents. They gazed at me so intensely, I was pretty sure they were trying to memorize each of my freckles.

"Sorry, dear. I thought you might want us to wake you," my mom said. "Grace is on the phone." She let go of my dad's hand as she passed the receiver to me.

My parents had come back from the missile station in

the wee hours of the morning. The launch had gone well, despite some minor last-minute glitches. In a way it was lucky the police only reached my parents by phone after the launch. With AmStar's team running around in a frenzy, the last thing they would have needed was my parents freaking out about me.

When my parents walked in the door, I couldn't remember ever being quite that happy to see anyone. Or quite that happy to hear an apology, for that matter. It turned out the single known acceptable case of parents repeating themselves ad nauseam was when they were gushing about how wrong they were. It was downright embarrassing. And the hugs! As if my ribs weren't already sore enough after Slater's tackle. I had to remind them I didn't escape with my life only to lose it in the first recorded suffocation by hugging.

There was decidedly less risk of dying from the awkward hug Jake gave me when he found out I'd almost been killed. Still, it was awfully sweet—especially considering that he'd gotten busted for not being home when the cops had brought me back. When he had finally traipsed back in, he looked like he'd had his own brush with death at his girlfriend's. However, upon closer inspection, the red welts all over his neck proved to be hickeys.

When Grandpa found out about Bain, he'd bunched up

his mouth and glared across the street. "I knew it!" he'd exclaimed. "Something about that woman never did smell right."

With some coaxing my parents finally left, glued at the hip, so I could talk to Grace.

"You got your cell back!" I greeted her.

"Nope. Calling from the landline."

"No way."

"Way. Laptop's still gone, too. But my dad is *loving* booking me all these interviews, so I guess I'm not grounded anymore."

"Interviews?"

"Sophie, go turn on the TV."

I stayed on the phone as I walked to the family room. Grandpa smiled and saluted as he made room for me on the couch in front of the television. PRETEENS FOIL TILMORE EIGHT FUGITIVE read the scrolling caption. A heavily made-up reporter stood in front of Luna Vista Middle School.

"In a shocking development late last night, two preteen sleuths helped capture a fugitive posing as a school counselor in the quiet coastal suburb of Luna Vista," she reported. A mug shot of a wigless Agford flashed on-screen.

"Whoa," I said.

"I know. It's been like this all day," Grace said.

"Former Tilmore, Texas, Assistant School Superinten-dent Deborah Bain—believed to have died in a fire two years ago—was very much alive when she was arrested by police," the reporter continued, her flimsy jacket ruffling in the breeze. "She faces charges of embezzlement, manslaughter, and—along with her brother, Daniel Slater—three counts of attempted murder."

"Now that's a victory," Grandpa said, patting me on the back so hard, I cried out. I had a feeling it was going to be a long time before my bruises went away.

We stayed glued to the set as newscasters summarized the details of the case. It was all just as Grace and I had figured out from the articles that night. Even most of what Agford had said in her melodramatic performance as "Cassie Ogden" had actually been true, I realized, as the news ran archival footage of the Tilmore Eight media frenzy. Except, of course, that Ralston was perfectly sane. Agford had simply taken on one of the Tilmore Eight mothers' stories as her own and twisted the facts about Ralston in an effort to throw us off her trail. I shuddered to think it had almost worked.

"FBI software programmer and Tilmore Eight mother Louise Ralston had long been trying to convince authorities to reopen the closed case," explained a reporter standing in front of an official-looking building in Texas. He described how police had repeatedly ignored Ralston when she had pointed to irregularities in the investigation of Bain's death by fire. Frustrated, she'd continued to investigate on her own. She used her high-clearance access to flag police background checks of people with fewer than two years' history under a name. Because Ralston had tracked Slater to Los Angeles after he was paroled, she was particularly interested when our call to police triggered an alert about Agford in nearby Luna Vista—especially since the first recorded use of Agford's name was so close to the time of Bain's supposed death. Ralston took an unauthorized leave to investigate. "Though Ralston has been suspended without pay, pending investigation, police have released her from custody," he finished.

Grace and I both let out sighs of relief.

"Told you she was real FBI," she said.

"Kind of real FBI," I corrected.

"But not crazy."

"At least not as crazy as we are." I smiled to myself. "You think our parents are ever going to let us hang out together again?"

"Yep," said Grace. "In fact, my mom and dad want to invite everyone to a banquet at Happy Family tonight. Lobster, abalone, egg-drop soup—the whole deal. I've already invited Trista and her family. Do you think you all can come?"

"I'll check with my mom and dad," I said. "They'll say yes to anything right now. Start thinking of stuff I should ask for."

"Get your phone back, at least," Grace said. "Better yet, get it upgraded. I'm so over the walkie-talkies."

"Ten-four," I replied.

Grace laughed. "Over and out."

Chapter Thirty

Walking Tall

After school on Monday, I stood at my booth in the gym as the science fair wound down. It was hard to believe that just days ago I'd been sitting in the gym bleachers surrounded by the same sweaty smell of old gym mats and varnish as Agford clip-clopped across those hardwood floors and leveled her cold stare at me. I wondered what sound her prison-issue shoes would make when she paced her Texas jail cell.

Though I hadn't gotten to the bottom of sugar's effect on teeth, people had been stopping by my booth in a steady stream to congratulate me on that *other* hypothesis I'd nearly died proving. My poster board left a lot to be desired, but it looked gorgeous compared to Marissa's disaster. She stood glumly a few booths down from me, her bangs looking as wilted as the houseplants around her that cowered in the roar of Beethoven's Ninth Symphony. "Do Plants Like Music?" her otherwise plain poster read in black marker. Then, underneath it, she'd written simply: "No."

S.M.I.L.E. had been devastated when they had learned the truth about Agford. If it all hadn't been bad enough, they'd discovered that the money they'd raised over the past two years had never been donated. Even the knitted Peshawar scarves were found stashed in the back of a closet in Agford's office. They apologized to me for everything and were shocked when I apologized back. I was truly sorry. I had never seen them as anything but extensions of Charlotte Agford—a single beast of rolling backpacks and fake smiles. In reality, they were victims.

We had all been victims. That much was clear, even if we were still learning some of the details of the case. The police suspected that Bain had come to Luna Vista to wait until her brother was free, falsifying her résumé to secure a position in a school so that she might be able to pull a similar scam again.

I folded up my poster board. It had been quite a first day back. High fives during passing periods. Ms. Gant coming up to praise me for my logic. Madame Tarrateau, her poodle curls bouncing, had spent half of French performing elaborate charades to teach us words like *fugitive* and *private investigator.* And Rod. I'd never forget how Rod looked when he asked if he and Peter could sit with Trista and me at lunch—nor, for that matter, the smile Trista gave me when she kicked me under the table. She finally got it.

The crowd had thinned, except for a throng of people clustered around a booth at the end of the row. Trista's. I smiled. I should go congratulate her on her first prize. I finished packing up, chuckling when I almost forgot the gift Mr. Katz had given me.

Trista bent over her solar panel as she animatedly explained its features to the crowd of kids and parents grouped around her, appearing oblivious to the big blue ribbon pinned to the display. I'd never seen her surrounded by so many people, let alone look so at ease among them. Someone's mom, who must have worked at AmStar, asked a technical question. As Trista rattled off an answer, I turned to look at the large white screen displaying captioned PowerPoint slides of her building process. I nearly fell over when I saw who stood there.

"Grace?" I asked.

Grace smiled at the crowd and clicked to the next slide, then gave me an open-palmed shrug. Her outfit was impeccably put together, from her tights and funky shoes to her cute skirt and updo. A single silver vintage watch graced her wrist.

"Trista needed a little help," she explained sheepishly as I approached. "She knew you were busy with your project. So . . ."

"Trista needed help?" I repeated.

"Happens more often than you think," Trista interrupted, stepping away from her crowd of admirers for a moment. "My slide themes were awful. And the place needed a little dressing up." She gestured to her booth, which was very stylishly decorated in earth tones and orbs suggesting suns.

Grace looked over at Trista's plain black T-shirt and jeans. "I made some fashion suggestions, too. But . . ."

Trista held up her hand. "This is my dress T-shirt."

I laughed. "Want to wear it out on the town? Let's all go to the Seashell."

Trista jerked her head toward the crowd. The AmStar mom was waiting for more details. "I need to stick around here a little bit. You two go ahead. But"—she pointed to the cardboard poster tube I held in my hand—"make sure you tell Grace all about *that*."

As Trista wheeled around to answer a question on semi-conductor materials, Grace looked at me expectantly.

"Oh, you're going to love this." I slid the poster out of the tube and unfurled it. Grace gasped and covered her mouth. It showed a mountain climber scaling the face of a snow-covered peak. COURAGE was printed in large, bold purple letters underneath. "Mr. Katz presented it to me at a Special Assembly today. You know, for my heroism and all," I explained.

"It's going to look awesome in your life-path *gua*," Grace joked as we headed for the exit. "Oh my God, you have to tell me *everything*. Trista gave me, like, zero details."

As we walked through the outdoor halls to my locker, I explained how Mr. Katz had practically gotten down on his knees in front of the whole school—as well as a group of angry parents who'd shown up—to apologize for not checking Agford's background. I did tell her everything, from S.M.I.L.E.'s apologies to Ms. Gant's congratulations and Madame Tarrateau's charades. Grace smiled but looked around apprehensively, no doubt remembering the last time she'd passed the same classrooms. When a couple of kids waved to me and she looked away shyly, I was startled to realize that she was nervous to be at school with me at all.

"Trent Spinner actually high-fived you?" Grace asked, trying to hide her unease. "He was probably thanking you for his three-day vacation from school."

"Probably. He did still call me Ay-nus, though." I shut

the rest of my stuff in my locker and waved my new blue Lightning iFlash at Grace. "Then there's this."

"Full data plan and unlimited texting?" Grace asked, beaming.

"Not quite. But close enough. And look who emailed." I handed it over. Grace read aloud as we headed out the doors, trying her best to imitate Louise Ralston's drawl:

Dear Young and Yang,

How can I ever thank you? You'd think there'd be a Texas expression up to the job, but I'm at a loss. I hope that someday you will find it in your hearts to forgive me for not trusting you with the truth. I should have known better than to sell you short. Sometimes, on the way to find justice, we can lose sight of what's really important. I bet you two understand that better than anyone. You're fine investigators—finer than hair on a frog's legs, as we like to say here. Steer clear of trouble. And be sure to stay in touch. Maybe one of these days I'll take a real vacation and come see you. I'll leave the

blue car at home . . .

Yours Truly,

Louise Ralston

"I'd forgiven her a thousand times already," I said as Grace finished. We stood outside school, about to make our way up the hill toward town. The sun shone low behind us, as always. Pink clouds looked raked across the sky.

"Me, too." Grace grinned. "Except for that hairy-frog-leg comment. I'm holding that against her." She fiddled with my iFlash. "Wait. Rod texted you?" She turned my phone sideways and squinted at it. "A code?"

My cheeks turned red.

"Oh, I hope this is really from him," Grace joked. "You break it yet?"

"It's a Caesar substitution code. 'Madame Tarantula is finally interesting again. Glad you are back safe.'"

"Aww . . . ," Grace said. "He totally likes you." As she handed back my phone, I saw something glimmer on her neck in the sunlight.

"Hey . . . ," I said. "You're wearing it!"

It was the little white teardrop pendant with a circle of black in it—the yang part of the split yin/yang charms that Mrs. Dr. Yang had given to us last year.

Grace broke into a smile. "You don't know what I had to go through to make it look right with this outfit."

I tried to keep it together. I really did. But I couldn't hold it back. I burst into laughter. Uncontrollable, hiccupping laughter—with maybe even a few snorts tossed in à la Charlotte Agford.

Grace shook her head at me, then flicked me on the shoulder—hard. "Watch it, shorty," she said.

"Hey, I'm four foot—"

"Four foot six. I know, I know. You're actually looking pretty tall these days." Grace grinned and took my arm. "Shall we?"

"We shall." I hooked my arm around hers.

We headed up the hill and turned down Luna Vista Drive, walking in silence past the clean-swept driveways and manicured front yards, past Mr. Valdez watering his lawn and Mrs. Stenwall calling for her cat.

All seemed peaceful in Luna Vista, California. Boring, even.

And for once we didn't mind.

Acknowledgments

Though Sophie Young merely imagined she possessed the strength of an entire army, I relied on a very real and embarrassingly large one to help me tell this story. I'm very grateful to my wise and hilarious agent, Jennifer Laughran, for leading the charge so passionately and for finding a perfect home for my young sleuths. Young & Yang may be clever, but they have nothing on editorial duo par excellence Rosemary Brosnan and Andrea Martin. This book (and I) benefited immeasurably from their patience, enthusiasm, and insight. I am so fortunate they were on the case.

My heartfelt thanks also go to the remarkable team at HarperCollins Children's—from editorial to design to marketing to publicity and sales—including Phoebe Yeh, Cara Petrus, Kim Vandewater, Patty Rosati, Renée Cafiero, and cover artist Marcos Calo.

I'm deeply indebted to Kara LaReau, who took me under her wing and not only taught me how to do this but also showed me that I could. She is a rare bird, indeed.

Tania Casselle and Sean Murphy, Young & Yang's earliest champions, helped me "Write to the Finish" in their fantastic workshop and gave me the confidence to share my writing.

My dear friends offered tireless support and welcome distraction. Thanks, especially, to Elena Ritchie, Elise Gibney, Jody Gibney, and Caitlin Thompson, who slogged through bad early drafts and cheered me on regardless, and to Sacha Howells, who channeled his inner twelve-year-old girl and gave me invaluable revision advice. Tim Terwilliger not only inspired me with his own creativity but always offered a sympathetic ear. A special shout-out to my fellow former sixth-grade spy, Heather McAuley Gilman, and to her very generous husband, Bill, who produced a trailer for the book.

I'm not sure what I would do without my brilliant (and tactful) writing partners-in-crime, who gave constant encouragement and feedback: Cynthia Mines, Maggie Parks, Sarah Skilton, Amy Spalding, Melle Amade, Ingrid Sundberg, Toni Sherwood, and Melanie Abed.

I'm also very grateful to my readers and advisers, Jane George, Elsie Chapman, Rachel Lee, Ryan Lee, Millie Shih, Lori Walker, Sophia Chang, Stefanie Tatalias, Amy Rigsby,

Katie Nelson, Angela Russell, Amy Chou, and Jenn Reese, who weighed in on everything from tai chi moves and FBI protocol to title suggestions and banquet menus.

Thanks to Cecil Castellucci, who lent me some of her boldness when I needed it, and who has helped create such a vibrant Los Angeles young adult/middle grade literary community. Connecting with writers and people passionate about books has been one of the best parts of this adventure. Thanks, also, to the LAYAs, SCBWI, Bridge to Books, and the Lucky 13s, especially Alison Cherry, Brandy Colbert, and Lindsay Ribar.

I owe so much to my family for all of their support: the O'Connors, the Cliff Island Cusbacons, particularly Agnes, Lavinia, and S.B., and, of course, the Altwaters and Fiedlers, especially my brother, Eric, my cousin, Konrad Thọ, and Bess and John Fiedler, who offered so much of their time, advice, and enthusiasm.

To my mom, my most trusted reader: I wish that I had half of your patience, kindness, and intelligence. (Dad was right. You *are* the best.) And lastly, to Kai. Ich liebe dich, mein Schatz. Thank you.

Read on for a sneak peek
at the next book in Yang & Young's
adventures.

Chapter One

Operation Winter Sun

I grasped the cold metal rung of the scaffolding and pulled myself up, the steel frame clanking and swaying beneath my feet like a wobbly ladder. The warehouse floor far below spun dizzily toward me and away again. I shut my eyes and took a deep breath. My mouth was dry. My heart hammered. But I couldn't stop now. Not with our target in reach.

Grace and I should never have accepted the mission. What had we been thinking? It was too dangerous, even for expert spies like us. It was too late. We were in too deep.

And up too high.

"T-minus one minute and counting!" Grace panted as she scrambled up behind me. "Keep going, Sophie!"

"Roger," I called back, my voice hoarse. In my free hand I held our mission supply box—a long, shallow, open cardboard container. I reached for the top rung of the scaffolding,

1

struggling to keep the carton level. If I spilled it, the mission would be doomed.

I heaved myself onto a narrow wooden plank stretched over the warehouse floor like a balance beam. The target was only twenty steps away, tops. Twenty steps across a splintery, wobbly board tied in place by a fraying rope—but still, only twenty steps.

"Approaching target. Prepare to take position," I said.

"Affirmative," Grace said. "T-minus thirty seconds!" Grace's watch beeped frantically. "Go ahead without me!"

My stomach churned. A drop of sweat trickled down the back of my neck. The mission was scary enough without having to face it alone.

"Roger," I said, trying to hide the quaver in my voice. "I'm going in."

I gritted my teeth and inched out onto the shaky plank, holding the cardboard flat in one hand. I took one small step, and another. Then I bent my knees and side-shuffled faster, hoping the momentum would make it easier to balance. It did—for a few steps. Then my ankle buckled. My weight tipped. I swayed and rocked on the board like a beginning surfer. But it was too late.

Wind whistled past my ears as I sailed into the emptiness.

"Sophie! No!" Grace's shriek echoed in the rafters.

Time really does slow down when you're about to die. Years fold up inside of seconds and your brain has time to replay every memory—twice, if they're awful. Laughing too hard and peeing on Stacy's down comforter at her sleepover birthday party. Getting caught giving my American Girl doll a buzz cut with my dad's shaver. Gagging down a cold heaping spoonful of liver-flavored Whiskas. (Tip: *Truth*, not *dare*. Never *dare*.)

I was starting to imagine Grace's teary tribute at my funeral when it hit me that, if time had slowed down that much, I should probably try saving myself.

I thrust up my hands and managed to catch the wooden plank one level below, my body jerking like a piñata as my arms nearly yanked out of their sockets. Our supply box cartwheeled overhead, sending thousands of red flower petals shimmering into the air. I tilted my head back, closed my eyes, and let them shower over me like confetti.

It was a Winter Sun Festival miracle.

Who knew that decorating parade floats could be so dangerous? My muscles burned as I tried to hold my grip. Splinters pierced my fingers. I opened my eyes again and stared at the giant fake ice cream scoop on Luna Vista's Root Beer float looming over me. I deserved a better final

3

sight. Something more noble. More meaningful. Something that wasn't an oversized imitation dairy product. I wondered if I should shout for Rod Zimball so I could finally profess my undying love. It wouldn't matter if he didn't say anything back.

I'd already be hurtling to my death.

"Hang tight!" Grace hollered. I cringed as my fingers started to slip. Over my head, a banner sagged from the rafters, counting down the happy moments I might never live to see: 6 MORE DAYS TILL PARADE DAY! it mocked.

"I'm trying!" I called back to Grace. The scaffolding rocked as she climbed faster to reach me. Below me volunteers dashed around, too distracted by their own float decorating to notice me dangling. Kids shouted for cranberry seed refills and lugged buckets of strawflower and silverleaf through the "float barn," as everyone called it. Once upon a time there had been an actual barn on the Ridley Mansion grounds where the Festival was headquartered. Now the "barn" was a big drafty white warehouse that housed the parade floats. Most of them still looked like oversized papier-mâché projects speckled with paint-by-number patches of color. Eventually, we'd decorate them all with fresh flowers, but for the time being we were gluing a color base of seeds and finely chopped petals onto them.

"Let yourself fall, if you have to!" Grace shouted. *Let myself fall?* Ten seconds was all it took for my best friend in the world to give up and let me die? Then I remembered. The nets! Relief rushed through my aching limbs. The town of Luna Vista would never let a bunch of seventh-grade volunteers prance around on rickety scaffolding decorating parade floats without at least *trying* to make sure we didn't kill ourselves. Marissa and Kendra Pritchard's dad would have already filed, like, ten trillion lawsuits.

As I loosened my grip and braced myself for the fall, Grace's footsteps pounded against the plywood scaffolding one level below. A second later, her arms reached up and wrapped themselves tightly around my hips. "I gotcha. Go ahead, let go," she said as she gently eased me down. I sighed as my feet met the solid, wide boards.

"All clear, Agent Yang," I said, trying to keep up our pretend spy lingo. My voice shook.

"Over and out." Grace smiled, but she kept a steadying hand clamped on my shoulder. "You're getting good at that."

"Dangling from ledges?" I grinned back. "Practice makes perfect." Two months earlier I'd nearly tumbled out of my second-story window while creeping out on one of our missions. Things had changed a lot since then. That was before our spy games turned real and we'd nearly gotten ourselves

5

killed trying to capture a dangerous fugitive who'd been hiding out right in Luna Vista. We were town heroes now.

Town heroes who were laughingstocks, apparently. A chorus of giggles had broken out behind us. I turned to see Marissa Pritchard covering her mouth and twirling a lock of honey hair around a finger as she huddled on the Root Beer float with the identical twins from my homeroom, Danica and Denise Delgado. Big puffs of cotton spilled from the box next to them as they worked on creating the "foam" on top of the giant root beer mug. For a while I'd thought Marissa and I had finally made our peace. We'd even been lab partners in earth science. But she'd figured out that I liked Rod Zimball, and since then she took every opportunity to embarrass me whenever Rod was within a five-mile radius.

Marissa wrinkled her nose. "Are you playing spy? What, are you, like, in preschool?" she asked loudly.

If Rod still had ears, he'd heard her for sure. He was standing on the float not far behind us, gluing flaxseed to the giant root beer mug. Marissa smiled slyly at Danica and Denise. "I thought Festival volunteers had to be at least twelve years old. Am I wrong?"

I felt my cheeks turn red as the twins erupted into giggles again. Ordinarily, I would have shrugged it off, but that morning we were on their home turf—Winter Sun Festival territory. In a few years they'd probably even be princesses in the Festival's Royal Court. I could already see them sporting sparkly tiaras as they waved from their parade float. In fact, Marissa's older sister, Kendra, was probably going to be chosen as a Royal Court princess that very afternoon. She'd already beaten out hundreds of girls in the interview rounds to be a finalist. And Marissa and her friends were shoo-ins for royal pages, the mini-princesses whose job it was to buff and powder and spray tan their royal highnesses. But just because they thought they were royalty didn't mean that *I* had to.

"Yeah, we're playing spy games. So?" I asked, puffing up my chest to look taller. "Maybe you remember when those little 'spy games' helped catch a killer?"

Marissa rolled her eyes. "Not that again. Please. How long are you going to ride that? 'Ooh, remember when I caught the Tilmore Eight fugitive?' Whatever. It was forever ago."

She shifted her eyes to Rod Zimball. His brown curls hung over his eyes as he painted a new layer of glue on the mug. My stomach sank. When I'd captured a killer, I'd thought I would capture his heart, too, but it hadn't worked out that way. Yet.

"Yeah, forever ago," I repeated, trying to stay calm. "Like when you threw up raspberry slushy all over the ice rink last weekend?"

Danica and Denise gasped, and Marissa flushed redder than, well, a raspberry slushy. Target acquired. Direct hit.

Marissa hooked arms with the twins and glared at me. She flashed a smile at Grace before they turned away. "Those jeans are supercute, Grace," she said sweetly. "You always look supercute."

"Thanks." Grace straightened in surprise. "You, too."

You, too? I was about to ask Grace what the heck she was thinking when a voice thundered from the warehouse floor below. "Young! Yang!"

Grace groaned. The Floatator—aka Ms. Barbara "Barb" Lund—had spotted us. I swear that woman had cameras sewn into every inch of her denim overalls, and possibly into the eyes of the Winnie the Pooh patch plastered on the front of them. There was a reason we all called her the Floatator. A direct descendant of Festival founder and former root-beer magnate Willard Ridley, she ruled Winter Sun Festival float decorating with an iron fist—and a totally unnecessary megaphone.

Her staticky voice blared through it now. "Sundae inspection in five!" she called.

Ms. Lund wasn't all bad, really. Her round, plump face peeked out below a goofy mushroom cloud of short dark-blond hair, and she looked almost friendly on the rare occasions she smiled. She even chuckled at her "Floatator" nickname and proudly made up new ones for herself like "Chairman Barb," "Barbarossa," and—Grace's favorite—"the Grand Pooh-Bah." She also thought it was fun to toss around what she thought were popular slang terms, but which we suspected were either from 1994 or made up entirely. Still, she flipped out if she thought someone wasn't living up to her crazy high standards for the Festival. That morning her face had actually turned purple when she saw that my petals on the ice cream sundae had clumped messily over the glue.

Barb lifted her megaphone again. "Quit yer chit-chattin' or I'm going viral on you two!"

Grace shot me a puzzled look.

"I really don't want her to go viral," I said.

"No kidding." Grace stifled a laugh. "I think I'd rather land on her Watch List." There were a lot of rumors about what being Barb's Watch List involved, and death sounded like a nicer option.

Barb narrowed her eyes at us, pointed her megaphone into the air, and whooped its built-in siren three times.

"Okay, Agent Yang," I called out, nudging Grace. "Sounds like it's time to wrap up this mission and head back to headquarters."

"Uh-huh," she said, distractedly. Her eyes flicked to Marissa and the twins gluing cotton root-beer "foam."

"What's wrong?" I asked, but as soon as the words had left my lips, I noticed her cheeks had turned a shade darker. I knew exactly what was wrong. She was embarrassed. Of me.

"Nothing," Grace said. Her eyes stayed locked on the girls as if she were memorizing the details of their too-short jean cutoffs to incorporate into one of her own outfits.

"Jeez, you think those cutoffs can be any shorter?" I asked. "They're like, loincloths or something."

Grace shrugged. "I think they're supercute."

I flinched. Heaviness settled over my chest as I wondered what else was on the list of things she and Marissa agreed were *supercute.*

"I can't believe I forgot to tell you," I said, trying to shove the feeling away and distract her. "I found out about the coolest code. Have you ever heard of a Polybius cipher?"

Grace sighed and picked up another empty cardboard flat. "I'm getting bored with the spy games, Soph. Aren't we beyond all that now?"

A couple of months didn't seem like long enough to be "beyond" anything, let alone something that'd made us heroes. Judging from the face she'd made, though, you'd have thought I'd suggested we drag out our old Barbie collections to play with in front of everyone.

I ignored her. "Anyway, it's this cool knocking code that prisoners used to communicate with. It's kind of like Morse, but everyone knows Morse, so with this one—"

Grace's eyes flashed. "Soph, seriously! Let's take a break on the spy stuff, okay?"

I snapped my mouth shut. A sick, sad feeling poured through me as Grace pressed the cardboard flat into my hands. "We'd better hurry on that petal refill. I heard that last year Barbarossa made kids on the Watch List scrub down the parade port-a-potties." She arched an eyebrow. "With *toothbrushes*."

I grabbed the box, trying to tell myself that Grace was acting strange because she was homeschooled and wasn't used to being around so many kids. Or that capturing a real fugitive had scared her off spying for good. Something told me there was a different reason she'd tossed out her FBI "Most Wanted" posters and had given away her walkie-talkies to the fourth grader down the street from us, though. She'd gotten really into browsing fashion websites and reorganizing her room—which was weird, because before, she was basically on track to be on one of those reality TV shows about people who can't leave the house because they're trapped behind all the old magazines and empty ramen packages and cat pee–soaked blankets they've hoarded.

Sometimes I wondered if she was changing faster than I could ever keep up.

Grace started for the scaffolding. "Come on, Sophie," she said, sighing. "I can't wait for you forever."

I stared at her, a sinking feeling in my gut, and for the first time it struck me.

Maybe she really couldn't.

Chapter Two

Festival Fever

Each year "Festival Fever" struck as early as November, when crews started setting up bleachers along the main boulevard. The Winter Sun Festival was like Luna Vista's Fourth of July and New Year's rolled up into one. Even though the parade was on the winter solstice, just days before Christmas, the only signs of our holiday spirit were a few door wreaths and a scrawny tree outside the shopping plaza.

Festival Fever felt doubly intense that year. Not only was it the parade's 125th anniversary, but Luna Vista had become a national joke when it turned out we'd been harboring a fugitive as a school counselor for *two years*. Everyone was determined to show off our town and make this Winter Sun Festival the best yet.

The truth was, I didn't know who Luna Vista was showing off for anymore. Until the 1990s the Festival was actually a nationally televised event. People all over the country would tune in to check out sunny Southern California and its bright, flowery parade floats in the dead of winter. It was just what the parade's founder, Willard Ridley, would have wanted. After all, showcasing California's warm December days was exactly why he and his hunting club had started the parade in the 1890s. That, and to advertise famous Ridley root beer, of course.

In the meantime America had become way more into Internet cats than parades, but Luna Vista still prepped for the Festival as if the whole world were watching. Marching bands from all over Southern California auditioned to appear in it. Hundreds of local high school senior girls competed to be selected as a princess or queen on the Royal Court. Designers worked months in advance on new fancy float plans. And kid volunteers like us swooped into the float barn to decorate them as soon as school let out for our winter break.

Grace and I had been dying for Prep Week to kick off—even more than most seventh graders. Not only was it the first time we were old enough to volunteer, but it was also the first time she and I and our friend Trista Bottoms would get to hang out together all day, as if we went to the same school. We even made our own special Winter Sun Festival calendar to count down the days. But as I stood there in the float barn trying to shake off the strange twisty feeling I had about Grace shutting me down on the spy stuff, I found myself wondering if the Festival was really going to be as much fun as I'd thought.

"Sundae inspection in FOUR minutes!" Barb Lund blared through her megaphone again as Grace and I hopped off the last scaffolding rung and scooted past her to get more chopped strawflower petals. "And Zimball!" she shouted up to Rod on the Root Beer float. "Where's your dad? I need him to help adjust the starboard confetti cannons, pronto!"

Poor Mr. Zimball. Rod's dad was very high up in the Festival ranks, but he was so nice that Chairman Barb was constantly roping him in to help with something or other. We'd only been volunteering three days, and he'd already fixed the flat tire on her golf cart, oiled her squeaky office chair, and sanded down a splintery scaffolding board. And those were just the things I happened to witness.

Grace linked her arm with mine and we headed to the flower refill station at the back of the warehouse, passing dozens of colorful floats that featured everything from giant cartoon figures to replicas of Ferris wheels and palm trees. Festival rules said that every inch of the float had to be covered with organic material of some kind, so buckets of bark, seeds, flowers, seaweed, and every type of plant you can imagine lined the aisles. Petals drifted in the air like snowflakes, and Barb Lund's favorite eighties oldies echoed through the warehouse.

"Have you asked Rod if he wants to sit with you at the Royal Court announcements yet?" Grace asked as Mr. Zimball hustled past us in his trademark Festival root-beer-brown business suit with another "Brown Suiter," as we called all the Festival officials.

I guess she thought I couldn't embarrass her with spy-game talk if we focused on my love life instead. "Not yet," I mumbled. "I think I should ask him to go to something else with me, don't you? It's too weird."

Grace didn't have any crushes, not unless you counted my older brother, Jake, who was a high school junior—and that crush was obviously the result of early brain injury and/or serious vision impairment. Being homeschooled meant limited romantic options.

"I mean, it's not like it's a dance or something," I explained. "He probably has to sit with his family. They'll be sitting on the terrace with all the VIPs, I bet."

Grace sighed. "He likes you. It's so obvious. He's just shy! If you ask him, he'll know you like him, too."

"And if he says no?"

"He's not going to say no. And if he did? He doesn't understand what he's missing." She hugged my arm closer to her side. Just then another Brown Suiter zipped past us on one of the motorized white Festival scooters, a clipboard tucked under her arm.

"Royal page sign-ups!" someone squealed from the Girl Scouts of America's Beary Happy Family–themed float. It was like someone had blown a whistle. Before the Brown Suiter had even slowed to a stop, a mass of khaki-uniformed girls streamed away from their decorating stations, their badge sashes flapping as they raced past a surprised Goldilocks and the Three Bears huddled around a fake Girl Scout campfire. *Just Right,* read the loopy cursive script at the front of the float underneath them. Nothing felt "just right" about it.

Our good friend Trista Bottoms got caught in the crush of the crowd. Wearing her own version of a scout uniform— a khaki cargo vest that she'd sewn all her Girl Scout badges onto—she stood in front of the Beary Happy Family float like a boulder in a rushing rapids. The big mop of dark curls that sprang from her head made her seem bigger than she was. As a second wave of middle-school girls from other floats jostled by her, she turned toward us with a helpless shrug. Grace and I shot her a sympathetic look.

"Exc*uuuu*se me!" an annoyed voice whined behind us. Grace had accidentally bumped into Marissa's sister, Kendra Pritchard, who was carrying a basket of sunflower seeds. Kendra brushed off her uniform and flashed us a death stare, which hardly seemed right coming from a Girl Scout.

Grace apologized, but Kendra was flouncing back to her station on the Beary Happy Family float, stopping to give Marissa an encouraging pat on the back as she waited to sign up for the auditions.

"I think she put some kind of a hex on us," Grace muttered to me.

"She's just afraid we'll audition for royal pages and beat out Marissa," I joked.

Grace clapped her hands together. "Oh my gosh, how perfect would that be?" she asked, a glint in her eye. The flyaway hairs that had broken free from her ponytail gave her a wild look.

"I was kidding!" I backed away. I couldn't tell if the drifting petals made the air feel hazy or if Grace's suggestion made me feel woozy. It was probably both.

"We can all audition together," she said, breathless. "Think of how much fun it'd be if we made it!" She turned to Trista, who'd finally waded upstream and made her way to us. "Right?"

Trista bumped her fist against ours in greeting. "How much fun?" she asked in her booming voice. "Let's see. Living in a mansion for a weekend waiting hand and foot on high schoolers who believe they are actual royalty." She pretended to do some mental calculations. "I estimate roughly *negative* 3.5 tons of fun. Possibly less."

I laughed. "What, you don't want to buff Lily Lund's toenails every night?"

"You guys," Grace scowled. "It wouldn't be like that! A whole long weekend together, twenty-four/seven. Festival parties. Cool traditions. Riding on the Royal Court float!" She practiced her pageant wave and blew a kiss to an imaginary crowd.

Trista and I traded a look. I think we both would've rather grated cheese all over ourselves and spent the night in a rat-infested sewer.

"I'm not sure we're royal page material," I said. The Festival claimed the Royal Court wasn't a beauty contest—that they were just looking for the "ABCs." That is, girls who were "articulate, bright, and charming." Still, I'd never seen a middle-school page as short as me or as wide as Trista. Not even once.

"Don't be silly." Grace rubbed red mum petal dust into her fingers, then swiped each of my cheeks. "All you need is a liiiiittle bit of blush."

"What're you talking about?" I smiled mischievously as I repeated the Royal Court judges' famous advice to contestants. "We just need to be ourselves."

"Ha!" Trista snorted, ducking out of the way as I grabbed a huge handful of petals and launched myself forward. I tugged on the collar of Grace's T-shirt and tossed the petals down her back. Grace squealed, then filled both her hands and returned the favor.

"Hey, there," a voice called out behind us. My heart skipped a beat as I turned to see Rod Zimball. He put down his flower bucket and gave a little wave. White petals were caught in the crests of his dark curls like whitecaps, and his hazel eyes shone. The only way he could've possibly looked any cuter was if he were cradling a baby panda.

"You call that a line, ladies?" Barb Lund's thundering question made us jump. She was waving her hands at a group of seventh-grade girls, trying to steer them past the Girl Scout float to the sign-up clipboard. "Now let's see those patooties in single file, PDQ!" she barked at them.

"Patooties?" Rod's forehead wrinkled. "I feel like I need a translator," he said.

"That would be bomb diggity," I said, imitating Barb's awful slang. Rod laughed.

"You think the Floatator would be in a better mood,"

Grace said. "Just three hours till Lily's crowning, after all."

"Unless Lily doesn't make the cut," I said.

"Passing over a Ridley in an anniversary year? Not gonna happen," Rod said.

"C'mon," Grace said. "We only have two more minutes until Lund—"

A bone-chilling shriek rang out next to us. We whipped around to look.

"What the heck . . . ?" Trista's mouth fell open in surprise.

There, beside the campfire feature of the Beary Happy Family float stood Kendra Pritchard, her face twisted in horror.

A wisp of smoke hovered over her head.